date.

Murder in the Woods

A detective novel

LUCiUS

Text copyright 2017 Bruce Beckham

All rights reserved. Bruce Beckham asserts his right always to be identified as the author of this work. No part may be copied or transmitted without written permission from the publisher.

This is a work of fiction. Names, characters, places and incidents either are the product of the author's imagination or are used fictitiously. Any resemblance to actual persons, living or dead, events and locales is entirely coincidental.

Kindle edition first published by Lucius 2017

Paperback edition first published by Lucius 2017

For more details and Rights enquiries contact:
Lucius-ebooks@live.com

EDITOR'S NOTE

Murder in the Woods is a stand-alone crime mystery, the eighth in the series 'Detective Inspector Skelgill Investigates'. It is set largely in the English Lake District, a National Park of 885 square miles that lies in the rugged northern county of Cumbria, and in particular to the west of Derwentwater, around an imagined wooded knoll not unlike Swinside, in the vicinity of Catbells.

BY THE SAME AUTHOR

Murder in Adland
Murder in School
Murder on the Edge
Murder on the Lake
Murder by Magic
Murder in the Mind
Murder at the Wake
Murder in the Woods
Murder at the Flood

(Above: Detective Inspector Skelgill Investigates)

Murder, Mystery Collection
The Dune
The Sexopaths

Glossary – Cumbrian dialect

Some of the local words used in *'Murder in the Woods'* are as follows:

Backend – autumn
Bletherin' – talking nonsense
Brocken – broken
Brossen – full up (eaten too much)
Chessin – chasing
Clap – stroke a pet (mainly Scots)
Deek – look, peek
Divvent – don't
Flaiten, flaite – frightened
Foily – smelly
Girt – great
How – rounded hill
Ken – know (also Scots)
Marra – mate (friend)
Ower – over
Reet – right
Yat – gate
Yon – that
Yowes – ewes

1. HARTERHOW – Monday

'Guv – was that a scream?'

Skelgill, not a man known for sunbathing, lies unmoving; he might almost be asleep. However, the stalk of grass that he grips between compressed lips twitches like a fisherman's float, indicative of some sub-surface activity. DS Jones rolls over and achieves a sitting position with considerable ease, wrapping her arms round her knees. Now she surveys the scene; they face south, and in descending order is the sun in its dome of azure sky, a bleached mountainous horizon (Skelgill would tell her the names of the tops, such as High Raise, Pike O'Stickle and Glaramara) blending into green foothills and dales, the shimmering plane that is Derwentwater, and finally a verdant canopy of oak that froths up from the lake. In fact there are two more features, between them and the woodland fringe a steep downslope to which cling patches of fresh green bracken and mauve ranks of straining foxglove and, closest of all, Cleopatra, Skelgill's Staffie-Boxer cross, who sits snapping at flies. Suddenly, and simultaneously, the dog and the detective sergeant turn their heads a few degrees; they concur on the bearing.

'There it is again.' Skelgill still does not respond, but the grass stem stops moving. A note of anxiety occupies DS Jones's voice. 'Guv – wake up! It sounds like someone's in trouble!'

'I'm not asleep.'

If he were he is now alert and on his feet. Indeed he pitches forward and sets off downhill at a canter, spitting the straw. Without looking back he barks his orders.

'Put in a call – might be quicker across the lake. Watch the dog.'

DS Jones shades her eyes with a salute. Skelgill's loping stride seems precarious, like a skier who leans into a steep piste and might overbalance. Brown butterflies rise and flutter in his wake amidst puffs of pale yellow pollen. She kneels and slips her mobile from the hip pocket of her jeans. It takes her twenty seconds to make the call. Now she considers Cleopatra.

'Sit. Good girl. Stay.'

The dog is vaguely bemused, but does as bidden. DS Jones casts it a stern look and sprints after her superior. In her natural athleticism she exhibits more grace than Skelgill but he is in his natural element. Sure-footed he plunges into the woodland, and his beeline does not deviate; he hurdles decaying trunks and ducks leafy hazel switches and sprays of sweet-and-sickly scented honeysuckle. His progress is unaffected by the lattice of fallen branches and twigs that booby-traps the forest floor. The yell is repetitive, in frequency and timbre; it could be a homing beacon.

DS Jones is forced to skirt around Skelgill's course; in the heavy air beneath the canopy the cry is resonant, and she reaches its point of origin only in time to see him slap a dark-haired woman across the cheek. It is a successful manoeuvre and the penetrating squeal ceases. He hears the crackling approach of his colleague and makes a face that means she should take over. DS Jones grasps the woman by the shoulders and turns her 180 degrees, intending to shepherd her away, but she pauses for a moment to watch Skelgill.

Close by a black-and-tan Lakeland Terrier is worrying some object that it has partially uncovered. Leaf litter sprays about. There is the moist mouldy smell of mulch. Skelgill experiments with a pishing sound; then clicks of the tongue; then a whistle – but the dog is preoccupied with its excavation. He steps over and left-handed hauls it off its feet by the scruff. There is the unmistakeable musky waft of a stinkhorn that evokes rotten carrion and lures blowflies to the sticky spore-rich gleba – except gleaming from the black earth are two rows of bright human teeth.

*

'Dang!'
'What is it, Guv?'
Skelgill does not reply, but flaps a hand in the direction of his dozing dog. DS Jones looks puzzled, but then she understands as Skelgill stoops to pick up a crackling cellophane

wrapper from the tartan rug. For an hour Cleopatra has diligently guarded their hastily abandoned picnic site, but at some point, overcome by instinct, she ate the uncooked Cumberland sausages. DS Jones is unable to suppress a giggle. And Skelgill is forced to simper resignedly; it is not a trial of temptation he could have survived, either. Out of sight beneath them on the lower slope of Harterhow the woodland 'grave' is now taped off, a sentry posted in the shape of young PC Dodd, the scene of crime team being hastily assembled and soon to be despatched. The woman who raised the alarm has been coaxed away for a medical check-up; DS Jones has the lady's dog on a length of blue baler twine produced by Skelgill.

'What about this one, Guv – hadn't we better give it a drink of water?'

Skelgill regards the handsome animal like he is noticing it for the first time. He tilts his head to ascertain its gender.

'Has he got a name?'

DS Jones bends easily at the waist and then rather gingerly she feels beneath the creature's chin and rotates its collar. She chuckles for a second time.

'It says "Morse", Guv.'

Skelgill raises an eyebrow. He straddles the cornucopia of camping gear that spills from his toppled ex-army rucksack. He rummages and extracts a clear plastic bottle, but it is empty. He jerks his Kelly kettle from its base; it sloshes encouragingly. He casts about for a suitable receptacle, but in vain – and so squats beside the dog and pours from the spout into a cupped palm, as is his custom for his own dog. The terrier seems to bear no hard feelings, and is quick on the uptake.

'What kind is he, Guv?'

'A Lakeland – they're bred to follow the hunt – tough little devils, run all day long.'

Skelgill scowls at the Bullboxer; her obvious talents lie in other directions.

'Could that be why he was digging, Guv – maybe thought it was a dead fox?'

Skelgill screws up his features, recalling the hot sharp reek of decay.

'It were foily, alright – happen if you're a dog it must be like Friday night passing the chippy – irresistible.'

DS Jones makes a face of qualified disapproval.

'There was long hair, Guv – think it's a female?'

'Aye, I shouldn't be surprised. They usually are, eh?'

He gazes up as though he expects her to recite a ready statistic that bears out this supposition; his expression hints at concern, and some regret that this inequality should prevail. They both know, however, that any speculation at this moment is futile – until big questions like cause and time of death are answered by forensic analysis.

DS Jones nods pensively. She watches in silence as Skelgill performs the improbable trick of feeding all the gear back into the rucksack. But as they begin to pick their way diagonally down and across the fellside clearing, questions probe at her consciousness, and she speaks her thoughts.

'If someone has hidden the body – it's a long way from the gate. The lake would be nearer.'

Skelgill clicks his fingers to make sure his dog, unleashed, falls in behind them. He turns his head to consider Derwentwater. The schools have not yet broken up for summer; most trippers are silver surfers – not literally, of course, but those affluent empty-nesters and still-fit retired folks for whom the Lake District's combination of stunning natural beauty and network of cosy inns and coffee shops makes it a child-free magnet during term times. As such there are not so many rowboats on the water, and no flailing oars or joyful shrieks and splashes, but Skelgill counts four packed pleasure cruisers plying their trade, sedately circling the lake, both clockwise and anticlockwise, a hop-on hop-off service that calls at seven jetties, the nearest half a mile hence, at Brandelhow. Not that he has in mind this mode of transport; indeed he inserts a caveat into DS Jones's hypothesis.

'Aye – but you're talking a good three-hundred-foot height gain from the shore. There's a six-foot wall, and no easy footpath.'

DS Jones has thought of this.

'What if it were two people, Guv?'

'What if she walked there herself, Jones?'

She grins; they have come full circle. Patience is called for.

'How about Morse, Guv?'

'I'll take him round later – once the medic's finished with his owner.' He glances somewhat sheepishly at his colleague. 'I know the woman.'

*

Marvin Morgan puts down his binoculars. The young couple and their dogs have disappeared from sight – rather oddly, he thinks, for there is no path that way, albeit they are heading in the right direction for the dead-end of the track where a handful of cars can be squeezed onto the verge. He has seen the man before – must be late thirties, rough looking, hard-faced, could almost be a gypsy with that fighting dog – it's probably a pit bull.

His girlfriend was a good bit younger. Attractive – nice face and a slim figure – *and* curvy, you don't often see that. Marvin's pulse had risen. He'd been reclining in his usual spot when they first came into the clearing two hours ago. The man had spread out a rug, and they'd cooked sausages – the smell had made his mouth water but he'd already eaten his own sandwiches. Then they lay down – but there was bracken and gorse between them and his 'hide' under the conifers and he caught only the occasional glimpse of a bobbing head. He'd thought about creeping around the edge of the clearing for a better angle. But that would have meant leaving his own dog tied up – and he might bark and give the game away.

Anyway – then the screaming had started and the man had dashed off, followed by the girl. He'd considered a casual inspection of their picnic spot – until he realised the pit bull might be lurking. He'd had to be patient – it was the best part of an hour before they returned – in fact he'd probably nodded off when he heard their voices. They'd straight away begun to pack up – he got a better view of the girl, and a photo of her bending over in her tight jeans. He'd wondered if the cries for help had interrupted them having sex – it was a good twenty seconds before the man had risen, and didn't he hitch up his trousers? But they weren't exactly intimate when they got back. Maybe they're married? And the girl had another dog on a rope – that must have been something to do with the screaming. What was that all about?

Marvin Morgan's bristly monobrow is creased at the centre – an unconscious contortion that only appears when he is significantly troubled. Broodingly, he packs away his own gear – sit-mat, thermos flask and lunchbox, notebook and pencil, camera, binoculars, paperback novel – and unhooks his dog's lead from the little branch cut off for the purpose. He begins to trudge upwards into the pinewoods, the opposite way from the young couple. Then he stops in his tracks and listens – there is a distant siren. The crease deepens.

2. JUNE COLLINS

'Sorry – I haven't yelled like that since I was a little girl – I didn't know I still had it in me.'

Skelgill reaches to clap the Lakeland Terrier, which seems disinclined to leave his side. Then he leans his elbows upon the kitchen table and watches the woman. She has her back to him as she disposes of teabags at the sink. The belt of her pink towelling dressing gown is tied tight about her waist, revealing a trim if thin figure, and drawing the short hem perhaps higher than she realises. Her black hair, still damp and slick and brushed straight between her shoulder blades, looks longer than before. Ordinarily he would have offered to come back at a more suitable time – but the woman stepped aside and the dog virtually pulled him through the front door. Now she turns and sets down two china mugs and takes the seat closest to him.

'Happen it did the trick. Sorry about the slap.'

She lifts a palm to her cheek – as if only now she remembers what took place. Her nails are carefully manicured, quite long – possibly artificial – and varnished in a deep ochre. And though he must have interrupted her bath or shower, he does not recall the mascara or lipstick from their encounter in the woods. There is something Mediterranean in her appearance, with full brows and a nose that is a shade too large for the surrounding proportions of her face; her eyes, however, are pools of sparkling kingfisher blue, they seem illuminated amidst her tanned complexion. She fixes them upon him; then she folds her hands reverently upon her lap and her expression is one of wide-eyed admiration. Her voice is silky, and her accent a curious amalgam of north west England and the mid-Atlantic.

'I never guessed you were a detective.'

Skelgill is half-expecting this observation, if not the manner in which it is delivered. Nearby is Crow Park, a Keswick lakeside attraction popular with local dog owners and professional dog walkers. His recent taking custody of Cleopatra – in the opinion of most observers a spectacularly out-of-character lifestyle decision – has seen him become acquainted with this woman (among others), albeit on purely nodding terms.

'I never guessed you were a landlady.'

Skelgill intends this as a compliment, but she lowers her eyes and has him scuttling for the cover of a banality.

'Aye – they're a great leveller, dogs. You meet all these folk out there – pass the time of day with them – but you never know if they're a High Court judge or a murderer on the run – or one and the same.'

The woman looks up with alarm, her eyes shining.

'And now there *is* a murderer?'

That Skelgill has inadvertently implied a main line of inquiry causes him to backtrack. He takes a drink of tea – it allows him to compose a reply.

'Let's not get ahead of ourselves – at this stage there's no saying what happened. It could have been a suicide, an accident – someone taken ill.'

'So the skull – it was human?'

Skelgill grimaces and nods reluctantly.

'Aye – an adult, if it's any consolation – but we'd appreciate your confidence for the time being.'

He watches as she intertwines her slender fingers around her mug. Hers do not look like the washed-out hands of a landlady. Nor indeed does she exhibit the intense demeanour of the profession; she seems far too easy going, too glamorous, too young, even – though he knows her age to be 43 from among the basic contact details she has supplied to his colleagues. She affects a shudder and dips her head.

'And to think how many times I must have walked past.'

Skelgill remains guarded, though he decides to explore the avenue this remark presents.

'You were well off the nearest path.'

June Collins looks extravagantly puzzled by his inquiry – if she were blonde he might say dizzily.

'Morse wouldn't come back. He can be *very* naughty once he picks up a scent. I'm always terrified he'll get stuck in a foxhole. And then what would I do?'

She stares at Skelgill and bats her long lashes rather helplessly.

'What took you to Harterhow? Not many folk know it.'

For a fleeting second a pained look crosses her features, and there is a perceptible delay before she replies.

'Spencer used to go there. He showed me the way. It was their favourite place – Rebus especially. Usually I don't have time – it can be a half-hour drive in high season.'

Skelgill holds up a palm, traffic-cop fashion. She is going too fast for him.

'Rebus? Spencer?'

Now she seems surprised – that as a senior detective he does not know all this. She turns towards him in her chair and slides one bare leg over the other; it strikes Skelgill that the rich uniform tan could be from a bottle.

'Rebus came before Morse. Spencer was my ex-partner. They're not with us now.'

She presents a forlorn figure, her gaze imploring. Skelgill affects sympathy, though his unforgiving countenance does not especially lend itself to the expression of such a delicate sentiment.

'Spencer died?'

She puts a hand to her mouth. 'Oh, no – not Spencer – Rebus. Rebus passed away and so I got Morse – from the same breeder. Spencer –' She gives a little nervous laugh. 'Spencer left by mutual agreement.'

Skelgill looks uneasy. Absently he pats a pocket of his jacket. He did not come equipped to take a statement – indeed it is a function that falls outside his comfort zone, especially when he can call upon the competence of DS Jones – but now he senses that information of some import might overwhelm him. He opts for a diversionary tactic.

'Unusual choice of names – I mean Rebus and Morse.'

June Collins smiles; she takes his observation as an encouragement to elaborate.

'I've always loved whodunits – the way the clever detectives solve the crime.' But now she sighs and shakes her head. 'If only the writers didn't give them such unpleasant personal habits. Why can't there be a hero that you'd want to sweep you off your feet?'

She regards Skelgill rather wistfully, and his expression becomes conflicted. Perhaps just in time a little voice tells him that there might be some chicanery at play – does she flatter to deceive? In his job one never knows. He shrugs reflectively.

'Happen it would put off male readers if the copper were too perfect.'

The woman looks a little disappointed and folds her arms.

'That's what Spencer used to say. He wouldn't watch American films because he said you always knew the ending.' A dreamy look crosses her features. 'A *happy* ending.'

Skelgill makes a little cough.

'We hope for that, too, madam.'

She shoots him a reproachful glance – aimed it seems at his use of 'madam'. Indeed, thus far he has avoided any particular appellation, although perhaps more by circumstance than design. By the time he arrived to return the terrier, they were acquaintances of a sort, and conventional introductions largely inappropriate.

'Please – you must call me June.' She sees that his mug is almost empty and reaches forward and her gown gapes open momentarily. 'Would you like some more tea? And there's cake and a sandwich? I have a little snack ready for my guests – it's just one couple tonight and they're arriving late – there's enough to go round.'

Though Skelgill remains implacable there is a glint approaching hunger in his eyes. But he steels himself and rather ostentatiously consults his wristwatch.

'Thanks – but I need to get along.'

Indeed he begins to rise. The Lakeland Terrier, which has settled watchfully in a basket near the back door, detects the change of tempo and makes a brisk skittering lap of the tiled floor. Skelgill determinedly heads into the hallway, stepping over the eager dog, which seems to believe a caper is nigh. He lets himself out and turns to face the woman, who is hot on his heels and remembers too late that she is wearing a short dressing gown – and what might the neighbours think to see her bidding farewell to a stranger at this time of the afternoon? She withdraws to the threshold and blinks candidly at Skelgill, as though they conspire together in this scandal.

'Someone will call round tomorrow to take a full statement – when would be convenient?'

There is something about the way she leans upon the door jamb, and then raises one bare knee across the other that causes Skelgill to look away. She smiles with satisfaction and slowly brushes a fallen strand of hair from her cheek.

'Guests leave at ten-thirty – and the earliest arrival is five o'clock. I'll only have one room to make up – the others are all ready and waiting – empty all day long, *hah-ha*.'

Skelgill is staring distractedly at the dog, which is burrowing vigorously beneath a rose bush in a corner of the small front garden.

'Shall I have the pleasure of your company, Inspector Skelgill?' She says his name with special emphasis, as if she is reading aloud the opening line of a crime mystery, savouring the anticipation of a literary adventure.

'Aye, well – we'll see how it goes, Mrs Collins – June.'

'It's Miss – but June is better.'

3. SKELGILL'S OFFICE – Tuesday

'DI Smart was asking how come you were on the scene so quickly, Guv – I reckon he's peeved you've got the case.'

Skelgill scowls disapprovingly at DS Leyton and folds his arms. He glances at DS Jones, who is settled in her usual seat in front of the window. 'Happen we'd stopped for lunch nearby – and not a penny at the taxpayer's expense.'

DS Jones grins, a little sheepishly it must seem to DS Leyton. Skelgill's explanation is doubly holed, given the isolated location, and that the taxpayer funds not only their incidentals but also their hourly wages. However, he continues undiminished.

'Possession is nine-tenths of the law, Leyton. Besides, you know Smart – give him half a chance and he'll put some melodramatic spin on the whole thing.'

'He reckons it's narcotics-related, Guv – he says there's Manchester drug lords who've invested in properties up here, hotels and pubs – businesses that deal in cash, just the ticket for money laundering.'

Skelgill makes an exclamation of triumph – as if this proves his point – but there comes a knock on his door, which is partially open and a young female officer from DS Jones's team makes a nervous entrance.

'It's the urgent report you asked for, sir – from Dr Herdwick.'

Skelgill slumps against his chair and jerks a thumb in the direction of DS Jones. He watches in silence as the junior does as bidden, DS Jones rising to accept the delivery and congratulate her subordinate. When she has gone, Skelgill indicates to DS Leyton that he should shut the door. DS Jones meanwhile is trying to make sense of several sheets of handwritten notes, torn unceremoniously from a spiral-bound reporter's pad. She strips off the untidy perforations and drops them into the waste bin close by. She sits calmly as she reads, her posture serene; her long lashes seem almost to brush her prominent cheekbones.

After a minute she glances up at each of her colleagues and begins to recite from memory.

'Female. Aged between 45 and 55. The body had been dismembered with a saw and cleaver. No clothing but two rings on the middle and ring fingers of each hand. Extensive dental work – expensive veneers upper and lower front teeth. The corpse has been in the ground between 6 and 9 months. Cause of death presently unknown.'

DS Leyton's expression seems to be one of great worry – when generally he is phlegmatic in the face of the unpleasantness and even horror that can be part of a policeman's daily fare. Skelgill snorts dismissively.

'Cheer up, Leyton – I had to breathe it in.' He turns to DS Jones and squints to signal his discontent. 'I know I asked Herdwick for the bare bones – I didn't mean him to take me at my word.'

Both sergeants look doubtfully at Skelgill – it is never easy to tell if he is being flippant – but he does not invite their approval and instead kicks his chair around to glower at the map of the Lake District National Park on his wall.

DS Jones exchanges a puzzled glance with DS Leyton. She clears her throat.

'At least there's enough to go on – as far as missing persons are concerned?'

Skelgill remains brooding for a few moments. He speaks with his back to his subordinates.

'Aye – put someone onto it.'

'It's in hand, Guv – I asked the team to keep a copy.' She flaps the loose pages. 'Start with local reports and then initially extend to Merseyside, Greater Manchester, Tyne and Wear, and Glasgow. Roughly two hours' drive time. They should have a list for us before lunch.'

Skelgill makes a half revolution in his chair.

'That could be a long list.'

DS Jones shrugs off the implied criticism.

'I thought – in case there's someone we don't want to warn in advance.'

'Don't worry, Jones – they'll be expecting us.'

There is a round of silence as the group – Skelgill included – consider his fatalistic prophesy. Perhaps they each put themselves in the shoes of the killer, imagining what it might be like to wake every morning to the knowledge of what they have done, and whether today will be their day of reckoning. A rap on the door: it is the police. A body has been found and they have made some connection.

DS Leyton fidgets in his seat – it is a precursor to asking a question.

'What about the lady with the dog, Guv – can we trust her to button her lip?'

Skelgill glances at DS Jones but she is re-reading the notes.

'She's not the problem. It's a public amenity – and the Cumbria Way runs along the shore. Folk are going to see us going about our business. As it is we've shut off the lane. We shan't be able to keep the lid on it for long – even if we wanted to.'

DS Leyton looks glum.

'The media are going to lap it up, Guv. Now that England's knocked out of the World Cup. Nothing like a good murder to cheer up the country.'

His tone is flat, lacking his usual ebullient stoicism. DS Jones has raised her head and is watching him closely. Skelgill – perhaps unhappy at being reminded of the dismal showing of the national side – is somewhat dismissive.

'There's no saying it's a murder, Leyton.' For a second time in as many minutes his subordinates regard him dubiously. It is his habit to play devil's advocate, and not always with good reason. Technically, however, he is correct: at this stage they face a case of the unauthorised disposal of a human body. 'It wouldn't be the first time some crank's decided to give their other half a natural burial.'

DS Leyton objects.

'But chopping 'em up, Guv – that's taking it to another level.'

Skelgill shrugs.

'All I'm saying, Leyton, is without the cause of death, we're shooting in the dark.'

DS Jones holds up the sheaf of pages.

'Dr Herdwick's still on site, Guv – that's where he wrote these. His assistant has added a note – they're sifting all the soil around the remains before they excavate them fully. They're hopeful that once they can conduct a proper examination in the lab the cause of death will become apparent.'

Skelgill rubs his hands together impatiently – although his subordinates recognise the gesture as one that often precedes a request for a cup of tea.

4. HARTERHOW

'I should have brought the Kelly. I'm parched.'

'Maybe that would have been pushing our luck, Guv?'

Skelgill grins wryly. The gravity of the discovery has enabled a certain amount of glossing over of the nature of their presence here yesterday. Skelgill glances up; from a bough overhead a woodpigeon coos, a timeless five-note incantation that evokes his youth and tells him there is a nest nearby, an improbably frail platform of brittle twigs that will support two pearly white eggs, sought after by squirrels and schoolboys.

'We'll stop in the café at Portinscale – if we time it right we can meet Leyton there.'

'They'll have to make some provision for the scene of crime unit, Guv.'

He pulls a disparaging face. DS Jones refers to the fact that the team assembled to work in the wood – a group that includes anthropologists, archaeologists and pathologists – will require sustenance and supplies, a service of which they can avail themselves. Indeed a small, tented village has sprung up, at its hub a translucent-sided gazebo that has been erected over the remains to provide shelter from the elements, and prying eyes. At the moment the weather is set fair, and it is the intention that the field operation will continue around the clock in order as soon as possible to extract whatever clues the ground will yield.

Skelgill stops to consult the large scale Ordnance Survey map he has folded into a clear plastic carrying case (though he declines to wear it on its strap around his neck, should he appear to be a novice walker). Having visited the grave – where progress is painstakingly slow – he has led DS Jones up through the oak woodland, past the site of their 'lunch break', and into the pinewood above. Harterhow is a modestly sized domed hill that stands proud to the west of Derwentwater. Designated as a 'Local Nature Reserve' by Keswick Town Council it is a peculiar hotchpotch of natural and manmade habitat (the oak representing the former, the pine the latter) that fell into council ownership shortly after the Great War. Public access is not easy

– just a winding single-track lane, a no through road that deters most drivers for fear of meeting a vehicle coming back the other way; it is a lonely terminus occasionally frequented by courting couples. Formerly common land, it was enclosed during the 16th century, thence a substantial dry-stone boundary wall has seen to it that random passers-by do not encroach, assuming it to be private property. A further discouragement to visitors is now becoming apparent to DS Jones, as she tracks Skelgill's uncharacteristically hesitant upward progress: the summit is swathed in Norway spruce; not only are there no paths to the top, but once there, no views are to be had.

'Do you know this area, Guv?'

'Knocked around here a bit as a bairn – once in a blue moon nowadays – the occasional short cut.' He pauses and scowls suspiciously at a semi circle of white-speckled red fungi that sprout from the barren forest floor. 'It's a decent spot to exercise a dog – what with the wall, and there being no sheep. Happen I should come more often.'

'It seems very quiet, Guv.'

Skelgill nods.

'Can't say I've ever seen anyone here.' He gestures with the map – ahead of them through the trees is a shadowy stone cairn, supporting tufts of moss and draped in straggling silvery lichen. Such crowning features are normally exposed, blasted by the elements and constantly rearranged by walkers who add gratuitously to their bulk; this one has the look of long abandonment. 'Harterhow's only 907 foot – doesn't attract the top-baggers – it's not on any of the lists – most are a thousand foot and above.'

DS Jones grins – she comprehends but is nevertheless amused by man's habit of collecting – mainly man's. From matchbox lids to electric guitars, from garden gnomes to romantic conquests, it is a trait expressed in hill country by what can become obsessive summiting, though in Skelgill's oft-voiced opinion at the expense of enjoying the surroundings. In Scotland exponents are referred to as *Munro-baggers*; in Lakeland there is a popular list of 214 peaks known as the *Wainwrights* (after Skelgill's revered draughtsman and biographer of the fells) – only one of which, Castle Crag, is below a thousand feet. DS Jones is further entertained by Skelgill's dogged insistence upon imperial units – though when pressed he stoutly defends them against an ill-informed foreign bureaucracy that imposes metric measures which bear no practical relation to human proportions.

'Think it'll be a dog owner, Guv?'

Skelgill turns sharply. Her question is perspicacious; she means the killer. He does not reply, but glances about – he seeks a spot to sit, and indicates what are natural 'armchairs' formed by the buttress roots of a great conifer, their 'cushions' dry pads of browned fallen needles. He lowers himself and waits for DS Jones to take the seat beside him; she is more cautious, though the needles are deceptively accommodating. There is no view of course; just ranks of scaly trunks, flaking pillars that descend the shady fellside. Beneath the canopy the air is warm and still, birdsong becalmed; flies hover, spotlighted in shafts of sunlight, tiny angels that populate the woodland cathedral, the infinitesimal beating of their wings perhaps contributing in a minute way to its background sibilance. At last Skelgill responds, if obliquely.

'Why would you put a body anywhere?'

DS Jones widens her eyes as though she is trying to get them accustomed to the dappled light.

'So it couldn't be found?'

Skelgill nods.

'Seems like it, doesn't it.'

'The rings?'

He nods again.

'It means if we identify the body we find the murderer.'

DS Jones is pensive.

'It's curious, Guv. He – or she – has had time to plan the disposal – the dismemberment – the location – you think they'd remove a clue like that. Why stop at chopping off the arms?'

Skelgill grimaces. He pictures a dank garage, a mould-ridden bathroom – an abattoir – was it a bloody scene? But his original thought prevails. If no one finds the corpse, then it doesn't matter. The dismemberment was simply a case of practicality.

'A walker.'

'Guv?'

'How often do you see someone with a whacking great rucksack – wild camping – you don't bat an eyelid.' He scratches his head vigorously; midges are biting. 'Leastways, most folk don't – I'm nosy myself, see what they've got if there's gear strapped on the outside. Tells you if they know what they're doing.'

She gets his point – a large rucksack would enable the body parts to be carried with comparative ease – and in plain sight. She waves a palm in front of her face

'I was thinking more from a point of view of knowing about this place, Guv – that if you were a dog owner – you'd be aware few people come here.'

Skelgill does not demur. Indeed his underlying – perhaps subconscious – desire to explore the area has its roots in such a sentiment. The locus might prove to be a vital indicator to the identity of the killer. But it is far from an exact science. Murderers have buried their victims in their gardens (usually a spouse) believing they will not be missed, while others have simply dumped the cadaver in the most convenient layby, believing they themselves will not be connected to the crime – there is no hard-and-fast rule – for the mind of a murderer is not always a logical domain. This location, however, implies a more considered rationale – and the non-removal of the rings an expectation that the corpse would not be discovered. But it might simply have been an oversight – and that haste and panic abounded post mortem.

*

It's definitely the same couple. The girl has changed her outfit – a looser top that's not so revealing, and more casual trousers that look better suited for being outdoors – but the man's red-and-blue check lumberjack shirt he recognises from yesterday. Marvin Morgan glances at his dog, but it is preoccupied with its nether regions; in any event it rarely bothers about humans. Today the couple don't have their dog – or dogs. At times they walk close beside one another, conferring quietly, their expressions serious. In places, though, they have to go in single file – the man first. If they've climbed to the top of Harterhow they'll have been disappointed – he came that way himself – there's nothing to see, is there?

Now they're heading back across the big sloping clearing towards the oak wood. It doesn't seem like there's going to be any fooling around. He wonders if they're connected with whatever's going on down below. He hasn't risked too close a look himself – only glimpses of white tents through his binoculars – and people moving to and fro. It might be an outward-bound school party – plenty of them come to the Lakes for the last few of weeks of summer term. Maybe the staff have arrived early to set up camp – perhaps these two are teachers having an affair.

Maybe he'll come back after dark, without the dog, with his night-vision gear.

*

'Do you think it was just a fluke that the terrier found it, Guv?'

Skelgill is staring into the woods, away from the tents. He points to a narrow path, barely six inches across that winds away through the undergrowth.

'See that – it's a badger track. There's probably half a dozen setts on Harterhow. You rarely see them – unless you stake them out at dusk – and even then they just get on their way. Folk think a badger's cute – but you wouldn't want to tackle one that's backed into a corner. It's Britain's biggest carnivore – make mincemeat out of your average fox. And they can dig like there's no tomorrow.'

DS Jones is nodding.

'So you think it was uncovered by a badger?'

'Likely as not – then the smell would attract foxes – and dogs.'

'Morse.' DS Jones grins. 'A bit ironic, Guv.'

Skelgill makes a clicking noise with his tongue.

'Aye – I reckon we'll skip that detail when it comes to the report.'

DS Jones gives him a casual sideways glance.

'What was your impression of the owner?'

'Interesting.' However the word does not match Skelgill's tone of voice; he sounds guarded and is distracted for several moments. 'She runs a B&B in Keswick – overlooking Crow Park – that's where I've seen her – it's popular with dog walkers. But I reckon we can rule her out. And I'll show you why.'

Skelgill now strides across to a trestle table upon which are laid various tools and implements. He selects a spade and returns to DS Jones, passing her and indicating she should follow. He leads, taking the badger track; it is not so easy as it looks, for in places it passes beneath fallen boughs and elder bushes and patches of ferns. When they are about fifty yards from the site, he stops and casts about. Then he hands the spade to a bemused-looking DS Jones and points with the toe of his left boot at the ground before them.

'Try digging.'

DS Jones grins.

'What – for badgers, Guv?'

'Who knows what we'll find.'

DS Jones does as bidden. She positions the implement against the leaf mulch and applies pressure with her right foot. The cutting edge breaks the soft surface but to her evident surprise penetrates barely an inch before it meets some obstacle. She glances at Skelgill and moves the spade to an adjoining position – but to no avail. She puts more effort into the task, first pushing down with both hands upon the handle, bending her back, and when that does not work she hops two-footed upon the shoulders, and balancing she attempts to transmit her body weight down through the tool. With a small shriek she topples off and has to let go.

'I don't think I'd make a gardener, Guv – or a grave digger!'

Skelgill is smirking with some satisfaction. He picks up the spade and begins to scrape away at the leaf litter. Immediately he reveals the source of the problem: a network of fine pale roots that lies just beneath. Once he has cleared a small patch he changes his grip.

'Stand back.'

Now he becomes a man possessed – for it is plain that to do this job requires considerable force. But instead of digging conventionally, he wields the spade like an axe, swinging it double-handed through a great arc to bring the blade on one side down at an angle of 45 degrees, slashing through the roots, or splitting them sufficiently for a second spearing downward thrust of the cutting edge to sever them. After maybe a minute of vigorous exercise and a modicum of cursing he has hacked out an area of about two square feet, to a depth of some eight inches. It is plain, however, that even this technique has its limitations, for he has exposed a much bigger root, as thick as his forearm, upon which the spade makes little impression other than scoring its surface and releasing a milky sap.

'You've done that before, Guv.'

DS Jones sounds impressed and Skelgill looks pleased with her compliment. Panting, and rather heroically, he wipes beads of sweat from his brow, and then shakes his head as more no-see-ums begin to home in on the static target.

'You should see my garden – you wouldn't think so.'

Now DS Jones puts her hands on her hips and adopts a rather insouciant pose.

'The landlady could have had an accomplice, Guv.'

Skelgill slings the spade over his shoulder and flashes his colleague a wry grin. DS Jones has understood the purpose of his experiment, and her thoughts have leapt ahead. He puts one foot into the hole.

'If you came here thinking digging a grave would be plain sailing you'd be disappointed. If you wanted to make it really deep – to minimise the risk of discovery – you'd need to know what you were doing – what tools you'd need – and allow plenty of time – maybe even prepare it in advance.'

'There'd be the risk of someone finding it, Guv.'

Skelgill looks about. In contrast to the coniferous woodland around the summit there is more undergrowth, a patchy herb-and-shrub layer that restricts visibility.

'Less so here, though, eh?'

DS Jones nods.

'The actual trench that the body's in, Guv – it isn't all that deep?'

Skelgill hops out of the hole and makes to retrace their steps.

'See what the boffins come up with.'

They walk in Indian file for half a minute. As they approach the camp bearded individuals are congregating at the tent designated for social purposes, pitched a respectful distance from the gazebo over the grave.

'Looks like it's time for their lunch break, Guv.'

'That makes us late for ours.'

While Skelgill returns the spade DS Jones checks her messages.

'Oh-oh.'

'What is it?'

'George on the front desk. As you foresaw, Guv – a reporter from the *Westmorland Gazette* has been asking what's going on in Harterhow Woods – how come the lane is closed.'

Skelgill tuts.

'Next thing some bright spark will be running pleasure trips across the lake for rubberneckers.'

DS Jones smiles; simultaneously she interrogates her inbox.

'We've got several promising names on the missing persons list.' Skelgill watches as she reads. She purses her lips; they look full and soft. Her hazel eyes become pensive. She glances up at Skelgill and catches him observing her. 'Perhaps I should head back and get onto this, Guv?'

'Aye, maybe.' Skelgill sounds momentarily disappointed; his eyes narrow. Then he inclines his head in agreement. 'Fair enough. You can drop me at Portinscale and I'll make a plan with Leyton. But you need to eat.'

DS Jones chuckles, and then she pats her taut midriff.

'I'll be fine, Guv – I'm still living off yesterday's sausages.'

*

'Sorry I'm late, Guv – bit of an issue at home early doors. Set me back all morning.'

Skelgill is accustomed to ignoring DS Leyton's protestations concerning matters domestic, on the grounds that hyperbole is inbuilt in proportion to the noise and disorder created by small unruly children.

'You should get yourself out first thing, Leyton – then you can't be roped in.'

DS Leyton looks uneasy, crestfallen in fact. It seems his boss is missing the underlying sentiment – and shows no inclination to ask what it might be – and that he himself feels unable to elaborate. He pulls out the chair opposite Skelgill and lowers himself down with a resigned groan.

'I had to take over the school run, Guv – it's a right old bun fight for parking spaces – flippin' ruthless those mums are – I pity the old lollipop lady, trying to keep 'em off the zigzags – like a pack of hyenas.'

Skelgill is regarding him rather blankly – but a young waitress approaches their table and pre-empts any response he might make. She seems a little overawed by Skelgill, though his reaction is oddly paternal.

'Same again I reckon, lass – times two.' The girl makes a little curtsey and backs away. Skelgill glances at DS Leyton, who is regarding him suspiciously. 'Some kind of cousin, once removed.'

DS Leyton forces a smile.

'You've got more contacts in your family than DI Smart has in his little black book, Guv – and that's saying something.'

'Aye – except I don't have to pay for information you can't trust.' Skelgill rubs his nose between the thumb and forefinger of his left hand – but if it has some implied meaning he lets it pass. 'Plus we get the staff discount here – that's another saving for the taxpayer.'

'Every little helps, Guv.'

Skelgill recognises his sergeant's platitude for what it is.

'How did you get on at the council?'

DS Leyton glances about, perhaps out of habit – but the café is patronised exclusively by well-to-do middle-aged and elderly couples occupied by carrot cake and cappuccinos, maps and guidebooks. There is subdued conversation and the polite clink of cutlery punctuated by the sporadic clatter of plates and pans from the kitchen. Notwithstanding he leans forward and lowers his voice a little. He pulls his notebook from inside his jacket, though he lays it aside on the table surface.

'I met with the officer for the Parks Department – by all accounts they're more stretched than we are.' (Skelgill scowls in disagreement, but holds his peace.) 'She didn't seem to know much about this Harterhow place at all, Guv. I reckon they're out of their depth with a nature reserve. She admits they ain't got the expertise – nor the budgets.'

'Someone must be in charge, Leyton. Surely they've got a management plan? Some kind of warden – park ranger?'

But DS Leyton shakes his head.

'Have you seen the size of the council offices, Guv? I've passed it times and not even noticed – I thought it was a pub. They're mainly responsible for what you'd call regular public parks – kiddies' swings and herbaceous borders and football pitches. There's a depot on the industrial estate near the pencil museum – where they store all their kit – tractor and trailer, mowers and line-markers and whatnot. All keys are kept there – there's a chain and padlock on the gate at the end of the lane that leads to Harterhow. If the emergency services needed access, they'd call the duty officer for the council.'

Skelgill looks unconvinced.

'Aye, there's a gate, alright. But beyond it's rough terrain. You'd want a tracked vehicle – or a *Defender* at a push – or you'd get nowhere. If there were a forest fire it would have to burn, Leyton.'

DS Leyton shrugs his broad shoulders.

'How do you get in on foot, Guv?'

'There's a stile beside the gate – dogs can just slip through – or there's a culvert beneath the wall.'

Skelgill's remark prompts DS Leyton to open his notebook.

'She did say that if we had an idea of dates she could check through their invoices – it might be possible to trace a subcontractor who's done some work – like repairing a wall or cutting down a dangerous tree.'

Skelgill's expression is one of doubt.

'How would they find out about that if there's no warden?'

DS Leyton raises an index finger, as if he has been holding back a more salient point.

'Apparently there's this local voluntary group, Guv. Keeps an eye on the place.' He consults a second page of his tidily written notes. 'Friends of Harterhow Hill.'

DS Leyton sounds rather formal, carefully pronouncing the initial 'H' of each word, going against the grain of his East London accent. Skelgill's frown deepens.

'Not *hill*, Leyton.'

'Come again, Guv?'

I doubt it's called "Friends of Harterhow Hill" – leastways not if they're proper locals. 'How' means hill – you don't need it twice – it's as daft as saying Lake Windermere.'

DS Leyton tries to look simultaneously interested and apologetic. His superior can be surprisingly pedantic for one so often disorganised.

'I'm just going by what she told me, Guv. There's a little committee – and they produce a newsletter. She gave me the secretary's phone number.' He turns the page. 'Lives in this neck of the woods. Want me to arrange to see him this afternoon?'

Skelgill does not reply at once – and now the food arrives – a bacon roll each, and tea in takeaway beakers. DS Leyton thanks the girl while Skelgill inspects the contents of his roll – a generous helping of streaky rashers – and reaches for the red sauce bottle.

'I'll tell you what, Leyton – we'll divide and conquer. You hop over to the B&B and get a full statement from the landlady – find out what happened to her ex if she doesn't volunteer it. I'll take your committee man.'

DS Leyton is again looking rather discomfited, though now the focus of his concern seems to be his lunchtime snack.

'Righto, Guv.' He sits back and folds his arms. 'To be honest, Guv – I've not got much of an appetite – I'll take the tea with me and get moving – if I could work through lunch and finish a bit earlier today it would help?'

'As you like, Leyton.'

DS Leyton is surprised by his superior's ready acquiescence. He tears out from his notebook the page with the telephone number.

'I'll email you all the notes, Guv.'

Skelgill is already tucking two-handed into his roll, and gives a cursory nod. As DS Leyton rises and turns away, he frees a hand and draws his sergeant's forsaken plate alongside his own.

31

5. COOT & FOX

'I didn't hear your car, Inspector – you gave me a right old fright.'

Archibald Coot leans to look past Skelgill and he seems perplexed that the curving driveway of the secluded cottage is empty; but Skelgill does not trouble to explain that a few minutes on foot has brought him to this leafy lane south of Portinscale. In fact he is processing the man's accent – it is not pronounced, but the vowels in *right* and *fright* suggest Merseyside. In appearance there is something hunched and gnome like – amplified in his manner, which is slow and unblinking. He is a little below average height, a little tubby, and largely hairless, a trait that extends to the absence of eyebrows. His complexion is noticeably pink, his skin almost opaque, and small watery blue eyes are subsidiary in a round face dominated by fleshy lips and a bulbous nose. His attire is that of the retiree – grey polyester trousers and a maroon pullover – but also a shade formal for regular indoor wear, in that he sports black slip-on shoes and a check shirt with an unevenly knotted tie: indeed he looks ready to attend a meeting of the crown green bowls club.

'You had better come in, then, Inspector.'

Skelgill's silence seems to unnerve the man, who shuffles backwards to admit him, before fastening the door and making a strange lurching dart to lead the way into a modestly sized beamed sitting room midway along the low-ceilinged hallway. Skelgill's first impression is of a certain fustiness mixed with cooking smells (possibly cabbage), but he finds respite in lush green foliage that presses up to the flank of the cottage, visible through small mullioned windows on either side of an exposed slate chimney breast. The room is accordingly shady, and to his surprise a tall angular man seems to rise out of nowhere – but in reality from a wing-backed chair in the corner to his right.

'This is our chairman, Inspector.'

The second man waits rather self-importantly, as if he is expecting Skelgill to come forward and shake hands, but Skelgill simply holds his ground, creating an awkward stand-off. Indeed

Skelgill stares belligerently – his appointment was with the secretary, who has apparently taken it upon himself to invite this 'colleague'. The latter is roughly of an age with Archibald Coot – Skelgill would guess early sixties – though he presents a clear contrast in appearance: short-cropped grizzled gingery hair and beard, a stretched narrow face with pointed chin and nose, and beady brown eyes that peer from behind thick horn-rimmed spectacles. His attire, however, is of the same smart-casual genre, characteristic of the generation. Archibald Coot meanwhile begins to bow fussily from one to the other, uncertain of what to do next. Eventually he gestures with an outstretched hand by way of introduction.

'Mr Lester Fox, Inspector.'

The taller man is immediately prompted to speak.

'That's *L-e-s-t-e-r*.'

This might almost be a reflex reaction to the sound of his name, but Skelgill only scowls – as if to suggest why should he think otherwise? However, the man seems to be anticipating some quip, and is disconcerted when it does not come. Archibald Coot makes more fussing movements, and humming sounds, and then he reaches to pat the back of a small chesterfield sofa that faces the fireplace.

'Why don't you have a seat, Inspector Skelgill?'

Rather than wait for Skelgill to settle he scuttles around to occupy a single chair on the left of the hearth, leaving Skelgill no option but the chesterfield. Skelgill looks disgruntled, suspecting he is being deliberately positioned where one can surreptitiously observe him whenever he addresses the other. Moreover he senses something unnatural about their manner. Neither appears to be surprised by his visit, neither has yet asked him what it is all about. And both exhibit a demeanour that he has witnessed many times in court – when the jury files back in and the accused anticipates its verdict with an expression of resigned inevitability.

Consequently Skelgill is swiftly reassessing what to tell them. As things stand the 'murder' has not been announced. A press conference is presently scheduled for 11am tomorrow, subject to developments as regards missing persons, and the forensic investigation. While, of course, he has no reason to suspect their involvement, there is something in the nature of his reception that cautions him about being overly candid. Rather ponderously he lowers himself into the centre of the sofa, and stares with mild interest at the tall-fronted wrought iron cup dogs that support a decorative summer pyramid of pine logs in the hearth. Then he turns casually to Lester Fox, who has now resumed his seat.

'Yesterday afternoon on Harterhow a dog walker came across human remains.'

Lester Fox reacts with the tiniest of jolts; a tremor that would be all but imperceptible had it not found its outlet as a twitch of his feet. Skelgill's gaze falls upon the man's footwear – carpet slippers – curious that he has brought them along for this meeting. Almost simultaneously there is a release of breath from Archibald Coot – which he tries to disguise as a nondescript mumble. It is plain to Skelgill that both men have responded to the news with some trepidation.

Lester Fox is first to compose himself. He folds his hands upon his lap and tilts his head to one side. It strikes Skelgill as the sort of thoughtful pose he would adopt in his capacity as chairman of the committee.

'Is this a find of archaeological significance? There are well-documented Iron Age ground formations – rock-cut ditches and artificial hut platforms, over towards Catbells.'

His accent carries the same regional brogue as that of Archibald Coot – but he takes more care with his enunciation. Skelgill glances at Archibald Coot. He is nodding enthusiastically, as though impressed by his colleague's suggestion.

Skelgill frowns disdainfully.

'I don't think I'd be knocking on your door if it were. The body was buried under a year ago.'

'Buried!' Archibald Coot's exclamation draws a withering look from Lester Fox. 'Y-you mean there's been a *m-murder*, Inspector?'

Skelgill folds his arms – he is irked by having to check constantly from side to side.

'It's looking that way.' He glowers at each in turn. 'You didn't know?'

Lester Fox appears defiant. Archibald Coot is alarmed. Skelgill's tone becomes more conciliatory.

'You weren't aware we've got a scene of crime team operating on the hill?'

Archibald Coot shakes his head with some vigour. Lester Fox remains circumspect; it is he that replies.

'Despite our 'professional' involvement,' (he makes inverted commas with long bony fingers) 'we can't keep abreast of everything that is going on – far from it. Our function is as much administrative as practical.'

Now Archibald Coot is nodding in agreement. Skelgill addresses him pointedly.

'What exactly do you do?'

The secretary looks flustered, but his chairman comes to his aid.

'Fetch a newsletter, Coot.'

The man pushes himself to his feet and obediently trots over to an antique bureau that was hidden by the door as they entered. He lowers the hinged lid – Skelgill gets a glimpse of two ranks of narrow pigeon holes, and it is from one of these that Archibald Coot extracts an item of paperwork.

'There you go, Inspector – this is our latest issue, ready for distribution – the Summer edition.'

Skelgill accepts the proffered bulletin. He scowls rather disparagingly – a response, it appears, to the poor quality of the production – though it is merely his chronic antipathy to the printed word. Nevertheless, it is an amateurish piece – at odds with Lester Fox's assertion – a sheet of A4 paper folded to make a rudimentary four-page A5 circular. An untrained hand has clumsily juxtaposed photographs and text, embellished with clashing typefaces for the headlines.

Skelgill turns the leaflet over in his hands, making a cursory examination. The masthead – much to his dismay –

reads "Friends of Harterhow Hill" – and he hesitates grim-faced, fighting the urge to take them to task. The front page seems to comprise a clichéd reprise of *Swallows and Amazons* (peculiar, since Arthur Ransome's fabulous tale was set on a fictionalised Windermere, not nearby Derwentwater). The back cover carries a section entitled, "Notes from the Chair" and is signed off by none other than "Lester Fox, BSc". The inside spread features on the left an anonymous "Guest Article" entitled "Lakeland Legends" and on the right a "Regular Feature" entitled "Spring Bird Report" attributed to "MM". Skelgill flaps the leaflet in the direction of Archibald Coot.

'So how does it work – Friends of Harterhow?' He cannot bring himself to say the superfluous word "hill".

To his irritation it is Lester Fox that again answers.

'In much the same way as any friends group.'

Skelgill glares at the chairman.

'I can't say I'm familiar with such things.'

In fact Skelgill is being more than a little disingenuous, for his mountain rescue team has a vital friends contingent, people that for various reasons cannot be active on the fells, but provide invaluable help in fundraising and at promotional events.

'We are a registered charity.' (Archibald Coot makes affirmative humming noises.) 'We can advise local groups who may wish to use the Hill – we can organise guided walks, for instance – and we promote the benefits to the wider public.'

Skelgill is looking sceptical – this has the ring of a well-rehearsed homily.

'So how would I find out about you?'

With an imperious wave of the hand, Lester Fox now passes the buck to Archibald Coot. The secretary lunges forward and jabs an index finger at the leaflet that Skelgill holds.

'You can pick up our newsletter at various places – such as the Town Hall – and the Moot Hall, the tourist office, you know?'

Skelgill notices that there are miniscule beads of sweat, almost invisible, coating the translucent skin of Archibald Coot's domed skull.

'What about a website?'

Now Lester Fox produces a distinctly patronising laugh.

'That would be a rather unsuitable medium for people of our target age group.'

Skelgill looks unconvinced; but it is not his job to persuade them otherwise.

'Have you got a list of members?'

Skelgill is looking at Lester Fox, but out of the corner of his eye he detects that Archibald Coot fidgets uncomfortably. Lester Fox rests his forearms upon his thighs and entwines his fingers, leaning forward in an avuncular manner.

'We don't offer membership, as such, Inspector – it would be an unnecessary administrative expense – and, you see, Harterhow Local Nature Reserve is public property; being a member would not confer any special rights of access.'

Skelgill has begun to gnaw at a thumbnail and look rather bored. He seems to be arriving at the conclusion that this is a tin-pot organisation, its troopless generals – Lester Fox in particular – revelling in their pompous titles. He taps the leaflet twice with the back of his hand.

'What about this – your bird report – who's "MM"?'

Skelgill suspects that MM does not exist – and further that they also pen the "Guest Article" – but to his surprise, and to Lester Fox's evident annoyance, Archibald Coot blurts out an answer.

'That's Marvin.'

Skelgill fixes his stare upon him.

'Marvin.'

'Yes, Inspector – Marvin Morgan – he's a local birdwatcher – well, naturalist, really – he's quite an expert.'

Skelgill puts down the leaflet on the seat cushion beside him and folds his arms.

'And is this Mr Morgan a regular, out on the hill?'

Archibald Coot nods – but now Lester Fox interjects.

'You might say Marvin is our eyes and ears.'

Skelgill nods distractedly – he is thinking that the "eyes and ears" has not yet reported back the presence of police on Harterhow – either that, or he has failed to notice them.

'Is he on your committee?'

Archibald Coot, under Skelgill's renewed scrutiny, shakes his head.

'He publishes a blog – on the internet – with photographs and videos.'

The reply is oblique, but Skelgill joins the dots and concludes that this is the source of their information.

'Where can I contact him?'

The men exchange glances – it could be alarm, or uncertainty – but Archibald Coot feels obliged to answer.

'He lives at Overside – it's very convenient for Harterhow Hill.'

Skelgill again rails at the tautology – though they must have no idea why he grimaces – they may speculate that it is stomach cramps.

'What about a phone number?'

Archibald Coot shakes his head.

'But it's the only property – along the forestry track after the sharp left-hand bend. It's called How Cottage.'

Abruptly Skelgill jumps up and strides to the door. A puzzled Archibald Coot stumbles to his feet.

'Inspector – are you looking for the –?'

However, Skelgill seems perfectly in control.

'We'll need formal statements from you gents – in due course.'

Lester Fox makes no attempt to rise, and Skelgill exits the room without a farewell. By now Archibald Coot is shambling after him and catches him up at the front door. Skelgill suddenly makes an empty-handed gesture.

'I left your leaflet.'

'Oh dear – hold on, I shall fetch it for you, Inspector.'

The older man turns and hustles away.

The instant he is alone Skelgill picks up a small pile of envelopes from a sideboard. He leafs through them, his eyes narrowed. But when a couple of seconds later Archibald Coot emerges from the sitting room brandishing the bulletin the mail is back in its place and Skelgill is politely viewing a framed picture that hangs above the dresser. Nodding with satisfaction, he bends forward, his hands clasped behind his back in the manner of a visitor to an art gallery. It is a Victorian-style cartoon illustration, in which a fox has evidently attempted to prey upon a waterfowl – a black bird with a white bill and white frontal shield – but unsuccessfully so, for the outsmarted fox is immersed up to his nose in the millpond, while the bird – a coot – circles triumphantly.

Archibald Coot emits a rather embarrassed chuckle. Pink-cheeked, he hands over the newsletter. Skelgill absently folds it into a pocket; he scrutinises the stone-flagged floor in the immediate vicinity of the door.

'You don't have a dog, then?'

'No, Inspector, we don't.'

Skelgill gives a casual inclination of his head. Archibald Coot once more seems unnerved. He glances down the hallway, and then bows towards Skelgill. His voice is lowered.

'Are we suspects?'

Skelgill grins.

'No more than I am.'

With this he takes his leave. As the front door closes behind him, Skelgill cocks an ear – for raised voices begin to emanate from the thick slate walls of the quaint cottage.

6. PRESS CONFERENCE I – Wednesday

'You're missing the star turn, Skel.'

'What?'

Skelgill glowers at DI Alec Smart's jaunty approach. Skelgill is arriving via the back entrance, the way in from the car park. He lets the door swing to behind him rather than wait and hold it for his fellow inspector. DI Smart appears undaunted by Skelgill's inhospitable manner.

'Our Emma's got those old hacks wrapped round her little finger.' Now he leers salaciously. 'Or maybe it's the miniskirt they're drooling over.'

Skelgill's expression darkens. Above DI Smart's proprietorial attitude towards DS Jones looms a more immediate cloud of doom: somehow, he is late. DI Smart plainly revels in his discomfort. Skelgill's mouth is dry and his voice cracks as he speaks.

'The press conference doesn't start until eleven.'

DI Smart smirks and glances casually at his expensive wristwatch. He flashes Skelgill the sort of knowing look that says, "Nice try – but it's obvious that you're wrong." Then he shrugs indifferently.

'She was in full flow last time I looked – the Chief's in there – and your Cockney oppo – go and see for yourself, cock – it's standing room only.'

Skelgill glares past DI Smart, and then takes a step forwards. DI Smart occupies the centre of the narrow corridor; he sways to his right but Skelgill in the same instant veers to his left – and for a moment there is the prospect of a bout of pavement dancing – but only for a moment: Skelgill lowers a shoulder into his antagonist and barges him out of the way.

'Sake!'

DI Smart's protest is in vain – for Skelgill storms off without a backward glance or gesture of apology. DI Smart watches him and a cunning grin slowly spreads across his chiselled countenance. He straightens the lapels of his designer jacket and reaches inside for his cigarettes, and saunters from the building.

*

So she's a police officer. A detective. She looks too young to be a sergeant – DS Emma Jones – that's how she was introduced by the top brass (another woman, older, red hair tied back, and armour-piercing ice-blue eyes that show no mercy – a latter-day Boudica, *hah-ha).* 'Emma' on the other hand could almost be French, with her nicely sculpted cheekbones, strong features, shoulder-length hair that's a kind of streaky golden honey colour. There's not so much to see of her now they're all seated on the stage. The TV cameras are concentrating on close-ups. But when the police filed in she caused a bit of a stir. The room went quiet – the journalists are obviously more used to characters like the overweight male officer in the ill-fitting suit.

Marvin Morgan reaches for his mug from the kitchen table and scrapes his chair nearer to the small television set on the worktop. He keeps his gaze fixed on the screen. She's made her opening statement and there's about to be a Q&A – the TV crew have got a microphone on a long boom. The local radio said there was going to be an announcement – when he'd heard mention of 'Harterhow' his ears had pricked up. That's why he's tuned in. So – the body of a woman has been found. By a dog walker who is not suspected of any involvement. Buried since maybe September, they say. Caucasian. Aged about 50. Height between five foot two and five foot four. Long dark brown hair. Wore two rings on each hand. Had a lot of work done on her front teeth. Funny how they always home in on the teeth. Wait – here comes the first question.

'How was she killed?'

'At this stage we don't know. However there is no indication of a trauma injury to the skull, or of broken bones.'

'What about stabbing, strangulation?'

'The state of decay means that any soft tissue damage will be difficult to ascertain. We are presently running tests for alien substances. There will be a comprehensive post mortem as soon as the remains can be transferred to the pathology lab.'

'How do you know it's not just some walker who's sprained an ankle – had a coronary?'

This elicits a cynical murmur of agreement from the audience. But she's not flustered, is she?

'The body was buried in a shallow grave that entailed the cutting of tree roots.'

Now there's a silence. Marvin Morgan licks his lips. He takes a careful sip of his tea; it is still too hot and he has to inhale simultaneously. The questions are coming from different journalists, but the director is choosing to focus upon the young female officer.

'So it's definitely a murder?'

'At this stage we have to treat the death as suspicious.'

'Aren't there bloodstains – on the clothing?'

'There is no clothing.'

This revelation causes a small frisson amongst the assembled reporters. The word 'naked' must be being hastily written on pads and tablets, added to 'decay' and 'corpse' and 'grave' and putative headline combinations tried out.

'What leads have you got?'

The young detective does not waver or look to her colleagues for support.

'As you would expect we are following several lines of inquiry. At this stage what is most important is to identify the deceased. She probably went missing between September and Christmas – she is somebody's mother, sister, daughter, wife or partner – we appeal to you to make this request of the general public – particularly if they know of someone who travelled to the Lake District around that time and did not return as planned.'

'So you have reason to believe she was not a local woman?'

'As you may be aware we get over 16 million visitors a year to the National Park – compared to a resident population of 40,000 and half a million in Cumbria. Statistically a visitor is more likely. Moreover, our initial investigations into persons listed as missing have not revealed a local match.'

'What about someone who's *not* been reported as missing?'

The young officer maintains her composure. Marvin Morgan watches unblinkingly as the camera zooms in closer.

'That remains a possibility – and again we would ask the public if such circumstances – someone they have not seen since the autumn – in conjunction with the description of this lady – might jog a memory – of a neighbour not seen in the last six-to-nine months – or perhaps a dog walker who is no longer taking their usual route.'

'Why do you say dog walker? You said the dog walker who found the body isn't implicated.'

'I give that as an example – there are many instances where people are acquainted by sight but not by name – shopkeepers, for instance, where a regular customer has stopped coming, or members of a society or social group.'

'Did she have a dog – the victim?'

'There's nothing to suggest she had a dog.'

'But isn't it a popular dog-walking spot?'

'I wouldn't say popular – it's quite inaccessible.'

'But someone could have been attacked while walking their dog.'

The officer just narrows her eyes slightly. Marvin Morgan shifts in his seat – the newsperson is angling for a scaremongering story. *"Maniac Stalker Buries Naked Dog Walker."* But the young detective sergeant is equal to the question.

'We have reason to believe the victim did not meet her death at Harterhow.'

'So the body was taken there? And buried?'

'Yes.'

'How do you know?'

'We'll be releasing more information once the forensic examination is complete. At this stage we stress that we don't believe there is any threat to the public associated with

Harterhow Local Nature Reserve – and bear in mind the victim died many months ago.'

Now there is a slight pause. Marvin Morgan rubs the two-day-old stubble on his chin; something tells him he ought to shave this morning, straighten a few things up. Now another correspondent has gained the attention of the boom operator – it is a more youthful-sounding voice. Unlike his predecessors he introduces himself.

'Kendall Minto – *Westmorland Gazette*. What do you say to the rumour that this was drugs-related? Some kind of revenge killing?'

For the first time the young woman glances to her senior officer, but although the camera pulls back it isn't quick enough to catch the latter's reaction. There is a rumble of discontent among the old hacks: that some cub reporter has a tip they don't. The sergeant moves quickly to head off the idea before it gains traction.

'We don't suspect any such connection. The profile of the deceased makes that extremely unlikely.'

The journalist has a follow-up question ready.

'Is it true that the corpse had been mutilated?'

Marvin shifts uneasily in his chair as he sees the senior officer glare at the questioner. Too right, you wouldn't want her on your case. The hubbub increases and the director cuts away to the agitator. He is seated near the rear of the pressroom; he has boyish good looks though he is probably mid-twenties, wearing a fashionable collarless leather jacket, his expression confident. Marvin Morgan presses an index finger against the screen – however it is not the journalist that he pinpoints – but a person standing at the back of the room – it's him! The 'boyfriend'. He knows it's him – he couldn't mistake the roughhewn features and unkempt hair. So – is he a reporter, too – or is he in the police, like the girl?

The top brass woman begins to speak and it's clear they're not about to answer this question directly. She says that's all they've got time for today – they'll schedule another press conference as soon as they have new information. She thanks them for their help and appeals for good coverage – well, they're already getting it on the telly, aren't they? Just as the three police officers are gathering their papers, the voice of the young journalist pipes up again. He still has the attention of the roving mike.

'I'll be burning the midnight oil – if there's late news you want to disseminate.' The director cuts back to him. He's now standing. Behind him Marvin can see the 'boyfriend-journalist-cop' (or whatever he is) – his expression is like thunder. The young correspondent's face is creased by an impertinent grin. Now he calls out. 'Detective Sergeant Jones – just say the word – your place or mine.'

There is a ripple of laughter among the journalists, most of whom are male, and probably a chauvinistic bunch, Marvin thinks. The director switches back to the police – they are leaving the raised platform with their documents tucked under their arms. But the young detective sergeant, rather than ignore the heckler turns and responds. She is too far away from the desk microphones – and perhaps she knows this – but the background effects microphone picks up her rejoinder:

'Both – you go to yours and I'll go to mine.'

There is a much louder burst of laughter as this put-down registers – but Marvin notices that as she exits she casts a sympathetic glance in the direction of the reporter. Marvin's breathing rate has increased. *What about Emma coming to his place?*

*

'Cor blimey, Guv – this girl played a blinder!'

'Just as well, Leyton – with a stuffed dummy sitting beside her.'

Skelgill, already installed behind his desk as his sergeants enter his office, has a tea from the nearby machine; he holds it rather broodingly at arm's length on the surface. DS Leyton winces theatrically in the face of Skelgill's slight, but DS Jones lowers her eyes as she settles by the window. Skelgill glares at the world in general.

'What's her ladyship doing changing the time – and nobody lets me know?'

Now DS Jones looks up from the papers on her lap. She and DS Leyton exchange meaningful glances. They would be correct to suspect Skelgill's frustration will be channelled into making their inadvertent complicity an act of wilful subordination. DS Jones gives a nervous cough.

'She only gave us ten minutes' warning, Guv. Her secretary told us that a senior contact in the BBC had offered to get the press conference broadcast live on the News Channel if we went half an hour early. The secretary rang round and got all the media guys to come in at short notice. We tried your mobile, Guv.'

Now Skelgill grimaces at his handset, which lies discarded upon a stack of *Angling Times* newspapers that occupy his in-tray. He has forgotten to switch it back on, having earlier desired not to be disturbed.

'Aye, well – happen the battery's knackered.'

DS Jones leans forward a little.

'We said you were at Harterhow, Guv – there'd obviously be no chance of getting here in time.'

Skelgill reacts with faint softening of his expression. DS Leyton seizes the opportunity of further mollification.

'If I'm being honest I was brickin' myself, Guv – in case the Chief asked me to take the lead – but I reckon she guessed Emma would have read all the reports. *Hah!*' His laugh is self-deprecating.

DS Leyton has up his sleeve the knowledge that his superior would be equally uncomfortable in the hot seat. Apart from likely *not* having read all the reports, Skelgill is a fish out of water when it comes to quick-witted banter – and pressurised by what he would regard as a "parasitic naysaying layabout" of a journalist, he is prone to flounder and respond by thumping the unfortunate questioner (or, at least, making it plain that is what he would like to do). To this extent, much of his anger this morning is directed at his own inadequacy. The reality is, circumstances have probably done him a favour – just that he does not want to admit it. DS Leyton presses home the small advantage for the benefit of world peace.

'Turns out the Chief was right – made your team look good, Guv.'

Skelgill scowls as he slurps from his tea. His expression may or may not reflect upon the quality of the machine beverage; accordingly, DS Jones recognises an opening.

'Shall I get some fresh-brewed from the canteen, Guv?'

Skelgill nods, rather grudgingly it must be said, and she slips away, flashing an unseen (by Skelgill) smile at DS Leyton.

'She's a natural, Guv – gives her a nice little leg up on the career ladder – the Chief seeing her in action like that. She knows how to dodge a question – and they'll think twice about heckling her again.'

Skelgill regards DS Leyton pensively as he digests his sergeant's observations – though the outcome does not appear to please him any better.

'I take it the Chief blocked any mention of the dismemberment?' He scratches his temples with the nails of both hands, as if the sensation of biting midges suddenly revisits him. 'And cause of death.'

And now for a moment DS Leyton becomes distracted – but he gives a little jolt and replies.

'She said the priority has to be getting an ID – to focus on the description of the live person, Guv – in the hope that someone will recognise her.'

Skelgill gnaws at a thumbnail.

'Aye – but we'd get twice the splash – it's the blood and gore that gets folk talking.'

DS Leyton frowns reflectively.

'You know the Chief, Guv – she ain't happy when it looks like things are out of control on her watch. She soon put a stop to proceedings when that little twerp from the *Gazette* started asking about drugs – I mean, where did that come from?'

'Smart.'

'How's that, Guv?' To DS Leyton's ears this is a contradictory adverb.

'Alec Smart – he'll have that hack in his pocket. Pound to a penny he put him up to that question. Let's just rock the boat, eh? Get the Chief thinking we're flailing about. Never mind her watch – what about my patch.'

'Don't you reckon she'd see through that, Guv?'

Skelgill makes a disparaging growl.

'Have you heard Smart when he's with the Chief? Butter wouldn't melt in his mouth, Leyton. What's worse, she laps it up – beats me why.'

Now it is DS Leyton's turn to exclaim.

'Maybe he knows something he oughtn't, Guv. He told me the other day what I was having for dinner – I got home and stone the crows he was right!' DS Leyton absently brushes back his mop of dark hair from his brow. 'Then the missus remembered some shifty character chatting her up at the butcher's counter in the supermarket.'

Skelgill is looking agitated, but at this juncture DS Jones re-enters bearing steaming mugs upon a tray. She distributes the drinks and settles down in her place. It is DS Leyton that joins her into the conversation.

'Guvnor reckons it was DI Smart that tipped that local journo off – and him acting all innocent and pumping George about the lane being closed.'

DS Jones momentarily bites her lower lip; she looks a little unconvinced. She seems to be making up her mind whether or not to respond.

'I was at school with him – he was in the year below – he was a chancer back then, thought he was God's gift.'

DS Leyton chuckles.

'So it's not the first time you've used that put-down on him, eh, girl?'

DS Jones forces a grin.

'Something like that.'

Skelgill is looking increasing unhappy with the direction of this thread. He deposits his mug with a clunk and extravagantly throws himself back against his sprung chair.

'So, what's happened to our promising leads?'

DS Jones regards him earnestly.

'We're still sifting through the Missing Persons Bureau list – it is producing some names nationwide – but for Cumbria there are fewer than ten females who have been gone for more than six months – and only three of those roughly match the profile. Two have turned up alive and no one has bothered to notify us.' She raises her eyebrows and spreads her hands in an exasperated gesture. 'The third we're trying to get more information from Social Services – they submitted the report.'

'How about DNA?'

'The samples from the deceased are with the lab – provided they get a successful extraction they should be able to run a cross-check against the national database no later than tomorrow.' Pensively DS Jones brushes a strand of hair from her cheek. It seems she still harbours reservations. 'There's a low likelihood that she'll be on the database – but a chance that it will throw up a familial relationship through which we can identify her. And the possibility that it would lead us directly to her killer.'

Skelgill is obliged to nod – even he can recite the broad statistics: most murdered females are victims of someone they know – and though the majority suffer at the hands of a partner or former partner, a quarter are killed by a relative. That some lengths have been gone to in concealing the body adds weight to DS Jones's prognosis. If the murderer happens to be a relative *and* a former offender, a DNA sample from the dead woman may well catch him. Skelgill, however, is reluctant to pin any hopes on such a straightforward outcome.

'How about the rings?'

'Again we're waiting for feedback, Guv. The lab has finished with them – detailed photographs have been sent to the Assay Office in Birmingham. We should have a top-line report this afternoon and some specialist feedback by close of play tomorrow.'

'No inscriptions on the inside?'

She shakes her head.

'Just hallmarks – but the rings are quite elaborate – and the four together make a distinctive combination – the sort of thing you'd notice if you knew the wearer – a unique identifier really.'

Skelgill is examining his own hands – ringless – although maybe it is something about their coarse texture that prompts a change of tack.

'Leyton – the landlady.'

DS Leyton looks up slowly, and has to rouse himself from some daydream that has evidently crept upon him.

'Guv?'

'June Collins – how did you get on?'

'Oh, right, Guv – she, er – she fancies herself as a bit of a dolly bird.' He glances apprehensively at DS Jones to check he has not offended her sensibilities, but she appears unperturbed – his assessment is sincere. He fishes out his notebook, but does not consult it immediately. 'Interrupted her drying her hair – bit odd for the middle of the afternoon – and nearly choked me with her perfume.'

Skelgill is watching his sergeant through narrowed eyes. He senses DS Jones is now looking at him, but he keeps his gaze fixed on DS Leyton. However he does not comment, and so DS Leyton continues.

'I took a more detailed statement about her visit to Harterhow. She reckons she walks her dog there about once a month. Proper little horror – bit me flippin' ankle, soon as I walked in.' DS Jones can't suppress an involuntary giggle, while DS Leyton shrugs resignedly, as if he knows this fate is reserved for him, some inexplicable karma. 'She has a regular circuit around the hill – saves climbing over the top.' Now DS Leyton hums to himself, approving of this method. 'Says the dog wanders off into the bushes, but generally keeps within earshot. This time it didn't come back and she thought it was stuck down a foxhole – an *earth*?' He looks to Skelgill who gives a little nod of expert confirmation. 'But she could hear it snuffling and that's when she saw the skeleton – she's still upset by that, but who can blame her – out for a nice stroll in the woods and there's a set of Hampsteads grinning up at you?'

Skelgill seems unmoved either by the rhetorical question or his sergeant's obscure rhyming slang, and nods for DS Leyton to carry on.

'You know the rest, obviously, Guv – seems like you made an impression on her.' Now the sergeant grins a little sheepishly, for he is familiar with the details of Skelgill's first encounter. He consults his notebook. 'As for background, she moved to Keswick from Liverpool five years ago. She had her own beauty salon – suppose that explains the looks – came and stayed at the B&B one Easter, and it was for sale – so she fancied the idea and bought it. Been there ever since. Unmarried and no kids – seems to like what she's doing – she's obviously making a go of it – tidy little place.'

'What about the ex-partner?'

'Yeah – I asked about him, like you said, Guv. Spencer Fazakerley, name of.' DS Leyton lowers his notebook onto his lap and leans forward. 'Reading between the lines, I'd wager he's done one.'

'Aye?'

'Well – couple of times she said they'd split by "mutual agreement" – I always think when someone tells you that it means they've had the old heave-ho.' He glances at DS Jones and she responds with a nod of encouragement. 'Seems she met him when he came and stayed at the guesthouse – turns out he was a bit of a handyman – fixed some plumbing – cut a long story short, he ended up getting his feet under the table. That was four years ago – and he slung his hook in the autumn – October, November time.'

DS Jones is alert to the possible significance of this date, and looks inquiringly at Skelgill. He appears less interested, however.

'Where did he go?'

'She claims not to know – she had to chase him up about some outstanding bill and his mobile number didn't work any more. Reckons he's from the Liverpool area, and that he might have gone back there. He was a long-distance trucker – freelance. He'd be away most weeks, three or four days at a time.' Now DS Leyton regards Skelgill apprehensively. 'Want me to organise some background checks, Guv?'

But Skelgill is also hesitant, his features somewhat corrugated. 'We can't get sidetracked harassing everyone who might have been to Harterhow – the Chief won't buy that.' He takes a drink of tea and waits while it has some lubricating effect. 'Just top-line, Leyton – in case he's got any form.'

DS Leyton looks relieved and nods.

'She seems happy enough without him, Guv – the place looks spick and span – wish my paintwork was in as good nick. Reckon she can afford to pay local tradesmen. She had her 'no vacancies' sign in the window – and a punter turned up just as I was leaving – she shoved him and his suitcase in the sitting room – said he'd come early – poor geezer looked a bit embarrassed – must have thought I was a hotel inspector, what with me taking notes and her acting all proper, like.'

Skelgill remains pensive.

'Anything strike you about her as odd?'

DS Leyton is more accustomed to Skelgill's straight shooting, and adept at dodging unfriendly fire. He makes a show of racking his brains via an assortment of facial contortions.

'Only what I've said, Guv – about her being a bit of a dolly bird – but there's no law against –' For a second he pauses and then he raises an index finger. 'There was one thing, Guv – as she showed me out she asked if you'd be seeing her.'

'What did you say?'

'I kept it vague – explained we never could tell if we'd need to interview a person again.' Now DS Leyton becomes a little reticent. 'Thing is, Guv – then she said you'd offered to walk her dog for her.'

Skelgill looks genuinely perplexed – although from his subordinates' perspective it could be a well-practised expression of denial. DS Leyton feels obliged to elaborate, lest their superior's evident discomfort becomes reflected upon him.

'I just wondered, Guv – maybe there's something she wants to tell you – that she didn't like to say to me?'

Skelgill scowls at his sergeant.

'Why would that be?'

'I dunno, Guv – but, since you found her in the woods – sort of rescued her – maybe she just feels more at ease.' (Skelgill is glaring rather belligerently.) 'Just the impression I got, Guv.'

Skelgill leans back and folds his arms.

'Happen I'll cross paths with her anyway.'

There is a small hiatus, and this becomes extended as DS Leyton receives a text message, which uncharacteristically he opens in the meeting. After a moment he looks up, blinking as though he is surprised to find himself with his colleagues.

'Sorry, Guv – just the missus.' He is plainly distracted, and looses off a question to Skelgill. 'How about you, Guv – how did it go with that secretary geezer?'

It would not come as any great shock to Skelgill's team to discover that he actually went to recce the fishing on Derwentwater. However, his response dispels any such latent cynicism.

'*Geezers*, Leyton.'

Both sergeants now look on with interest.

'I gave the secretary ten minutes' notice, and in that time he managed to invite the chairman to the interview. Messrs Coot and Fox. They come as a pair.'

DS Leyton makes an exclamation.

'Blimey, Guv – sounds like *The Wind in the Willows* – I was only reading that last night – one of the nippers was having a job getting to sleep.'

Skelgill declines to become diverted by his sergeant's domestic travails.

'Appears they live together – which explains the other one being on hand. I reckon it's just a little hobby they've cooked up to keep themselves busy. Not the outdoor sort – no dogs – no boots in the hall – they more or less admitted they don't go out on the hill. Look like they've drawn their slippers as well as their pensions.' He runs his fingers through his hair. 'I got the feeling they were expecting a visit from the law – but a body was a bit more than they bargained for.'

Skelgill is of the view that most folk have a skeleton or two in their closets and become uneasy in the presence of the police. Accordingly he is wary of reading too much into a person's reaction; he might be asking about a bloody murder, when all they can think of is the untaxed car with a bald tyre parked outside. He swills the last of his tea around in his mug and swallows it in one.

'This newsletter they produce – there's a birdwatcher they get their information from – lives in a cottage at the back of Harterhow – Marvin Morgan.'

DS Jones sits forward.

'Someone you know, Guv?'

Skelgill shakes his head.

'Doesn't ring a bell.'

'What are you thinking, Guv?'

Skelgill repeats the words of chairman Lester Fox.

'They called him their "eyes and ears" – happen he ought to be more observant than most. He might have seen something that could help us.' However, it is with an unreasonable degree of expectation that he fixes his gaze upon DS Jones. 'But first we need this date nailed down.'

DS Jones makes a brave face of it.

'I'm confident by this time tomorrow we'll be getting closer, Guv. I plan to see Dr Herdwick this afternoon – to stress the importance.'

Skelgill notices that DS Leyton is again glancing at his phone and simultaneously yawning.

'Leyton – if we're boring you –'

DS Leyton jolts and looks rather flustered.

'Sorry, Guv – if you don't mind there's just a couple of things I need to sort.' He rises and looks to his superior for permission to leave the meeting. 'I'll get on and run that check on the Fazakerley cove.'

Skelgill shrugs and DS Leyton takes this as consent. He departs and closes the door – but almost immediately it reopens

– however it is not the returning sergeant, but the wily features of DI Alec Smart framed in the narrow gap.

'Nice one, Emma – showed a few old stagers a thing or two.' Pointedly he switches his leer from an embarrassed-looking DS Jones to an irate-looking Skelgill, and then again to DS Jones. 'If you want any tips on early promotion – you know where to come.' He taps the side of his nose and then swiftly pulls away, winking at Skelgill. He closes the door and is gone before Skelgill can summon a retort.

DS Jones looks discomfited on behalf of her superior: that DI Smart has cleverly fired off a little barbed compliment and made a hasty retreat. She gathers her papers and rises, perhaps deciding that to leave is the most diplomatic course.

'I'll chase Dr Herdwick, Guv – get back to you as soon as I can.'

Skelgill does not reply, and indeed sits obdurately with his arms folded as DS Jones opens his office door. It is only when she is halfway out that he calls her back.

'Jones.'

'Guv?'

Skelgill's expression is at once pained and appreciative.

'That press conference – well done, lass.'

7. MARVIN MORGAN

'Mr Morgan?'
'Yes?'
'DI Skelgill, Cumbria CID.'
'Oh.'
'May I come in?'

The man pays particular attention to Skelgill's warrant card, and leans forward to read it; he might be short sighted – or perhaps he has never seen one before and now takes his opportunity. Skelgill is struck by his facial appearance: closely shaved receding hair, dark crescent brows that meet above a hooked nose, prominent cheekbones, pointed ears, large fleshy lips, and almost black eyes that are sunken and strain from their sockets; it is a sinister countenance. Marvin Morgan must be in his fifties, but looks fit – wiry and no doubt strong, like himself, though a couple of inches shorter, perhaps average height – and wears a newer, freshly laundered version of the outfit that he would 'kick around' in, loose black hiking trousers, slip-on trail shoes and a fawn multi-pocketed outdoor shirt. He is clean-shaven and Skelgill detects a hint of cologne.

The man turns to look over his shoulder.

'Stay.'

That he utters this command is explained as he steps away from the door to admit Skelgill, and to reveal halfway down the stone-flagged hallway an excited-looking though mostly obedient dog. As Skelgill enters, however, its enthusiasm gets the better of its training and it makes a couple of friendly passes at his legs, and Skelgill a couple of largely unsuccessful attempts to clap it, for it is slippery, a wriggling wagging blur of wavy chocolate coloured fur.

'What is it, a –'

Skelgill is about to venture "Cockerpoo" – but he finds the name somehow distasteful – and in any event Marvin Morgan, like all dog owners, is ready to supply the relevant information.

'Miniature Australian Labradoodle.'

Skelgill drops down on one knee and unobtrusively collars the creature; it seems happy to accept a scratch behind the ear before he allows it to trot away.

'Not so miniature. I didn't hear him bark.'

'He wouldn't make a guard dog – unless the burglar were a fellow canine – he's less amenable when they enter his territory – he even sets up an invisible no-go zone for dogs the minute I settle somewhere with a flask.'

Though Skelgill nods comprehendingly as he stands to face Marvin Morgan he is actually thinking that the man's unkind physiognomy belies his apparent nature – he is softly spoken and plainly erudite, his accent perhaps grammar school with some underlying regional burr; and his manner is accommodating.

'On which note – can I offer you a cup of tea, Inspector?'

'Never known to refuse one.'

'Please – continue straight ahead to the back kitchen.'

Skelgill does as bidden. There is the bite of bleach as he passes the slightly ajar door of what must be a downstairs toilet, and the kitchen too has its own smell of some pine-fragranced proprietary cleaner. He settles upon one of two chairs at a narrow oak breakfast table that occupies a space beside a wall. The room, low ceilinged and beamed like the hallway, has a small mullioned window that gives on to a bright green bracken-covered slope, a little rectangle sampled from the north west flank of Harterhow. Marvin Morgan empties and then refills a kettle with freshly drawn water. Once the splash of the tap ceases, he speaks with an inquiring tone while he lights a gas ring and reaches for two mugs from a mug tree.

'How might I help you, Inspector?'

Skelgill hesitates for a moment – perhaps it rails with him that the man might make the running, when it is for him to decide – and in consequence his response is rather terser than the tenor of their interaction to date.

'You mean you don't know?'

Marvin Morgan swivels at the waist. His expression demonstrates concern, without trace of guilt.

'It sounds like I should.'

Skelgill makes a little inclination of the head towards the window. 'I believe you're a regular out on the hill – Harterhow. Doing your birdwatching.'

Now Marvin Morgan turns fully, cradling a mug in each hand.

'That's right.'

Skelgill is watching him minutely – and the man must sense that.

'On Monday afternoon a dog walker found human remains – it's been on the news this morning.'

Marvin Morgan glances at an old-style portable television set on the worktop opposite to where Skelgill sits. There is also a transistor radio. When he looks back at Skelgill his eyes might be fractionally narrowed.

'I haven't been over – I mean – the last few days I've been staking out a family of Sparrowhawks – just up the fell in the nearest stand of larches – they're ready to fledge and I'm hoping to get some shots of them as they leave the nest.'

Skelgill sticks to his script.

'We've got a scene of crime team working round the clock – in the oak woods that run down to Brandelhow – do you go that way, sir?'

'I go all over, Inspector.' Marvin Morgan turns away – it may be that the adjunct "sir" prompts some reassessment of Skelgill's intentions towards him, although the kettle is now boiling and he lifts it and fills the mugs. He swings them onto the table, followed by a screw-top carton of sterilised skimmed milk, and spoons and a ramekin for their teabags, and then as a second thought he retrieves a sugar bowl from a cupboard. 'Yes – I roam about – but the reserve extends to 250 acres – that's a lot of ground to cover. The oak woods are at their best in spring when the migrants arrive.'

Skelgill shovels several sugars into his tea, scowls at the milk but nonetheless adds a splash, and then stirs methodically, leaving the teabag in. Marvin Morgan watches evenly.

'You take photos – for your internet blog.'

The man is extracting his own teabag, taking care not to drip onto the tablecloth. Skelgill's observation brings a humble grin to his goblin-like features.

'I'm impressed that you know, Inspector – I've been blogging for the best part of three years and in that time I've acquired only seventeen followers.'

Skelgill appears neither impressed nor unimpressed.

'Between last September and Christmas – that's when we think the body was buried. A female – about your age, sir.'

It is somewhat provocative of Skelgill to make this connection with Marvin Morgan, albeit a tenuous one. But if he is fishing for a reaction he does not succeed in even inducing a nibble. The man places his elbows upon the table and intertwines his fingers. He looks Skelgill in the eye, and his demeanour is earnest.

'How does my blog fit in, Inspector?'

Skelgill gives his teabag a poke with a finger.

'You don't just take pictures of birds, sir.'

'That's right – you might say I shoot whatever's in season – I'm coming across a lot of butterflies at the moment – fungi in autumn, that kind of thing. My output would get a bit monotonous if I solely featured birds – there are only so many species, and they're the hardest of all to photograph.'

Skelgill folds his arms and leans forward on the table.

'It was scenery I had in mind.'

Marvin Morgan inclines his head – it seems he gets Skelgill's point. He is already nodding before Skelgill has finished his next question.

'I take it you have more images, sir – not just those on your blog?'

'I tend to post the photogenic ones – generally close-ups – they're just the tip of the iceberg – two or three a week. I can certainly show you the rest.'

Skelgill takes a couple of gulps of his tea. It does not seem to trouble him that the teabag is bobbing about in his mug. Then he pushes off from the table as though he considers Marvin Morgan's invitation to mean right away.

'You could be the next best thing to CCTV, sir.'

Marvin Morgan rises, and smiles obligingly, revealing a set of rather long and uneven teeth.

'Bring your tea, Inspector – we'll go through to my study.'

As Skelgill passes the portable TV set he places a palm upon it – it is something of a relic from times past, and Marvin Morgan recognises Skelgill's interest.

'Had it since my first job as a sales rep – I won it in an incentive – it was state-of-the-art back then, can you believe? I keep it for its sentimental value.'

He leads the way into a small cosy room tucked partially beneath a staircase that has an enlarged picture window overlooking a typical Lakeland cottage garden, shady and lush and damp underfoot, with a border of straining rhododendrons backed by mixed deciduous trees. A rustic bird table stands directly opposite the window, it is heaped with grain and a family of Chaffinches is making hay, while Blue, Great and Coal Tits acrobatically dispute a feeder of mixed sunflower seeds and peanuts. To Skelgill's eye the garden is well tended, and this orderliness is reflected in the study's interior. The walls are lined with bookcases, their contents arranged with the precision of a newly merchandised bookshop. Volumes of the same height are neatly aligned, and those that are not taper in descending size order from the centre of the shelf to the edges. Skelgill notes distinct sections: birds (there must be 300 books alone, about half of them antiquarian), trees & wild flowers, butterflies & moths, walking guides & maps (a collection to rival his own, though in superior order and condition), general reference, a business section, and finally – perhaps as many as the rest put together – paperback fiction; names mostly unfamiliar to Skelgill: John Fowles, Patricia Highsmith, Thomas Harris. Placed in recesses between books are a striking exotic stuffed bird, vintage brass field glasses beside their scuffed leather case, and several bleached animal skulls: Skelgill recognises fox, badger and a species of owl. In somewhat jarring contrast, arranged like a jagged coronet around the top shelves is a fantastic haul of metal trophies – Oscar style – fashioned from brushed aluminium, chrome and gold, of various sizes and shapes: cylinders, inverted cones, spirals, shining stars and gleaming globes.

On the back of the planked door a row of hooks holds a winter parka-type jacket, a beige cotton gilet, and a small black rucksack with a water bottle protruding from one mesh side-pocket and a tennis ball bulging in the other. On an oak desk before the window stands an open laptop. Skelgill's sweep also takes in a printer on top of a multi-drawer steel filing cabinet, the latter's slim drawers neatly labelled with the letters of the alphabet. On the window sill stand a pocket *Lenser* torch, a matching thermos flask and mug, a new-looking pair of binoculars – *Leicas*, no expense spared – a pocket-sized camera, an atomic clock that displays the time of 3:59, a similar device that monitors electricity usage, and a small grey plastic bottle labelled "Cod Liver Oil 500mg". Beside the laptop is a mesh desk-tidy, in which the items of stationery are impeccably organised, even by desk-tidy standards.

Marvin Morgan indicates that Skelgill should take his seat, a well-appointed wheeled office chair upholstered in tan leather. From a corner he pulls across what looks like a child's high stool, made of ash perhaps – it is a clever space-saver and Skelgill admires it with interest. Marvin Morgan perches on the stool and politely reaches over to pull the laptop towards him.

'There's a new album for each month – but if we go to the main directory I can find the beginning of September and run a slideshow from there.' He is adept with the trackpad and Skelgill notices that his nails are clean and neatly trimmed, and the backs of his hands tanned from exposure to the sun. 'That's it – just press the arrow keys if you want to go quicker – or to reverse.'

To the accompaniment of some light background jazz a series of photographs now begins to unfold. Skelgill watches as the images dissolve one into the next, each lasting about three seconds. Occasionally there is a shot that he recognises from the blog, but mostly they are unfamiliar, and trace the gradual progression of autumn into winter. There is a late red admiral basking in rich golden sunshine on the trunk what might be an oak; the striking yellow foliage of a maple; damp grass with a crop of pointed-hat mushrooms that look to Skelgill suspiciously like the magic variety; a skein of geese against a dawn sky, skimming above the darkened silhouette of Catbells; a Scots pine trunk, snapped clean off at six feet by a ferocious gale; a spider's web, frosted with dew; a huge yellow full moon hanging like a Chinese lantern amongst bare treetops; and animal tracks in the snow, five-clawed which tells Skelgill they belong to a badger.

Skelgill does not avail himself of the arrow keys, but sits motionless and rarely blinking, like he might watch a float from his boat, moored in a quiet bay on Bassenthwaite Lake. Only once does he exhibit any reaction – and that must be imperceptible to Marvin Morgan – for it is an urgent flicker of his eyes as his gaze darts about, hurrying to take in the detail. The particular image is a telephoto shot of a roe deer in a hillside clearing, framed by blurred foliage in the foreground; Skelgill recognises the location as the picnic spot patronised by himself and DS Jones, though on this occasion the surrounding bracken is brown and decaying.

Into the contemplative silence Marvin Morgan inserts the occasional explanatory remark, however he seems to sense that Skelgill will not take kindly to being treated as some novice naturalist in need of constant edification. After five minutes' watching – perhaps a hundred photographs – he gestures with an outstretched hand towards the screen. The shot is a close-up of a daffodil, a bright yellow star set against a powder blue sky.

'We're into February now – that one's on my blog – I always remark if they flower before St David's Day.'

He pauses the slideshow and the music stops with it. Skelgill gives the chair a quarter turn, so that he can look directly at Marvin Morgan. He leans back, as they are rather close.

'Are you Welsh, then?'

Marvin Morgan makes a noise in his throat; it is a chuckle of resignation.

'Just by name – my father's family were from Glamorgan – I was born and bred in the East Midlands.'

Skelgill purses his lips; this perhaps explains the man's hard-to-place accent.

'What brought you here?'

Marvin Morgan indicates loosely towards the trophies.

'For over 20 years I ran my own advertising agency – based in on the Wirral. We were reasonably successful and I was able to retire – in a modest fashion. It's a young person's game – I sold it on to the next generation of management. Let it go for a bit of a song, really. But I'd always promised myself I'd pack in at 50 – come to the Lakes for good. I managed to make it permanent at 52 – five years ago.'

'You don't work now, sir?'

'I do some occasional lecturing and tutoring – I'm still affiliated with my old industry institute, non-executive director – I set and mark some of the questions for their post-graduate diploma in advertising practice.'

'So it's mainly your photography that keeps you busy, sir?'

Now the man makes a self-deprecatory gesture, raising both palms.

'Oh, well – the photography's incidental, really.' He reaches for the camera from the windowsill. 'I mean – it's just this compact I use – tremendous zoom they have on them these days. It's more about having it handy in my pocket – with birds you only get a couple of seconds before they're gone. The resolution can be variable – but it does the job. My only skill is being outdoors often enough for things to happen.'

The photographs on the blog do in fact exhibit a greater level of talent and a better eye for composition than Marvin Morgan is admitting to, but Skelgill is not one to bestow compliments blithely, or without some ulterior motive, so he makes no attempt to gainsay the man. He swivels the chair further around, to look at the Labradoodle, which has unobtrusively trailed them and settled in a tartan-lined basket.

'Aye – that's the thing about having a dog.'

'Yes – rain or shine – he gets me out – and it is a luxury to be able to stride directly onto the fell, no car journey needed.'

'Happen he takes a bit of work – with that long coat – what with the mud and the wet.'

'Oh – I have a hose and a tub at the back – then I let him dry off in the little scullery before admitting him into the house proper.'

Skelgill nods reflectively. It does not smell like a home with a scruffy dog.

'You must get to know the other dog walkers?'

'On Harterhow?'

'Aye.'

Marvin Morgan inhales in a way that suggests he realises his answer will disappoint Skelgill.

'What few there are, they come in from the end of the lane, right over the far side from here. It's unusual for me to meet anyone – I tend to keep off the paths – it's better for finding birds, and the dog's happier that way.'

Skelgill cannot argue with this explanation, it is in line with his own preferred dog-walking strategy. But he persists with his point.

'Over a period of five years, though – you'd recognise the regulars?'

After a pause for thought Marvin Morgan nods.

'Yes – I would say so – but my impression is that people come and go – you know, they frequent the place for a while, six months, a year, eighteen months – and then drop off?'

'What about in the last year – anybody you've seen that would strike you as unusual?'

Marvin Morgan squints pensively out of the window; the creeping afternoon sun is beginning to slant into his face.

'I can't honestly say there's anyone – anything, even – that springs to mind. If I sat and pondered long enough, I might be able to conjure up a list of vague descriptions – but I believe I'm more likely to have noticed the dogs than the people themselves.' He shakes his head rather ruefully. 'You may be better off with the friends group – there's two chaps that run that – they copy material from my blog for their newsletter.'

Skelgill does not appear enthused by the idea; however he declines to elaborate.

'Do you do guided walks for them?'

Now Marvin Morgan looks rather blank.

'It's not something I've been approached about.' He ponders for a moment and his eyes drift to his ornithological books. 'I suppose I could – but birds are notorious for not showing up when you need them – it wouldn't be easy to please the paying public.'

Skelgill nods rather broodingly – this is something he knows all too well in relation to fishing. Whenever police work is going through one of its troughs and the rebellious notion of setting up as an angling guide infiltrates his thoughts, he is quick to remind himself of these twin perils – their corollary being the substitution of one form of enchainment for another. He casts about somewhat fractiously and then indicates towards the stuffed bird on the shelf.

'You could always stick that one in a tree – that would set the cat among the pigeons.'

Marvin Morgan grins – but then he makes a reproachful clicking noise with his tongue.

'I probably shouldn't have that, Inspector – I picked it up on my travels in my student days.'

Skelgill responds with a disinterested shrug.

'If we confiscated everything that contravenes some new law or other we'd never get our day job done. So long as you've not got an egg collection tucked away in your attic.'

Marvin Morgan responds with a little laugh that confirms the improbability of Skelgill's half-joke, though his gaze drops away and there is a slight furrowing of his brow. Skelgill on the other hand rises as though he means to leave. His sudden movement causes dog to rouse itself and it patters out into hallway, Skelgill and Marvin Morgan following. Skelgill notices that it makes no attempt at a break for freedom as he opens the door. He turns on the threshold.

'Thanks for your assistance, sir. We're at an early stage of the investigation. It's always possible that there'll be something in your photographs that might help us in due course. Perhaps I could take a telephone number for future reference?'

Marvin Morgan grins; his manner is somewhat self-congratulatory.

'I'm afraid I don't have a phone – mobile or landline – it was something I promised myself after 30-odd years at work, slave to the device.'

Skelgill seems to disapprove of this state of affairs, though his reaction may be tainted by a certain amount of envy.

'Well – we know where to find you, sir.' He begins to step away – and then hesitates and turns back. 'You're on your own, I take it?'

Now Marvin Morgan looks doubly contented.

'It has ever been thus, Inspector.'

*

So he's not a reporter – but a police officer, too. CID – Coppers In Disguise. That's what they are. And they were on Harterhow before the screaming started – *before* the body was found – why? Was it just a coincidence – did they come along like all the rest do, because it's a secluded spot? The inspector sounds like he's a local – he must know the place better than he makes out. Makes out – *hah!* Why wouldn't he pull rank on his sergeant? Detective Sergeant Jones.

Marvin Morgan stares greedily at the enlarged image on his screen. *Emma.* His lips seem to mouth the word – the name – several times over. After half a minute he clicks onto the close-up he took of the two of them – they're standing just inches apart – but they're conferring about something serious – they'd found the body by then, of course.

What does she see in him? He must be a good ten years older – and he looks more than that, while she looks younger. And hardly the sharpest knife in the drawer – he'd glazed over when he watched the slideshow. What did he expect? A shot of someone sneaking into the woods with a rolled-up carpet over their shoulder! It was like he was going through the motions.

Did he come to see the photos just so he could nose around? Is that how he operates – by blundering?

But what of his joke about birds' eggs? Was it an off-the-cuff remark – or a little tester? If he's from around here he might have been in the cottage during the tenure of a previous owner. He might notice the alterations.

Cautiously Marvin Morgan straightens up; he has to keep low to avoid the rusty copper tile nails that protrude from the sarking boards. He peers through the slit of the air vent that overlooks the front. The driveway is still empty. But who's to say that the inspector won't abruptly return – to catch him out – on the ruse of having remembered another question and not being able to phone him. There's a downside to that – maybe a few extra precautions are called for.

One last look at the laptop. *Emma*. Was that where the inspector was off too in such a rush? Another little rendezvous with Detective Sergeant Jones. A tryst in a back lane before going home to his wife – if he has one, that is. He'd not hung about, that's for sure. *He'd jumped into his mud-encrusted shooting brake and roared off, seatbelt unfastened.*

*

Skelgill leans into one bend after another. He throws caution to the wind, threading his car through these tight curves in the tourist season, when the traffic trebles. Never mind that confronting him around the next turn there might be a flock of sheep, or a broken-down tractor, or a ponderous trudge of tramping ramblers.

His eyes are unblinking and his jaw set, his nostrils flared and his knuckles white on the steering wheel. His faculties might be focused on the road, but his mind wrestles with a conundrum: why has Marvin Morgan just lied on at least three counts?

8. DOG WALKERS – Thursday

Skelgill is a man troubled by the protocols of in-groups. It is bad enough that he might be considered part of any such coterie without his consent. But to add insult to injury there is the matter of the in-group determining *how he ought to behave*. Fisherman, fell runner, occasional motorcyclist, Skelgill plainly errs towards lone pursuits. But even these hold their perils. For instance, the minute he rolls out his old *Triumph* from the garage he becomes a 'biker'. His hoped-for hour of solitude is continually invaded by passing strangers – for he is obliged to perform the 'biker's nod' to fellow enthusiasts – half of whom he would probably lock up were he ever to get to know them.

And now, an inadvertent recruit to the cynophile community, his patience has been tested further. At least on a motorbike he can sail blithely by, affecting not to have noticed the oncoming 'blood brother' (or sister) – and they are hardly likely to perform a U-turn and come after him for his surliness. But dog walking offers no such easy escape (although it is not unknown for him to pretend Cleopatra is up to no good and take off at a tangent). Generally he must endure the requirement to be in good humour, optimistic about the weather, and prepared to bluff convincingly upon subjects ranging from the exorbitant price of grooming to the hidden pitfalls of pet insurance exclusion clauses.

That said, one particular aspect of dog walking has aroused Skelgill's interest: what he regards as its shift system. The early shift, he observes, runs between 6am and 7am. It is staffed mostly by men: purposeful, dour, head down and legs pumping, keeping close control of their hounds and plainly on a mission to get the job done in good time for work. Skelgill admires this group, and sees himself in their image – ascetic by nature, religious in their adherence to the daily task. Greetings are rarely expected or exchanged. Dogs tend to be lurchers, whippets, terriers and other working breeds.

The next distinct shift begins around 9am, shortly after the school run, and there could hardly be a more vivid contrast.

The personnel are predominantly female: gregarious and loquacious they converge with designer pooches – the likes of Muggins and Puggles – that gambol unsupervised, copulate freely, and terrorise the local geese. Skelgill was recently called upon by one such 'yummy mummy' to free a Bichon Frise from a barbed wire fence with the minimum of lost fur.

Finally come the professionals. *'The Dog Whisperer', 'Doggy Daycare', 'Bark 'n' Ride'*. Rolling up in their air-conditioned vans at around 10am – having spent the last hour collecting – they disembark with practised aplomb. There is perhaps a commanding *"Charlie, quiet!"* or *"Willow, sit!"* – until calm prevails and the pack moves off as one, a fistful of leashes. An occupation equally divided between males and females, many of this group know of Skelgill in his own professional capacity; if asked, he would say they are law abiding and take their responsibilities seriously.

Today Skelgill has beaten every shift to the draw – even the most dedicated of the ascetics. He arrived on Harterhow on foot just after 5am. By the time a yawning PC Dodd appeared two hours later to resume his post at the end of the lane, Skelgill was long past his second breakfast.

He has stationed himself in the now familiar clearing. It is 9.45am and he is brewing his umpteenth tea, eking out the last of the water in his Kelly kettle. The weather is holding fair – for more than a week an unseasonal easterly drift has brought sea fret and frustration to holidaymakers on Britain's North Sea coast, but no such complaints over here in the west. Skelgill squints at a scolding Meadow Pipit that parachutes out of the morning sun and reminds him he has forgotten his hat.

While he waits for various experts to provide what may prove decisive forensic evidence, his strategy is to stay close to home. This morning's tactic is to 'stake out' Harterhow, and see just whom he intercepts. While PC Dodd's presence is ostensibly to reassure the public, he is equipped with a two-way radio in order to alert Skelgill to any arrivals via the main point of access. Skelgill is anticipating that the dog walkers' grapevine will be abuzz with the news of "The Body in the Woods" – and is intent upon witnessing what effect that has upon visitors to the underused local amenity. The clearing offers a good vantage point for him, and public utility as one of the few open spaces on the hill where it is possible to toss a ball or a stick.

However, if he had hoped for a stream of early arrivals he has thus far been disappointed: not a soul has come his way, and – unless PC Dodd has suffered battery failure (or fallen asleep in his car) – no one has yet entered through the gate. Indeed, now at long last that Skelgill espies through the steam wafting from his mug a figure emerge from the woodland fringe, he sees that it is DS Jones. Looking tanned and suitably summery in a sleeveless top, the sun's rays glinting off her fair locks, she makes her way lightly through the long grass. As she nears, Skelgill rises – but in doing so he seems to aggravate his troublesome back, and he turns away to face up the slope and flex his spine. He grimaces – but then, fleetingly, another expression takes possession of his features – it is more akin to alarm, and his eyes narrow. But it passes as quickly as it comes – and now it seems to be the catalyst for an entirely unexpected action. He swivels to face DS Jones; he steps close and grasps her upper arms. In the same movement he bends to kiss her. Whatever her feelings – taken unawares she acquiesces, and for a moment sinks at the hips into the forced embrace – but two, maybe three seconds pass and propriety descends upon her and she hops backwards from his grip. Staring wide-eyed at Skelgill she makes a frantic fanning motion with a hand in front of her face and simultaneously puffs air from flushed cheeks.

'Guv!'

But there is more than just a note of surprise in her tone – and she urgently jerks a thumb over her shoulder. Skelgill, whose expression is a conflicted mixture of glazed determination diverts his gaze to look in the direction of her warning. Not twenty yards away, and rapidly closing, arm outstretched by the pull of her eager dog comes an open-mouthed June Collins. A pair of aviator sunglasses hides her eyes.

'Oh – good morning, Inspector – I hope this is not a bad time?'

A new kind of alarm occupies Skelgill's countenance.

'We're surveying here this morning.'

That this explanation has little practical meaning does not seem to trouble June Collins.

'Well, I'm so relieved to encounter you, Inspector.' Skelgill finds himself tongue tied, but she approaches him directly, right up close until she can take a grip on his sleeve. 'I decided to *brave it*, you see?'

'Brave it, madam?' Skelgill's focus is divided between the intimate attention he is now receiving from June Collins, and DS Jones, who has edged away and is making surreptitious adjustments to her blouson.

'Inspector – I thought if I didn't come back straightaway I should never be able to do it – and that would be such a shame for poor little Morse.' She pushes up the sunglasses onto her forehead and gazes soulfully at the dog. 'But I've been *followed* through the trees – I heard the *crackling* of twigs – and someone *coughed* – so I dashed out of the woods and into this clearing – and here you were –' She breaks off and casts a conspiratorial glance at DS Jones. 'Both of you. Thank goodness.'

Skelgill has thus far ignored the Lakeland Terrier, persistent about his knees. But now he avails himself of the excuse it provides and squats down to appease the creature. A frown creases his brow.

'Miss Collins – you saw our constable on the gate?'

Now the woman seems bewildered.

'It wasn't *him* – following me?'

Skelgill pats his breast pocket, from which protrudes the aerial of a two-way radio.

'You're the only person so far this morning to have come to Harterhow. If you heard something in the undergrowth – happen it was a roe deer – they're rutting this time of year – they can make a barking sound.'

June Collins appears disappointed that Skelgill would de-escalate her crisis and substitute some mundane natural explanation. She looks imploringly to DS Jones.

'Well – you know how frightening it can be for a lone female, Inspector – even when you do have your dog for protection.'

Skelgill is still crouching and he stares rather doubtfully at the terrier – the suggestion calls to mind the whereabouts of his own dog. She has remained curled up (though with one eye on proceedings), half hidden in a shady nest beneath a clump of bracken. Skelgill rises and rather theatrically staggers backwards as if he has stepped in a divot.

'I'll tell you what, Miss Collins – Sergeant Jones will escort you back to the gate. I'll take a wander down through the woods.'

Skelgill detects a raised eyebrow from his subordinate; meanwhile June Collins looks rather crestfallen. Then suddenly she has an idea.

'Would you like to take Morse? He's barely had any exercise this morning – I didn't dare to let him off the lead – after last time, you know?'

To DS Jones's evident surprise Skelgill consents to this request.

'Aye – why not.' He accepts the leash and draws the willing canine to a patch of gorse bushes. He ties a half-hitch to a leathery stalk and returns to begin packing his gear. He glances up to address DS Jones. 'I'll meet you back at the office – couple of things to do on the way.'

DS Jones looks a little sceptical but nonetheless nods obediently. They say their goodbyes and the two females begin to pick a path down the hillside. Skelgill watches them out of sight. When they have gone he gingerly pushes his way into the middle of the clump of chest-high gorse. Standing stiff to attention, he quickly casts about on all sides. Satisfied that he is unobserved, he complies with the call of nature – an occupational hazard for a man who drinks so much tea.

He rouses Cleopatra, swings his rucksack onto his back, and then promptly lets the potentially errant Morse off his lead. The joyful terrier makes a couple of random sorties into the bracken, perhaps in the hope of picking up a scent or surprising a rabbit. However, as Skelgill has anticipated, it soon falls in with the older dog, and they seem content with a degree of mutual indifference.

At the edge of the oak wood Skelgill parts the overhanging foliage of an elder, displacing a myriad of tiny cream flowers, miniature stars that cluster in great galaxies all over the leafy firmament and infuse the air with their delightful muscat effervescence. Ahead of him an unruly band of corvids – he recognises the calls of Jackdaws, Jays and Magpies – has set up a raucous cacophony. As he nears the spot they begin to disperse, casting vengeful backward cries. Twenty feet up, a venerable oak has lost a limb, and there is a dark rent in the trunk. Skelgill claps his hands – and as if by magic a Tawny Owl pops up from within; it leans forward on the rim and fixes him with a malevolent stare before launching itself silently into the wood. The dogs, their attention momentarily attracted by the handclap, show no interest in the avian contretemps – flocks of birds, preferably overfed ducks, are for scattering when there is nothing better to do.

But the incident is not irrelevant, for it tells Skelgill that no one has passed this way in the last short while. The site of the grave is another hundred yards off, downhill, but now the Lakeland Terrier appears to pick up a scent – for it darts ahead, leaping with tremendous agility over fallen debris, dodging ferns and flattening nettles. Catching up, Skelgill discovers that the creature has homed in directly upon the target. The soil might have been sifted and sorted for every last clue, but Morse still finds something worth sniffing. Cleopatra, sedate at heel, is probably more intent upon securing the uneaten sausages in his rucksack.

The forensic team has done its best to restore the site to its original condition – no doubt with a view to deterring 'ghouls' and souvenir hunters. But to Skelgill's eye the disturbance is still evident – and in any event he has Morse's powers of olfaction to provide corroboration. There is no indication of an interloper, but he halts and listens; this time of summer the songbirds fall mute, and only a distant Wren, the tiny troglodyte, half-heartedly trills from some mossy bank. All about, the tall oaks, their leaves unmoving, stand silent witness to events past.

And then a sudden sharp yelp from the Lakeland Terrier ends his moment of reflection. The dog has recoiled – and as Skelgill strides across he sees upon the grave, armed with crescent thorns, a spray of wild roses, delicate pink and yellow blooms possessing the damp sheen of a just-brushed watercolour.

*

Back in his cottage, Marvin Morgan stares pensively at his latest batch of photographs. Where to file them? A kiss is 'level 2'. But then it – and the shot of the inspector urinating in the gorse – they could be "PC" – Potentially Compromising. They're not for posting on the blog, not yet – but they might have their uses. He grins and begins to hum, it is not especially tuneful, but it could be *'Watching The Detectives'*.

9. FORENSIC FINDINGS

'You've caught the sun, Guv.'

Skelgill flops flamboyantly into his chair; his colleagues are already seated in his office, and they notice immediately that he seems to be in good spirits.

'I might as well have been sunbathing, Leyton. Five hours on the fell and only June Collins turns up.'

He grins a little sheepishly at DS Jones. She returns his smile.

'How did it go with Morse, Guv?'

Skelgill makes a so-so face – but his reply refers to the terrier's owner.

'What I want to know is how she got under the radar. Did you ask Dodd?'

The trusty if somewhat accident-prone local constable is another of DS Jones's contemporaries, and it is plain she seeks to mitigate his lapse.

'Reading between the lines, Guv – I think it was a – a comfort break. He said he'd climbed over the opposite wall to investigate a strange noise – and in the time it took him June Collins had pulled up in her car and disappeared into the reserve.'

Skelgill tuts ostentatiously.

'Aye, same roe deer as spooked June Collins, eh?' But he is joking. 'It looks like it's right what everyone says about the place – it's too much trouble to get to, to be popular with dog walkers from Keswick.'

DS Leyton is looking pensive.

'In that case, Guv – reckon there's anything in June Collins coming back?'

Skelgill contorts his features into a benign scowl. He understands that DS Leyton refers to the propensity for killers to 'find' their missing victim; in the way that a crowd watching a great blaze will contain the arsonist, they ought at least to have June Collins on their list of suspects.

'I can't see it, Leyton.'

But Skelgill's definitive response prompts a rather terse intervention from DS Jones.

'She seems to like the attention.'

Skelgill shrugs.

'Like she said, lone female.'

Now he beams affectedly at his colleagues – it seems to be an invitation to move the conversation on – and the act prompts DS Leyton to check his wristwatch.

'Guv – I've got to nip out for half an hour at ten-to-four – if I could have first dibs?'

Skelgill holds out a palm, his expression amenable. It is as though his underlying thoughts are running with some other, more satisfying, scenario and for the time being leave no room for his customary recalcitrance.

'Aye – as you like.'

DS Leyton nods and brings up his papers, squinting until he finds his focal length. Skelgill seems to think that he is bothered by the sun, and stands briefly and reaches above DS Jones to adjust the window blind.

'Well – sticking with June Collins, Guv – in a fashion. Her former partner, Spencer Fazakerley – so far no trace of him. Nothing on the police computer – nor the missing persons database – even the checks we've done on the electoral register haven't come up with a match for the name.'

Skelgill looks unconcerned.

'If he's got no previous, Leyton – are we bothered?'

DS Leyton seems a little flustered by his superior's rather casual indifference – he might wonder if Skelgill is playing devil's advocate, despite his offhand manner. And likewise DS Jones seems unwilling to let the matter pass without comment.

'Guv – what if Spencer Fazakerley isn't his real name? We only have the woman's word for it. We know he went to Harterhow with the dog – and he disappeared within the time frame of the death.'

Skelgill remains phlegmatic – and he concedes the point without further contention.

'Keep it open at the moment – let's see how things develop.'

DS Leyton nods and refers to his notes.

'The only other thing I've got, Guv – about that committee – Friends of the... Flippin' How's Your Father – it seems there was another member – a woman called Veronica Crampston – used to be their treasurer.'

The additional revelation does not trouble Skelgill; instead he seems amused by his sergeant's stumble over the name of the society.

'And where is Veronica now?'

'Only just got the information, Guv – the officer I saw at the council contacted us – seems she's been doing a bit of digging, herself – er... no pun intended. The name has sprung out of that.' (Skelgill raises his eyebrows but does not comment.) 'She's compiled a list of all the notifications for council work on the Harterhow reserve in the past 18 months, plus invoices for jobs done by sub-contractors. I was going to drop in and pick it up before close of play.'

Skelgill considers his sergeant equably.

'You'd better shoot off, then.'

DS Leyton is surprised – but clearly decides he should not look a gift horse in the mouth. With a groan he raises his bulk and flashes a thankful grin at DS Jones.

'I'll be back after five, Guv.'

Skelgill waves him away with a dismissive palm. When the door is closed he turns to DS Jones.

'What's that all about – coming in later?'

DS Jones looks like she is wondering whether to answer frankly – but perhaps she detects that Skelgill, despite his rather blithe manner, is watching her more closely than he might like her to believe.

'Er – his wife's got a hospital appointment – there's no one else who can meet the kids out of school. That's all it is, I think, Guv.'

Skelgill scoffs, but not in a disparaging manner – he slides back in his chair and folds his arms – he produces a look of wistful nostalgia.

'They should be so lucky – when I was a bairn we got the bus. If you missed it – eight mile walk and no one would come looking for you.'

DS Jones regards him thoughtfully for a moment – but then she bows her head and considers her notes.

'I've got some feedback, Guv.'

Skelgill is still reclining, and he casts his eyes up to the ceiling, where in a corner a daddy longlegs is hopelessly trying to make an escape – a mummy, in fact: he notes it has an ovipositor.

'I take it I'd know by now if there was a result on the DNA?'

DS Jones sighs audibly – of course – they both know – that had a match been struck this news would have been transmitted through more urgent channels.

'Nothing, Guv – I suppose the only thing we can say is that from a familial point of view she's no relation to the watch list of local offenders.'

Skelgill looks pensive.

'We don't know she's British.'

Now DS Jones turns a couple of pages, with more urgency.

'Ah – that's one interesting thing, Guv – the report on the rings.'

'Aye?'

'They're not especially valuable – nor particularly uncommon – they're probably of quite recent Chinese manufacture – but made for the European market. Low-grade gold with non-precious stones. One of them is quite distinctive, though.' Now she folds the sheaf of notes and presents to Skelgill a page showing the four rings separately photographed and enlarged. 'This one – it's called a Claddagh ring – it's a traditional Irish design – see how the clasp is two hands holding the heart in the middle.'

'Irish.'

'Most popular among Irish people and the Irish diaspora.'

'Never heard of it – not that I would have.'

DS Jones nods eagerly.

'There are traditional ways to wear a Claddagh ring. To show what kind of relationship the person is in.' Now she pauses. 'The victim – she was wearing the ring on her right hand with the point of the heart towards the fingertips.'

Skelgill looks at his own right hand, something he has often joked he could manage without.

'What does that mean?'

'It indicates she was single – or looking for love.'

There is another pause while DS Jones scans her notes. Skelgill watches her.

'I'm guessing that doesn't rule out that she could be married?'

DS Jones glances up – it takes her a second to cast aside some preoccupying thought. 'No, I believe not.'

Skelgill sets his jaw and broodingly scrapes at the beginnings of a beard with a bare knuckle.

'So where does it get us?'

'I suppose your point, Guv – there's around half a million Irish-born citizens living in Britain.'

'That just makes life more difficult.'

DS Jones places the papers on the corner of Skelgill's desk.

'I still think the combination of the four rings is the best clue, Guv – on top of what we now know about the Claddagh ring – surely it's just a matter of getting a picture in front of the right person?'

'What are you suggesting?'

'I recommend we put them on *CrimeTime*.'

Skelgill makes a sudden explosive exclamation.

'The Chief won't buy it – you know what she reckons to that programme. She takes the hump – as Leyton puts it – if her officers are on the telly getting too big for their boots.'

DS Jones knits her brows and sits in silence for a few moments.

'Maybe if *I* asked her, Guv – it wouldn't seem like that?'

Skelgill's expression becomes introspective. Certainly DS Jones has achieved favour with her performance in the press conference. She has a point. But his antipathy towards cowardice overrules his common sense.

'If there's any asking to be done – I'll do it, lass.'

DS Jones nods rather meekly.

'We've got a reasonable description of the victim, Guv – and the cosmetic work on her front teeth is also quite distinctive – it's the sort of thing that friends or relatives would know about. All we need is a lead – a name and locality – and then the dental records would confirm the ID.'

Skelgill looks doubtful.

'What about Ireland? What if she's from over there?'

'I've checked, Guv – *CrimeTime* is also screened on RTE – it goes out the following night – but these days with digital, the BBC has a big audience in the Republic, plus they watch BBC Northern Ireland. And the broadcasters will post the images on their websites and social media feeds.'

Now Skelgill grins contritely – as usual his sergeant has not just come up with a spur-of-the-moment suggestion – she has thoroughly vetted the idea.

'If I'm to sell it to the Chief – we need it to be our best bet. What's the story on the post mortem?'

DS Jones is already nodding and flicking through her notes.

'Again it's more a case of what it isn't, Guv – if you get my meaning.' She glances up and Skelgill raises an eyebrow. 'There's nothing definitive regarding cause of death – Dr Herdwick thinks strangulation is most likely.'

'That's his standard get-out.'

'I know, Guv – but in this case his report states that there is a fracture of the hyoid bone – it's consistent with fatal strangulation – found in a third of adult cases.'

Skelgill, leaning on his elbows, seems to be digging his thumbs beneath his chin to test this hypothesis.

'Aye – except there's a but.'

DS Jones nods.

'The fact that the body was dismembered – the hyoid may have been damaged at that stage.'

'Whatever caused it – it doesn't look like it's going to help us much.'

'Strangulation at least suggests a male assailant, Guv.'

Skelgill now gives a shrug of his shoulders. He is already satisfied on this score: the dismemberment, the removal of the corpse to the distant grave, the heavy digging.

'What about time of death – what do they reckon?'

Now DS Jones leafs further through the report. Skelgill can see yellow highlights in places in the text and red comments in the margins. After she has refreshed her memory she speaks without the notes.

'The soil analysis – they measure the levels of phosphorous and nitrogen that leak from the cadaver and compare it to the surrounding earth – indicates concentrations of both elements were well past their expected peak – and that's roughly 100 days – but that was strongly suspected, anyway. There's a similar difficulty with the forensic entomologist's and microbiologist's reports – they can be most accurate within the first couple of months when the process of decay is at its most active. So we're not really getting any closer than 6 to 9 months ago. In fact the absolute outside limit they're stating is last June – that extends the original estimate.'

Skelgill watches in silence as she checks again for some salient detail. He looks relieved that this job has not fallen to him. Now DS Jones stops and reconsiders a highlighted paragraph.

'A couple of points that struck me, Guv – more to do with the description of the burial itself. The grave was dug to a maximum of eighteen inches – not very deep – and it seems to me there was a kind of ritual aspect.'

'What do you mean, *ritual?*'

'The grave was about five feet long. But when you think about it, the murderer had dismembered the body – he – or she – they didn't need a hole that big – some kind of square pit would have been sufficient. But it looks like the body parts were laid in their correct positions. Also, the alignment of the grave had the head facing east.'

'And your deduction?'

'Doesn't it suggest that the murderer had some inclination to provide a Christian burial, Guv? And – therefore – *cared* about the victim – which is supported by the fact that the rings weren't taken.'

Skelgill pulls a face – she could be right. His thoughts hark back to the tribute of wild roses. But DS Jones's theory, while informative, is not revolutionary – most victims knew their killers. DS Jones observes his doubts and taps the report with the back of one hand.

'The other thing, Guv – and this could have a bearing on timings – beneath the corpse and also to some extent mixed in with the back-filled earth, there was an unusual number of oak leaves that were still in a relatively fresh condition.'

'What – like the grave had been deliberately lined with them?'

'Not to that extent, Guv – it is an oak wood, after all – but it could suggest the burial took place earlier in the year – in the summer, even.'

Skelgill rests his chin on his knuckles and closes his eyes. His features now contort rather alarmingly – it is an expression that has a corresponding effect upon DS Jones and she watches him with trepidation. But Skelgill is merely picturing the scene that he visited earlier: the oaks are all mature trees – towering bare trunks with hide like a rhino's, there are no oak leaves to hand – just shrubs of hazel and elder and the occasional downy willow. He presses his fingers against his temples and bows his head. Now he slips into a moment he has envisaged since first encountering the exposed skull, its fateful smile a glint of white in transient moonlight; of cloaking blackness and howling wind that descend to smother the senses; of driving rain and intermingled sweat; of bursting lungs and burning muscles; of the ghostly fingers protesting against his face of leaves ripped from a storm-tossed canopy. Sharply, he sits upright, and stares unseeingly for a moment at DS Jones.

'Wait a minute.'

He reaches for his mobile phone and calls up a number, engaging the loudspeaker function and leaving the handset on the desk between them. Then by way of explanation he makes a hand gesture at the device.

'My old fishing mucker, the Prof – he's a bit of a birder on the quiet.'

DS Jones nods – not quite understanding – but now the call is answered.

'Hello – Daniel?'

'Jim – sorry to trouble you.'

'It's always a pleasure, Daniel.'

'I'm with a colleague – DS Jones – we're investigating the body found on Harterhow.'

'Ah – I saw the news – and your young lady in action – a very competent performance, if I may say so.'

DS Jones makes a suitably self-deprecating cough. But Skelgill does not want to dwell on this, for some idea is boring a hole in his head.

'Jim – oak trees – correct me if I'm wrong – but they don't cast their leaves until it's nearly winter?'

'That is right, Daniel – it is often December before abscission occurs. The leaves may remain green well into November.'

Skelgill pauses.

'We found leaves in the grave that hadn't gone brown – they'd not naturally withered and fallen – remember there was a heck of a gale last autumn?'

'I think I can help you, Daniel – my log. One moment.'

There is the sound of a chair shifting and a grunt and then pages being turned.

'Here it is – the first Fieldfares came down on a strengthening northerly on the 25th of October – a tail-wind all the way from the Arctic. Gusts touched hurricane force 12 overnight.'

Skelgill glances at DS Jones; she is writing down the date.

'Are you thinking it would be a good night to dispose of a corpse, Daniel?'

Skelgill makes a sound that smacks of reluctant agreement.

'It would explain the leaves.'

'They would have been falling like confetti – there were trees down all over the county.'

Skelgill nods grimly. Then he sits more upright.

'On a separate note, Jim – there's a twitcher does a blog for Harterhow – birds and wildlife.'

'I have seen it.'

'Is he bona fide?'

'Oh – I should say so, Daniel.' Now the professor allows for a diplomatic pause. 'He is not your prime suspect, by any chance?'

Skelgill produces a somewhat nervous chuckle.

'If you'd told me he was a fraud I might have considered it.'

'Ah, well – one never knows – strange lot, birdwatchers.'

'Nearly as mad as fishermen, Jim.' Skelgill ahems meaningfully. 'On which note – I'd better get weaving. Tight lines and all that.'

The professor seems to understand Skelgill's hint, and they exchange farewell pleasantries. Once the call is over Skelgill folds his arms and looks pensively at DS Jones.

'Marvin Morgan's got a photograph of a pine snapped clean off – taken last autumn. Suggests he was out on the hill the next day, at least.'

DS Jones delays her response for a moment, perhaps choosing her words with care.

'*Is* he a suspect, Guv?'

Skelgill rises and walks round his desk to the window. He stands beside his sergeant and parts the blinds with the fingers and thumb of his left hand. It is apparent he does not want to get ahead of himself. His reply is oblique.

'I've let him know we might want to requisition his photos – copies at least.'

'If he's using a modern camera each image file ought to have location and date tags – date, certainly.'

Skelgill is staring at the midsummer countryside – the foliage is past its spring-green best – the cornfields are already straw yellow, and lone hedgerow trees cast lengthening shadows in the late afternoon sun. It is hard to imagine an autumn gale in such benign conditions. He mumbles.

'Fancy a pint.'

'A *pint*, Guv?'

DS Jones's tone carries a hint of amused indignation.

Skelgill looks at her sharply, as if he has not spoken at all and she has just read his mind.

'It wasn't a question – I meant *I* fancy a pint – but you're welcome to come. Tonic water, whatever.'

DS Jones shakes her head with mock exasperation.

'I got the impression you were going fishing.'

Skelgill taps his temple with an index finger.

'I'm always fishing.'

10. CRIMETIME – Monday

She's got nice hands – smooth tanned skin and slender fingers – nails not too long, not too short – a delicate pink pastel varnish. Has she had them done for this programme? He's seen Inspector Skelgill's hands – kept biting his thumbnails while he watched the slideshow – ragged nails and rough skin – callouses on his palms – it's hard to imagine Detective Sergeant Jones approves. *Emma.*

Looks like she's not getting a speaking part – though the anchor introduced her alongside the boss-cum-boyfriend. Wonder who knows about them – or is he the only one? The director's had his eye on her once or twice – he knows what makes viewers sit up. Is this a live broadcast? It must be – they'd edit it otherwise. Inspector Skelgill sounds like he's reading – disjointedly from a script. There's a tremor in his voice that makes his accent sound even more plodding – he's not doing Cumbria Police any favours. They should have given the job to Emma.

Marvin Morgan leans closer to his laptop. The broadband is not so good today and the stream keeps pausing. The anchor has asked Skelgill a question about the rings, and the screen has frozen on a close up. DS Jones is wearing them, two on each hand, her palms resting gently on her bronzed knees. Skelgill clears his throat loudly. The audio is now running ahead of the image.

'Aye – we believe it's the combination of the four rings together that someone might recognise – including the Irish Claddagh ring on the right hand.'

'And that can have a special meaning – worn with the point of the heart towards the fingertips?' The anchor has obviously been briefed in advance.

'Aye – it can signify that the wearer is single – or that they are seeking a partner.'

Ah – the picture is catching up – now an extreme close up of Emma's right-hand ring finger. She must be calm, there's no trace of nerves – not like Inspector Skelgill – he doesn't sound like he's enjoying it at all. Back to the anchor – she's wrapping up the show – they're only giving them a couple of minutes' airtime. She repeats the appeal – more eloquently than Inspector Skelgill would – the camera cuts to him – he looks like a rabbit in the headlights – and then to Emma – she's gazing into the lens – her expression sincere – she's reaching out...

Marvin Morgan pounces to screenshot the image. *As the programme ends and the theme music strikes up he leans back with a growl of satisfaction.*

*

'We don't know the rings have anything to do with it.'

'Come again, Guv?' DS Leyton glances across from his role as chauffeur – alarmed by his superior's statement.

'What if they were planted – to throw us off the scent?'

DS Jones – also troubled – leans forward between the two front seats of the car.

'But, Guv – we've just been on *CrimeTime* and told the whole nation.'

'Aye – and we've told the killer that he's got us barking up the wrong tree – if that's what he wants.'

DS Jones is pensive.

'You've not mentioned this, Guv.'

'Came to me while I was speaking – on the programme.' Skelgill shrugs jauntily. 'I considered saying it.'

DS Jones now looks more disconcerted – but at the same time relieved. Meanwhile there is something Skelgill has patently been itching to mention.

'How did I do?'

'You were great, Guv.'

It is DS Jones who is quick to reply – and DS Leyton backs her up with vigorous nodding. He clears his throat.

'It weren't such a clear picture on my mobile, Guv – but I liked the way you casually covered up your flies being undone – with your clipboard.'

'What?'

'Er – only joking, Guv.'

There is something in DS Leyton's less-than-convincing retraction that endows his original statement with a certain verisimilitude, and Skelgill glowers at the motorway ahead of them. It is true that nerves had prompted him to visit the bathroom both before and after the broadcast – and – could he remember the state of his dress? He and DS Jones had taken the dawn train down to the television centre in Manchester – DS Jones was already smartly attired, impeccably so, but on arrival at the studios he had been asked if he had brought anything to change into. He had not. But now he shrugs – the ordeal is over – and they already have leads coming in by telephone to their call handlers. Indeed, he picks up on this point.

'What's the latest?'

DS Jones has been monitoring updates via her mobile.

'Sixteen names so far from the general public.'

Skelgill nods. He is torn between celebrating the positive response and lamenting the open invitation for cranks, pranksters and batty pensioners to occupy precious police resources. But at this moment the sign for Burton-in-Kendal services comes into view and Skelgill presses a hand to his stomach. The time is approaching 11.30am. There is a barely perceptible hunching of DS Leyton's broad shoulders and the car seems to pick up speed – indeed he makes what appears to be a premature overtaking manoeuvre, for the next vehicle in their lane is some way ahead. Ominously, Skelgill leans across and checks the dashboard clock.

'Happen we've just timed it right for a mash at Tebay.'

DS Leyton suppresses a sigh. Skelgill's stated intentions to have a 'mash' – a pot of tea – rarely go without some form of calorific accompaniment.

'Righto, Guv.'

Skelgill seems satisfied with this arrangement; now he gazes contentedly at the countryside, industrialised though it is, hedges neatly trimmed and fields liberally bathed in agrochemicals that leave little room for real wildlife. After a few moments' reflection he speaks.

'How did you get on with the Scousers, wack?'

He makes a bad falsetto attempt at the Liverpool accent, and it comes out sounding more like Brummie. Regardless, DS Leyton understands the reference to his mission, first thing this morning, to confer with the Merseyside police, a trip that has enabled him to collect his colleagues by car for their return journey.

'Local bobbies seem a decent enough bunch, Guv – after giving me grief for being a soft southerner – and that's the printable version.'

'Could have been worse, Leyton – you could have had a Manc accent.'

'They certainly took more of a shine to me when I told 'em I was a Millwall fan.'

'Nobody likes a glory seeker, Leyton.'

'Too true, Guv.'

DS Leyton seems to ponder this point – or some other – and Skelgill now has to prompt him again.

'So, Leyton?'

'Yeah, right, Guv – well, they've assigned a detective constable to the inquiry – seems a decent geezer – he's a local lad. He's going to do his best to track down Spencer Fazakerley – he had a look on the computer while I was there, but nothing doing. I also gave him the names of the other people we've talked to – since they've all got Liverpool connections – just in case one of them crops up in relation to Fazakerley. June Collins, obviously, Guv – but also the Coot and Fox characters, plus that Morgan chap you've interviewed.' DS Leyton raises a hand absently to ruffle his hair. 'I realised then that we don't have a whole lot on them – previous addresses, employment and whatnot.'

Skelgill has been listening without seeming too interested.

'So long as you tie up the Fazakerley loose end, Leyton – it's bugging the Chief – on paper he looks suspicious.'

There is a further silence – a reasonable interpretation of "on paper" is that Skelgill regards the vanished Spencer

Fazakerley as a red herring – though he does not trouble to explain why.

'When I was briefing the DC, Guv – it did strike me as a bit of a coincidence – I mean, what's the odds of four people – five including Fazakerley himself – all coming from the Liverpool area?'

Skelgill shrugs indifferently.

'You tell me, Leyton – you're the one with the bookie for an uncle – but remember one in ten folk in the Lakes are from Lancashire.'

DS Leyton makes a ruminating noise in his throat as he counts with his fingers, lifting them sequentially from the steering wheel. 'That would be one in a hundred thousand chance, Guv.'

The bald figure might be thought provoking – but Skelgill responds with a shake of the head.

'Aye – except Coot and Fox – they've moved up together – so there's no coincidence there – and what if June Collins knew Fazakerley beforehand and isn't telling us? It's not like they're all complete strangers.'

DS Leyton adjusts his calculation.

'That would bring it down to one in a thousand, Guv.'

Skelgill turns to DS Jones, to find her watching him with anticipation. It appears his subordinates feel this matter should not be swept under the carpet, whatever else is going on in Skelgill's head. He yields and sits back in his seat and folds his arms.'

'Aye – fine – while we're twiddling our thumbs waiting for these *CrimeTime* leads to be vetted we'll have another little chat to them – do it this afternoon. Leyton, you can take June Collins and the committee men.'

DS Leyton grins.

'They sound like a folk band, Guv.'

DS Jones is holding DS Leyton's *A-to-Z of Liverpool*, which she has picked up from beside her on the back seat. She pats the cover.

'There are a lot of Irish people in Liverpool – two cathedrals and all that.'

It would seem that DS Jones makes a salient point, Liverpool – with its accent exceedingly rare – is the most profoundly Irish of English cities. But Skelgill is inherently wary of jumping to conclusions just because convenient patterns emerge. Coincidences can usually be found if one looks hard enough, but that doesn't make them connections. To illustrate his unease he leans forwards and cranes up at the gathering sky.

'Look at that – a cloud in the shape of Ireland – we must be on the right tracks.'

Now more severely he regards each of his colleagues. DS Jones is plainly frustrated.

'What about Marvin Morgan, Guv – will *you* see him?'

His answer is not what she expects.

'No, Jones – *you* will – but I'll explain nearer the time.'

'Sure, Guv.'

That Skelgill says no more might be construed as him not actually having a plan – however there is no way of knowing this. After a few moments it is DS Leyton that speaks.

'There is one other person, Guv – that woman Veronica Crampston – if I'm following up with Coot and Fox I can ask them about her. Would be a bit remiss if she turns out to be our mystery lady.'

'Happen we'd know if she was reported missing, Leyton. She probably just had her fill of the pair of them. I shouldn't blame her.' He rubs distractedly at a mark on the windscreen with his cuff. 'Make sure you interview them separately – otherwise you might as well speak to a ventriloquist and his dummy.'

DS Leyton nods thoughtfully.

'How should we approach this business of the date, Guv – 25th of October?'

At Skelgill's behest they have agreed to "park" the possibility that this was the night of the interment. While a forensic botanist has pronounced that Skelgill's theory about the semi-preserved oak leaves is indeed feasible, it will remain a card tucked up the sleeve.

'Just work around it – don't make it obvious. Ask folk when they were out of the area – holidays taken in the last 12 months.'

DS Leyton settles rather broodingly over the wheel – their speed has crept up to a rate that might just about evade the attentions of a police patrol. After a short while he speaks in rather subdued tones.

'So you reckon we're on a bit of a wild goose chase with these locals, Guv?'

'Not necessarily, Leyton – but we could spend months tracking down every last person that's ever set foot on Harterhow and still not get close.' He turns over his shoulder to DS Jones. 'What would you say to the Chief – if she asked you for a status report right now?'

DS Jones leans forward. She has on a short pencil skirt and a sleeveless white blouse; she is holding open DS Leyton's *A-to-Z* and now she presses it two-handed to her breast in the manner of a chorister receiving instruction mid-recital.

'Well – it's true we don't have any suspects as such – the local people are merely witnesses to the location – they may have some role to play in due course. We have to approach it from the perspective of what we know. We've got a pretty good description of the victim, and with the rings and the dental work we would be able to corroborate her identity.' She pauses to brush away a strand of hair from her face. 'But then there are the things that "might be". She might be Irish or of Irish descent. She might have been strangled. The killer might have been someone she knew – a partner or a relative – someone who might have cared for her – or at least who felt remorse for what they'd done. She might have been killed on or before the night of 25th October last year. That the body was dismembered suggests a single person – in that they were able to conceal the murder and the disposal. Quite likely a male – someone fit, and competent with tools – the dismemberment, the carrying of the remains, the digging of the grave. They probably own a vehicle.

And probably know Harterhow – that it's a rarely frequented place. A dog walker – hiker – birdwatcher.'

A silence ensues. DS Leyton's eyebrows have gradually risen – perhaps he is surprised and impressed by his younger colleague's grasp of the case. When the facts are added to the reasonable assumptions a solution seems tantalisingly within their grasp. If this is so it, it causes a release of emotion and his features crease into a pained mask. Skelgill notices his subordinate's distress.

'You alright, Leyton?'

DS Leyton looks somewhat blankly at his superior.

'You what, Guv?'

Skelgill stares at him for a moment – but then he turns to the road ahead and extravagantly flings out a hand at the oncoming motorway sign.

'Take this junction – scenic route.' He glances back with a frown at DS Jones. 'The M6 does my head in.'

DS Leyton complies and swings the car across to the inside lane to reach the off-slip.

'You'll need to direct me, Guv – this is bandit country, for all I know it.'

'Just follow your nose, Leyton.'

'Easy for you to say, Guv.'

Skelgill darts a suspicious glance at his sergeant – but DS Leyton's countenance has resumed its usual mask of phlegmatic innocence. It is possible that DS Jones suppresses a chuckle, but she might just be recovering her breath from her little soliloquy. Skelgill lets it go – though after half a minute or so he rubs an itch from the bridge of his nose. They sink into contemplation, punctuated by the odd grunt of encouragement from Skelgill for DS Leyton to take the turns he guesses will lead them eventually to the service road into Tebay. DS Leyton is subdued, his driving sedate by his usual standards. The lanes are quiet and as they pass through hamlets and farmsteads they scatter frequent flocks of birds, family parties of sparrows and finches that feed on spilled grain, and wagtails that mine invertebrate roadkill from the tarmac, leaving late their escape from a similar fate beneath the wheels of the car. Occasionally a swallow hawks ahead of them, twisting and turning and taking out flies that otherwise explode upon the windscreen – from time to time DS Leyton engages the washers, but the splats just smear and this seems to disconcert Skelgill, and he turns to watch from the side window, which he lowers halfway. He blinks at the blooming verges, an alternating cream and purple blur of meadowsweet and rosebay; a young buzzard on a post, mewing for a meal; a heron loping across a water meadow; multi-coloured birthday balloons affixed to a cottage gatepost; honeysuckle draped over a dry stone wall; a war memorial with its desiccated wreaths of paper poppies.

'Look at that, Guv – strange name for a place – sounds like it's out of a whodunit.'

'What?'

'There, Guv – "Hidden Dip" – that sign.'

Skelgill looks askance at his sergeant, and then around at DS Jones, but she has her gaze discreetly buried in DS Leyton's *A-to-Z*.

'That's a warning, Leyton – you donnat – not a settlement. What – do you think it's twinned with Blind Summit?'

DS Leyton's eyes roll and he puffs out his cheeks.

'Cor blimey – *hidden dip* – so it is, Guv. I thought it was the village! Seven years and I'm still showing my ignorance.'

'I don't believe it.'

This remark comes from DS Jones. Skelgill is baring his teeth, grinning gleefully – he swivels in his seat to share his amusement – but he finds his female colleague frowning at the open Liverpool street directory.

'You won't find it in there, Jones!'

DS Jones looks up.

'It's not that, Guv – it's Spencer Fazakerley.'

'What is?'

DS Jones turns the guide and offers it to Skelgill.

'I think it's an *address* – look.' She points carefully with an index finger. 'Fazakerley is a district of Liverpool – and here's Spencer Avenue – right near the centre.'

Skelgill takes the book and glowers at the page – he has to extend his arm before it will come into focus.

'I thought from the beginning it was a strange name, Guv – and it would explain why we haven't been able to trace him.'

Now DS Leyton chimes in – though his tone is rather downbeat.

'That'll make a right old monkey out of me – when those Scousers realise I've got them looking for a geezer whose name is a postcode.'

Skelgill tuts.

'Leyton, if they were on the ball they'd have noticed as soon as you mentioned it.'

DS Jones is animated.

'They ought to be happy – it will help us find him. If that's his address – we just need a photograph – a neighbour will surely recognise him?'

Skelgill and DS Leyton are long enough in the tooth to join up the dots in DS Jones's supposition: that 'Spencer Fazakerley' – for reasons best known to himself – one day visited June Collins' guesthouse and checked in with a false name. If it was a whim, conjured up on the spur of the moment, then his home address of course could spring to mind – or perhaps he was in the habit of using an alias. Why he might have persisted with it is unknown, but it has certainly facilitated his disappearance more latterly.

'Leyton – you'd better get a photo from her – she must have something if they were together four years.'

Skelgill turns and hands back the *A-to-Z* to DS Jones.

'Miss Marple strikes again.' His tone is charitable – but now he adds a caveat. 'Let's not get carried away – as far as we know this couple are a sideshow to the main event.'

'Sure, Guv.'

'And keep the lid on this – we don't want the media getting hold of it and declaring that a non-existent Spencer Fazakerley is the prime suspect.'

DS Leyton raises a hand from the steering wheel and points an index finger skywards.

'That reminds me, Emma – that reporter, the Minto geezer from the *Gazette* – he was hanging about in reception early doors – making a nuisance of himself – wanted a word with you. Seemed to recognise me and collared me as I left.'

DS Jones reacts with apparent disinterest.

'What did he want?'

'*Hah* – a date I reckon. Gave me his card for you – for old time's sake, he said.'

DS Leyton glances at Skelgill, to see that he is scowling.

'He tried the usual reporter's blag, Guv – reckons he's got some clever idea he wants to bounce off've Emma.'

Skelgill shrugs casually. 'You should have bounced him out, cheeky little git. It's a scoop he wants.'

DS Leyton can sense that Skelgill's annoyance runs deeper than he admits. He casts about, in search of inspiration to change the subject. Then he gestures at a black-and-white bird that bobs buoyantly, crossing in the air ahead of them.

'Look, Guv – I've learned that one, at least – it's a Pee-Wee!'

'It's *Pee-wit*, Leyton, you lumpheed.'

11. ALWAYS FISHING

The gradual change in the weather sees gentle July rain pluck at a stippled Derwentwater. Skelgill sits becalmed. He has borrowed a rowing boat from his friend Harry Cobble at Portinscale marina, for his own craft lies landlocked in the secluded inlet of Peel Wyke on Bassenthwaite Lake. A fellow fisher would notice he is under-equipped – in fact vastly so by his usual standards – he wields a six-piece, eight-foot fly rod, and has just a small black rucksack tucked in the bow. Nowhere to be seen are his bristling array of pike rods, his big green plastic tub of tackle boxes, his scale-spangled landing net, or his clanking ex-army backpack that smells of soot and methylated spirits and holds his Kelly kettle and *Trangia* stove. His own boat has a mackled bracket that accepts a capacious fishing umbrella, and takes on the appearance of a Chinese junk when it is unfurled – but this afternoon he is protected from the elements by what for Skelgill is a rare extravagance – he has splashed out on a brand new set of lightweight black *Gore-Tex* waterproofs. "Neither use nor ornament – wouldn't last ten minutes on Bass Lake – a treble hook would have 'em in shreds," had been his retort to the terrified shop assistant. Nonetheless, he had steeled himself to the price ticket and the prospect of quips such as, "They saw *thee* coming, Skelly, lad" from his drinking pals. Given the doubtful utility of the outfit, a certain conclusion can be drawn about his activity now: he is fishing only for appearances' sake.

Indeed, as he casts, and drifts minutely towards the western bank of the lake, he does not look at the water. His eyes seek neither rises, those ripples more prominent among the raindrops, nor promising wind lanes to target; he merely goes through the motions. There is the occasional drip of rainwater from the tip of his nose. His gaze is elevated. The gathering cumuli that marked the journey up from Manchester this morning have coalesced into a grey blanket of stratus, a sinking cloud base that has already decapitated Causey Pike and now threatens the distinctive peak of Catbells. Bright in the gloom he can see the red cagoules of plucky walkers on the zigzag path up to Skelgill Bank.

But the majority of his attention is reserved for the distinctive wooded cone of Harterhow. From this angle it looks perfectly symmetrical, its slopes a patchwork of simple greens in the flat light: medium green for the oak woods that creep up from the lakeside, pale green for the big clearing, midnight green for the spruce plantations that cap the little hill. In the three-quarters of an hour that he has lingered on the lake, he has seen no movement on Harterhow, though the occasional group of ramblers meanders along the water's edge, following the route of the Cumbria Way.

At twenty-four minutes past three – slightly later than he has anticipated – he receives a text message. He tussles briefly with the unfamiliar zip of his breast pocket. He checks the display and engages silent mode before he replaces the handset. He winds in furiously, the reel protesting like a cicada on amphetamine. He catches the nylon leader – he has been using a tiny lead shot in lieu of a fly (lest he get seriously distracted by the temptation to fish). Now he bites it off and spits it away. He dismantles the rod with a succession of pops that ascend in scale from butt to tip, and slides the pieces into his backpack. Then he begins to row purposefully for the shore.

*

Emma!

Marvin Morgan swallows as he watches DS Jones slip her mobile phone into a trendy canvas shoulder bag – the sort students use to carry their laptops. She has plainly heard him scrabbling at the door – it's a trick he uses when he wants to buy a few seconds to see who is there – at the rattle of the key a visitor tends to look up and face the spyhole. He takes off his spectacles and slides them into the pocket of his shirt. He licks his lips. He smiles. He turns the handle.

'Mr Morgan?'

Marvin nods – there's an unexpected lump in his throat and no words can get past. She's holding out a warrant card – he has to lean closer to read it without his glasses; he can smell her perfume! There is a small unmarked car parked beyond her in the driveway; he notes it is empty.

'You met my superior officer, DI Skelgill?'

'I did – that's right.' Marvin gives a polite cough. 'About the unfortunate discovery on the other side of Harterhow.'

She's looking at him very calmly. No nerves again – either that or she's good at concealing it. And now she's smiling back at him. He feels his heart make a little bump.

'You offered to provide us with copies of your photographs – we'd like to take you up on that – if it's convenient, sir?'

Sir. He is dizzied – he has to resist the scenario that wants to play like an illicit movie, dark and sinister, grainy and crackling across the little screen deep in the recesses of his subconscious. He regenerates the smile.

'Of course – of course – come in, please.'

'Thank you. It shouldn't take long, sir.'

As he steps back to admit her and she passes so close he feels his eyes widening and has to wrestle with a sudden urge to reach out.

'Don't mind the dog – he wants to lick you to death.'

Who wouldn't? She's stooping to pet the doodle. See how she's dressed – changed from this morning – assuming that *was* a live broadcast. Now she's wearing tight black stretch jeans and a fine long-sleeved cashmere top that clings to her figure. He can hear his pulse in his temple.

'Can I get you a drink? Tea, coffee – sparkling rosé – *hah-ha!*'

She doesn't take offence. Imagine if she said yes.

'Tea would be fine, please. Just as it comes – no milk or sugar, thank you.'

That's a surprise.

'Do you want to get straight on with the computer – while I make it?'

She stands up – such poise – like a gymnast.

'It's okay – you're my last call of the day.'

And then a little rendezvous.

'Straight ahead to the kitchen.'

The kettle seems painfully slow. He senses her watching – then no girl should accept a drink blind from a stranger, should they? He strains for small talk. Should he say he saw her on TV – he feels an urge to ingratiate himself – but that might be a bad idea – why would he be watching *CrimeTime* or, before that, the press conference?

'I'm pleased to be of assistance.' He wants to call her Emma. He feels like he knows her – in the way of knowing a celebrity. But what should he call her? Sergeant? Officer? Miss? Remember to smile – in a self-deprecating way. 'As I told your Inspector, I'm stranded on seventeen followers – perhaps I'll get a few more if you publicise one of my photos.'

She understands the irony in his tone; she seems interested.

'They're very good – you must spend a lot of time waiting to get some of the shots.'

'You're too kind – but, really, more often than not it's just a matter of having the camera ready in your pocket.' You have to grasp the moment.

That's the tea ready. Carry her mug.

'Shall we go through? My laptop is set up in the study – in fact I'm in the middle of a project organising pictures into themed folders.'

'Sure.'

This is a carbon copy of Inspector Skelgill's visit – except it's chalk and cheese, really. The inspector – dull-witted and intimidating – not good at pretending to be friendly – makes you want to back off. Emma – she's the complete opposite – her magnetism is almost irresistible, her aura of femininity could swallow him like a dark whirlpool. She steps softly – she's wearing stylish trainers – each movement showcases her graceful form. No, chalk and cheese is all wrong. It's more akin to that analogy about the ridiculous and the sublime.

'Please – have my chair.'

She ducks out of her shoulder bag – she pulls it round onto her lap and begins to unfasten the buckles. At the same time she shakes her hair – so fine and glossy – disturbed by the strap and now restored. He could do that. At least he has reason to lean in close – tap the trackpad – wake it up. Such a delicate fragrance – applied for whose benefit?

'That's it – the main library file – everything is in chronological order – you can see how it's divided by the date bars. Can I give you a memory stick?'

She doesn't recoil. She's relaxed, taking her time. He must point out the downstairs loo – it's freshly cleaned – they appreciate that, females. What would Inspector Skelgill's place be like? A tip, at a guess.

'It's okay, thanks. We can't accept files on flash drives or attachments by email. IT anti-virus rules. I have a portable drive and disks – if you've no objection to that, sir?'

He shakes his head. She could drop the "sir" – but that's probably just her training. What now? Pull the other chair over? That's appealing. But maybe she'll be suspicious. Look – those slender fingers – this morning on television – their delicate movements now here before his eyes. Mesmerising.

'Shall I leave you to it –?' *Emma* almost came out there. 'I was just preparing a bolognaise when you arrived – I ought to get it seasoned and in the oven.'

Sucking spaghetti between those full rosy lips. Red wine and candlelight.

*

Skelgill beaches his craft and in the same moment leaps from the prow onto the shingle. Given his attire he bears a small similarity to the intrepid 'Man in Black' from the *Milk Tray* adverts; he differs in that he would certainly have eaten the chocolates by now, and the lady in her boudoir would go hungry.

He fastens the painter to the exposed roots of a gnarled stump and makes his way swiftly into the trees that line the shore. It is now apparent that his protective lightweight garments will facilitate speed of movement.

The rain as such does not penetrate the wood, but instead drips sporadically from the canopy, larger droplets that have him wiping his brow whenever they strike. Underfoot, the going is still dry, and he makes rapid progress, first reaching and scaling the stone perimeter wall – a momentary hiatus when midges move in – and then striking uphill in a north westerly direction. It is clear that he has a destination in mind, and no fears that he might be observed, for he makes little effort to move with stealth or in silence.

He becomes more circumspect, however, when he encounters the large clearing. He meets it on its east side, nearest to the lake; the site of the grave is to his left, back down through the oak woods in a southerly direction, while the exit gate at the dead-end of the lane is diagonally over towards the south west. For a few seconds he lingers under cover and surveys the area. He is encouraged by a handful of crows that rise silently from some murderous business; one upside of the adverse weather, it deters the casual visitor. He picks his way across the sloping fell, wading through waist-high bracken that wets his new waterproofs. He reaches the 'clearing within the clearing' – the circle of rabbit-cropped turf backed by the clump of gorse.

Rather curiously, the first thing he does is to sit, looking in the direction of DS Jones's approach four days ago. Then immediately he rises, and turns about to face uphill. It is apparent that a small reconstruction is going on, and that Skelgill is now scrutinising the thick coniferous woodland fringe fifty yards off, his grey-green eyes steely, his features straining into a grimace. It is an expression he reserves for those hunting moments, when he waits for a float to bob, or a rod tip to twitch, sensing there is some interest. Now he finds his mark and sets off, rounding the gorse and keeping his gaze fixed upon a particular spot where the overhanging foliage is broken by a small shadowy slit of a window into the wood.

As he nears he takes care not to flatten the vegetation; it diminishes at the edge of the wood, and merges into a carpet of needles. He stands for a moment, squinting into the darkness of the gap, which is a rough diamond about four feet wide by eighteen inches high at its extremities. While at a distance it looks just like a natural break in the branches, close up he can see their tips have been trimmed. He backtracks several yards along the edge of the wood until he can force an entry. Once inside the going is relatively easy; scaly trunks bristle with vestigial annual rings like the spokes of busted cartwheels; little light penetrates, next to nothing grows.

Cautiously he makes his way back towards the 'window'. It is opposite a particularly thick bole, the same tree whose upper branches sweep down to contribute to the dense woodland fringe. Skelgill recognises immediately a rudimentary seat between two buttress roots: the pine needles have been scraped up to form a raised platform that has an unnatural vertical edge. He kneels and scrapes away a little of the debris: driven into the earth is a row of wooden pegs, a miniature palisade that holds back the cushion of needles to make a level base. Carefully he restores the displaced mulch. He pulls from his backpack a concertina-fold sit-mat and spreads it upon the seat. Then he lowers himself into position – now he sees there are two heel-marks in the leaf litter – a shade short for his longer legs, but nonetheless they produce a stable stance on the downslope. He rests his right elbow on his right knee, and makes a Director's frame with the opposing thumbs and forefingers of each hand. Directly in his makeshift viewfinder is the clearing with its little patch of gorse.

Now he closes his eyes. The picture he conjures – perhaps surprisingly – is not one that includes himself, despite his knowledge that he has stood in the line of fire. It is the autumn shot of the roebuck, framed by blurred foliage – of conifers in the foreground – undoubtedly photographed from this exact spot.

When he opens his eyes he is confronted by an equally stirring vision – and he has to blink to convince himself it is real.

A woman – perhaps three or four years his senior, fortyish – tall and well proportioned and dressed in brightly coloured exercise gear has materialised in the clearing. That she is soaked to the skin appears to be of no concern to her – nor any suggestion that she may be being observed. Dark hair tied back in a severe ponytail, she bends and stretches in an uninhibited manner that leaves little to the imagination in terms of what she wears beneath the ensemble of tight-fitting yoga pants and vest top. And then – as swiftly as she has appeared – she sets off at a sprint, down and across the clearing in the direction of Derwentwater. Now Skelgill realises she is accompanied – for a graceful Weimaraner bounds after her, leaping like a dolphin from the bracken to keep her in sight.

*

She's taking longer than he expected.
What should he do? Whereas Inspector Skelgill gave the impression that he'd leave at any moment, break off mid-conversation and up sticks and go, Detective Sergeant Jones – *Emma* – seems content to take her time. She must be able to smell the bolognaise cooking? The piquant aroma of oregano is all pervasive, mouth-watering. Dare he suggest she should join him? Is that what she's waiting for? Does she cook for herself? She must be single – she wears no rings – unless she took them off for the television programme and hasn't replaced them. And she seems to like him. She compliments him on his photography each time he goes in. And he can tell she's impressed by the neatness of the cottage. Hadn't he better check upstairs – make sure everything is shipshape, everything ready that he might need? Do it now.

He comes down – alas! – she's standing in the hall. There's some change in her manner. She looks anxious – and ready to go. What's wrong with her? Has she seen a photograph that has alarmed her? One that's slipped through the net? Or is it something else? Is it now or never – or should he bide his time? Call her another day – tell her there are more photographs that he'd forgotten about? Why is she looking at him like that? It makes his thoughts race and his head spin – how can he be calm or coherent? Wait – now she's smiling. She likes him again. But she's moving towards the front door. She's thanking him. She's trying the door. She's realised it's locked.

Bang! Bang! Bang!

*

From the secluded 'hide' above the clearing Skelgill has followed the faintest of paths, so faint in fact that at first he was not entirely convinced of its existence. If one desires to move about undetected, a pinewood is the place, for the dry carpet of needles expediently accepts few if any tracks. But to his trained eye there was a path, a line of compression caused by regular tread. And its direction stacked up. It threaded its way to the afforested summit of Harterhow and skirted the mossy cairn, a looming edifice in the twilight beneath canopy and cloud like some eerie monument to long-dead hillfolk. Thence it led him down the northern flank, whereupon reaching the edge of the plantation unfolded the present view of Marvin Morgan's cottage.

From the back gate of the angular slate-built dwelling a dark hairline of shadow strikes up the rough pasture towards his position. He notices a distinct branch that splits off to the west, to the left as he sees it, and hugs the contour of Harterhow. It might be a dog-walking alternative – a change of scene – or a less demanding low-level route for poor weather days, avoiding the mist. Or something else? Skelgill checks his watch – he ought to be getting Harry Cobble's boat back to him – he'll want to lock up the marina and go home – or, correction, he'll expect a couple of pints in return for his favour; a debt the fulfilment of which does not unduly trouble Skelgill. But what does disturb him is this new path. His mind's-eye-map of Harterhow tells him the contour is that on which the end of the lane will be found – and the public access – maybe one third of the way anticlockwise around the hill. He plunges at a tangent into the wet bracken; Harry shall have to wait.

Sure enough, when Skelgill meets the path he finds it hugs the inside of the wall that encircles the nature reserve; ten minutes' brisk walking brings him to within a couple of hundred yards of the gate. Now the path turns abruptly and climbs into a stand of larches that begins to run parallel to the wall, some twenty yards higher up the fellside. As soon as it enters beneath the trees it vanishes underfoot – but by now Skelgill knows what is going on. He moves watchfully along the edge of the little copse until he spies the path as it begins again, a short section that reconnects with the wall, a dozen yards short of the gate. It is a clever trick: anyone finding this path, having turned left instead of taking the more obviously trodden route to the right towards the lake, will only discover it peters out almost immediately amongst the dense conifers. The trail to Marvin Morgan's cottage is neatly covered.

Cautiously Skelgill picks his way down to the wall. Being on the slope it is only four-and-a-half feet high on his side, but there is a drop of six on the other, to a tyre-rutted verge where there is space for three or four vehicles, provided they park close to the wall – requiring the passenger to shuffle across and exit from the driver's side. Right now, interestingly enough, there is one parked car, apparently empty; from his elevated position Skelgill can see a pink-and-grey tracksuit on the back seat and a dog's bed in the boot. The vehicle is a trendy hatchback; it calls to mind the athletic amazon, perhaps still braving the elements to exercise her pet. He notes the distinctive personalised plate.

Skelgill leans his elbows on a convenient sill. He is not wearing a hat and is a man that eschews a hood on the grounds that it would impair his hearing. His face is wet and his hair soaked, but he seems not to care as he rests his chin pensively upon his interlocked knuckles. Then all of a sudden he jolts and takes a couple of steps back. His questioning gaze is fixed not on the car but the flat rock upon which he has been resting. Then he notices – maybe ten feet along – another of a similar form. His glistening brow shows him to be perplexed – the copings of a dry stone wall are typically pitched at 90 degrees, like the uneven crest of some ancient reptile, or crocodile teeth. And now he sees that the turf on his side of the wall is eroded beneath the position of each horizontal slab. This is not some chance arrangement – the wall has been deliberately reshaped into a pair of comfortable stances, effectively concealed from the road – something that would suit a birdwatcher, to enable binoculars to be held steady, or a shooter with their gun... or a photographer with a camera.

12. KESWICK COFFEE SHOP – Tuesday

'You went for a drink with him – was that wise?'

DS Jones gestures at the mugs of frothy cappuccino she has only this minute placed before them.

'Just a coffee, Guv – I was driving.'

'Never trust a reporter.'

Skelgill's scathing words perhaps mask another sentiment – disapproval at the implication that had she not been driving she would have enjoyed something stronger.

'I know he's a bit of a Walter Mitty character, Guv – but I thought I should find out what he was doing turning up at Marvin Morgan's cottage – if he had some information we ought to know.' She looks at Skelgill and gently combs back her hair with the fingers of each hand. 'Remembering what he'd said to DS Leyton.'

Skelgill is obliged to relent.

'And does he – have something on Morgan?'

Now she shakes her head and her hair slips forward again to brush across her prominent cheekbones.

'It wasn't exactly that.' She lowers her gaze – as if she is contemplating the merits of what she might say, weighed against Skelgill's interrogative manner. 'To be honest, Guv – I rather suspect he'd followed me. This murder's obviously a big story for the local press – especially now we've been on national TV.'

Whether Skelgill notices that she has avoided answering is not entirely apparent; now a resigned expression comes upon his features. On the table he has a copy of this morning's *Westmorland Gazette*. The case is not the lead news item, but nonetheless Kendall Minto's latest piece graces the front page: "Body in the Woods: Cumbria CID Make Public Appeal on BBC *CrimeTime*." Skelgill has skimmed the article. It is at least factual – when a reporter might be tempted by sensational clichés, "Baffled detectives scratch their heads" – ammunition for the likes of gunslinging DI Alec Smart. Perhaps Minto wants to stay on the right side of them – or of DS Jones, at least. And the article does not contain anything that she might have let slip to favour the local journalist – nothing about the Liverpool connection – nor thankfully is there any reference to the contentious questions he had raised at the press conference, about drug-running and dismemberment. Maybe that was all show – to get himself noticed.

'So what happened?'

'It was just as I was leaving, Guv. There was a knocking on the door. Hammering, really – a bit embarrassing. Especially when it turned out to be someone I knew. I wondered if Marvin Morgan suspected I'd tipped him off.'

She hesitates – pensive for a moment. Perhaps something now strikes her as odd for the first time. She had instinctively reached to open the door – lest there be more enthusiastic banging – she had assumed the postman, or a courier in their usual hurry – only to find it was locked. Marvin Morgan had darted forward, apologising that it was just his habit – something about having found an intruder in his hallway last year. The incident had become immediately subsumed in the somewhat awkward melee in which Kendall Minto had possibly feigned surprise at finding DS Jones present, and then presented himself to Marvin Morgan, who had declined to speak with him, though in perfectly respectful tones.

'Kendall explained he was writing a feature about Harterhow, and that he'd heard Marvin Morgan was the local expert. Marvin Morgan said he wasn't free – that he had to attend to his dinner. You wouldn't blame him for not wanting to be interviewed.'

Skelgill frowns that she is on first name terms – but if she and the journo were contemporaries he can hardly expect much else. As for her account, he knows something of this. Indeed, more than he lets on. Yesterday afternoon, from the viewpoint overlooking How Cottage he had observed the second car arrive. Its driver lingered for a while – maybe ten minutes. Then, apparently, he went to the front porch – out of Skelgill's line of sight. Shortly afterwards DS Jones and he emerged into view – Skelgill was unsure as to his identity. The pair stood beneath an overhanging yew tree to shelter from the rain. They conversed for a minute or two – their body language was relaxed, friendly. The man offered her a cigarette; she declined. And then they departed in convoy – he lost sight of them in the trees – they may have headed right for Portinscale, or gone left for the pub at Swinside – certainly no vehicles used the clear stretch of road visible beyond that.

Skelgill releases the breath he has been holding.

'And what about Morgan – how did that go?'

'He seems a nice guy, Guv. He was very charming. And the place was spotless, really tidy.'

Once again Skelgill is discomfited. That DS Jones – reliably perceptive (more so than he, though he wouldn't admit it) – seems to harbour an opposing sentiment undermines his self-assurance. Is he prejudiced by the extra knowledge he possesses?

'OCD – or whatever they call it.'

DS Jones smiles patiently – a reaction that suggests she feels Skelgill is coming from another place altogether.

'I just mean he was accommodating, Guv – without giving the impression he was trying to cover up anything. He allowed complete access to his computer – and left me to it. If he was worried, surely he would have watched me like a hawk – to see which pictures I wanted?'

Skelgill has not yet touched his coffee.

'I'd like to know if he's deleted any since I saw them. Did you get the one of the snapped-off pine?'

She nods. 'There were several shots featuring storm damage.'

'And what about the date?'

'Sure enough it's the 26th of October. The image files have data labels – in fact his photos application displays them by date.'

'So it confirms he was on Harterhow the next day. What about the 25th?'

She shakes her head.

'Naturally I didn't ask him directly. He admits he goes out every day – with his dog – but that if the weather's bad he doesn't walk far – and there's not always something to photograph. If you look at his blog, he only posts items once or twice a week.'

Skelgill regards her doubtingly, and then more aimlessly he casts about the café. That she does not share his suspicions regarding Marvin Morgan is perhaps the cost of his taciturnity. She does not even know why he had instructed her to confirm by text Marvin Morgan's presence at the cottage. Skelgill checks his watch.

'Where the heck's Leyton got to?'

DS Jones seems a little guarded.

'I think he's calling back to see June Collins this morning – there was some domestic problem yesterday afternoon. I gather he tried to see her in the evening – but she was busy with her guests.'

Skelgill ferociously stirs the froth into his coffee.

'I'm getting a bit worried about his commitment lately.'

DS Jones hesitates to reply and is saved from doing so when a panting DS Leyton bursts through the café door, and peers blindly into the gloom, plainly thinking he has missed his colleagues. It takes a shrill whistle from Skelgill – to the consternation of several elderly hearing-aid-wearing patrons – to orientate the poor sergeant, who apologetically squeezes his perspiring bulk between occupied tables to reach them at the back of the room. He recognises Skelgill's patent disenchantment.

'Got the photo, Guv – Spencer Fazakerley.' He brandishes his mobile phone. 'I got her to forward it to me. Have a butcher's, Guv – I'll get you a top-up. Emma?'

Despite that Skelgill has barely touched his coffee – and that DS Jones flashes him a smile and gives a shake of the head – DS Leyton makes a diplomatic retreat to the serving counter, apologising once more to the only-just-settled senior citizens. It is a couple of minutes before he returns, and when he does – with two coffees and an Eccles cake, which he has bought as a peace offering for his superior ("Don't mind if I do, Leyton") – Skelgill is still examining the photograph. A composition taken from the waist up, it shows what might be a tallish man, gaunt, with lank brown hair, long cadaverous features and dark sunken eyes. By contrast the backdrop is a summery garden, a blur of blue and white delphiniums. The man has his bony hands pressed upon the handle of a spade or fork, and is looking up with an expression that suggests he has been surprised by the photographer – presumably June Collins – indeed there might be an element of protest in the shape of his mouth, and the beginnings of an objection in the cast of his eyes.

'Recognise him, Guv?'

Skelgill is chewing pensively.

'Aye.'

'Really, Guv?'

Skelgill grimaces.

'Aye – I've seen him before.' But now he gives a dismissive flap of a hand. 'Couldn't tell you where.'

'Maybe walking the dog, Guv?'

Skelgill shrugs.

'There's hundreds of folk hereabouts I'd know by sight, Leyton. Work in bars, tackle shops, Post Office – folk you pass in the street with their paper or their chips – on the fells, fishing.'

'June Collins reckons he'd be 40 in that photo, Guv – she said she took it not so long after he moved in. That would make him 44 now. He don't seem her type, really – I'd have expected someone a bit more suave-looking.'

Skelgill considers this proposition, but then his mind moves on.

'Any paperwork?'

'Not a scrap, Guv – no mail – nothing.' DS Leyton's jowls droop in a hangdog manner, as if he feels this is an oversight that could be attributed to him. 'I asked her if she'd cleared it out – thrown it away – but she reckons he didn't get any post. He told her he had no family to speak of – never married, only child, parents dead – and that he did all his banking and whatnot online.'

Skelgill becomes introspective – he is reminded of his own sparse mailbox – and that this morning Cleopatra got to his *Angling Times* before he did.

'What about junk mail – how do you avoid that?'

'I wish I knew, Guv – but it seems he did.'

DS Jones has been spooning froth from her coffee; now she speaks up.

'He must have another address. If he were employed as he'd told June Collins, the Revenue would correspond with him. There's also DVLA – if he worked as a truck driver there'd be a correspondence address relating to his licence – as well as tax for his private vehicle.'

The others are nodding. It fits what they now suspect about his name being false – and the idea of an address in Liverpool.

'Didn't you say June Collins told us he was away three or four days most weeks?'

DS Leyton nods.

'Reckon she just took him at his word – suppose she had no reason to believe otherwise.'

Skelgill is scowling. His contribution is more cynical.

'Happen it suited her to believe it, Leyton. Ask no questions, tell no lies.' He looks again at the photograph on DS Leyton's mobile. 'Is that the best she's got?'

'She says it's *all* she's got, Guv.'

Skelgill passes over the handset.

'Figures, eh? Better send it to your Scouse oppo.'

'Done it, Guv – he's going out on the knocker around Spencer Avenue – teatime today, when most folk are home.'

Skelgill leans back – he and DS Jones share a boxy leather-upholstered settee tucked into an alcove, but its seat cushions are too deep and he would have to sprawl excessively, so he is forced to sit upright again.

'And what else from the lovely June?'

Now DS Leyton inhales – abruptly – as if he has remembered something – and indeed he raises a palm to indicate there is some important matter before he can move on.

First off, Guv – here's a strange thing. That Lester Fox.'

'Aye?'

'I called on him and his sidekick yesterday afternoon – like we'd agreed?' (Skelgill is nodding, impatiently.) 'Well, Guv – Fox is *only* the geezer I'd seen at June Collins' guesthouse last Tuesday – the one she told me was a visitor that had arrived early.'

Skelgill contorts his features as though he doubts his sergeant.

'Straight up, Guv – you can't miss a queer-looking cove like that.'

Skelgill considers this proposition; certainly Lester Fox is of distinctive appearance.

'So what was his explanation?'

Now DS Leyton looks alarmed.

'I didn't ask him, Guv.'

Skelgill's frown deepens.

'Why not?'

'He didn't recognise me, Guv. I thought it was better to keep my powder dry. I mean you never know –'

Skelgill interrupts.

'Hold your horses, Leyton – what do you mean he didn't recognise you?'

'At June Collins' place, Guv – when she let him in, I was further back down the hallway, it was a bit shadowy, and he never actually looked at me. I think he realised someone was there – he was acting a bit embarrassed, like. She said something about just finishing off an inspection. I assumed she didn't want to mention the police to a guest – fair enough. She sort of bundled him into the lounge with his case. He went in without any protest. It seemed a bit odd at the time.' Now DS Leyton leans forward across the table, at least as far as his long-suffering belt will permit. 'And another thing, Guv – she called him *Mr Smith*.'

DS Leyton looks inquiringly at his colleagues as they take in this curious fact. He may rather be hoping that Skelgill doesn't ask why he has waited until this morning to impart this news. However, it is DS Jones who is first to offer a response.

'We know they're indirectly connected through Harterhow – maybe she's a member of their friends group?'

Skelgill pulls a disdainful face.

'Doesn't explain why she pretended he was a paying customer. And what was he doing with a suitcase?'

DS Leyton shrugs.

'I suppose it'll be easy enough to find out – they can hardly deny I saw him.'

Skelgill looks irritated – that this is another twist in the tail – and quite likely a diversion that may waste their time. He eats the last of his Eccles cake and gazes searchingly across at the counter as though he might fancy another.

'Sit on it for now. Remember which investigation we're conducting – else we'll be up one garden path and down another.'

DS Leyton appears a little crestfallen. However he pulls out his notebook and offers to press on.

'Shall I finish on June Collins – and then the committee men?'

Skelgill nods.

'She can't remember the exact date Spencer Fazakerley left – she thinks early November, definitely after Halloween. She said it drove him crackers kids knocking on the door – this American trick-or-treat malarkey they do nowadays – he insisted they put all the lights out and pretended they weren't in – she'd wanted to get into the spirit of it – her to dress up as a vampire and him as Frankenstein.'

While DS Jones's eyes register a little sparkle at this suggestion, Skelgill is looking like he is firmly in the lights out camp. DS Leyton continues.

'Seems the geezer didn't talk about his past and she was happy to let sleeping dogs lie. He palmed her a generous wedge every week for food and bills.' The sergeant performs the action, passing an imaginary wad of cash out of the side of one hand. 'Lived a quiet life – told her he needed to take it easy because the

HGV driving exhausted him. He'd spend a lot of time during the day taking the dog for walks. And at night he used to stay in and watch the telly.'

'And what about them splitting up?'

'She's still being cagey about that, Guv – I wouldn't be surprised if she wanted to tie the knot and he weren't having none of it. She said he'd mentioned going away for a while – getting a job delivering on the continent. But I don't reckon they ever actually sat down and said "right, that's it over" – like I said before, I think he just did one and she don't want to admit it. He left behind some clothes – she's saying that's because he was hedging his bets – but it don't exactly fit with there being some clear arrangement between 'em.'

'Any trouble that she knew of?'

DS Leyton shakes his head.

'What about neighbours?'

Now he nods.

'One side's a holiday home – no one there. There's an old bird on the other – she was in. Said he kept to himself – would say hello but wasn't one for a chat – said he was polite enough. With them being terraced properties and the car parking at the back – folk can come and go without the neighbours noticing. She said he took the dog regular – early morning and late at night on the street. But she can't be that observant – she didn't know he'd slung his hook.'

'Got the details of the car?'

'Silver, Guv.'

Skelgill stares with exaggerated patience. DS Leyton hunches his shoulders.

'It's all June Collins can remember. Might have been Japanese.'

'That narrows it down.' Skelgill makes a scoffing sound. 'It went when he left?'

'She thinks so.' Rather in the style of Stan Laurel, DS Leyton plucks at his thick dark hair. It might be for effect, or it could be an unwitting gesture. 'She's quite scatterbrained, eh, Guv? It's not easy to get sense out of all that hair and nails and make up. Then there's the dressing gown – bit off-putting – seems every time I call she's been having a shower. No wonder she's as thin as a rake.'

DS Jones is amused, but Skelgill remains brooding on this point. It is a few moments before he speaks.

'And what about Tweedledum and Tweedledee?'

'Coot and Fox, Guv?' DS Leyton chuckles; the allusion is apposite despite the disparity in their appearances. 'I spoke to them individually – like you said.' Now he harrumphs. 'Waste of time – for all the difference I got in their answers. Same previous address in Liverpool – eighteen years – and the pair of them employed by the council. Only, Archibald Coot worked in the marketing department – that's how come he produces their newsletter – and Lester Fox was in the finance section – seems to be the more educated of the two. Moved up together about six years ago when they took early retirement. Claim they haven't been away since they got here.'

'Did you ask about Fazakerley?'

DS Leyton nods – but his jutting jawline portends of an inconclusive report.

'No joy there, Guv – though you might have thought one of them would have mentioned it sounds like the place name. They just clammed up. Coot, mind you – when I said, doesn't your blogger bloke Marvin Morgan come from Liverpool an' all – he said no, he's from the Wirral – admitted he'd talked to him once or twice in passing.'

DS Leyton now gazes at his notebook. His expression is such that he seems to be willing it to spout more facts – but the well appears to have run dry.

'Anything else?'

DS Leyton optimistically turns the page – and then starts as he sees there is another entry.

'Oh, yeah – the treasurer woman, Veronica Crampston. Seems she's not been around for at least two years – they were surprised when I mentioned her – but both of 'em came up with the same story – she had to drop it due to other commitments – WI, church, local magistrate. Apparently lived in Keswick. They didn't have a postal address. I thought I'd put one of the team onto it once we're done with the *CrimeTime* leads?'

He looks at his superior a little apprehensively. But Skelgill takes this as cue to turn to DS Jones – and she correctly reads his segue. She licks melted chocolate powder from her lips as though she can tell it draws his eye.

'In all, Guv, twenty-five names have been put forward – mostly by the public, but the UK Missing Persons Bureau has now suggested three more possibilities. There's still a handful to be investigated, so far twelve have been ruled out, including the remaining local woman. We've sent packages with photographs and descriptions to four of the forces where more promising individuals have been reported missing. We've also sent the same information to the police in Northern Ireland, the Irish Republic, and Europol. It's probably going to be a couple more days before next of kin can be contacted, and for any new leads to come in from the media coverage in Ireland.'

Skelgill is grim faced – an onlooker would judge him to hold a pessimistic view of the likely success of the television appeal. That 24 hours after their broadcast the tactic has not yielded a clamour around a particular name might be disappointing, but it is not grounds for dismay. For a man prepared to sit for hours and *not* catch a fish – and then return the next day and do it again – his impatience seems unreasonable. Moreover, as DS Jones points out, there are leads being followed up and still a significant audience to be reached, over the Irish Sea. Skelgill ought to think of the exercise as more akin to the baiting of a swim, such that it will produce the right result a few days hence.

DS Leyton, too, appears somewhat downcast, his usual genial optimism tinged with some underlying malaise that gradually surfaces when silence prevails. It is he that remarks next upon the lack of a newsworthy response.

'You'd think we'd get dentists calling us up, Guv – all that work she'd had done – what, four implants and six veneers – must've cost thousands. I had to have a crown sorted a few years back – one of the nippers coshed me with a *Barbie* doll – dentist stung me good and proper, just for the one tooth.'

Skelgill is fortunate enough to have no idea what would represent value for money in the crown department. He shifts irritably in his seat and runs his fingers through his hair.

'There must be something we can do to speed this along.'

DS Jones might just have been waiting for such an opening – for purposefully she turns to face her boss.

'I've got a suggestion, Guv.'

Skelgill folds his arms, his body language immediately contradicting his stated desire.

'Which is?'

DS Jones does not answer directly, but instead she reaches for her mobile phone. After a few dexterous taps she turns the screen to Skelgill. She has conjured up the image of a face – it is a lifelike waxwork bust of a man, at once stern and regal, wearing a mediaeval beret emblazoned with a jewel-encrusted brooch.

'Are you familiar with this, Guv?'

'Richard III.'

DS Leyton is craning to get a look.

'Cor blimey, Guvnor – how'd you know that?'

'Because it says underneath the picture, Leyton.'

'Oh – I can't read that far, Guv.'

Skelgill turns back to DS Jones. 'They dug him up from under a car park in Leicester – from beneath the letter 'R' marked on the tarmac.' He has a peculiar note in his voice – whether it is cynicism at the improbable act of divination that preceded King Richard's exhumation, or indeed some awakening of interest in this regard, it is hard to tell. But DS Jones is eager to press on with her point.

'It's not exactly that, Guv. There's a university that has developed a new technique – from a 3D scan of a skull they can reconstruct the face. They can produce a computer-generated image. In the case of Richard III it closely matched the most credible contemporary portrait. We could do that for –'

'Rose.'

It is strange, but in the split second that DS Jones hesitates, Skelgill supplies a name. For a few moments his colleagues look at him open-mouthed – and he realises he must be more forthcoming to correct the false impression that he knows who she is. He rests an elbow on the arm of the sofa and leans sideways to cradle his brow in a gesture of discontent. His other hand he flicks dismissively, but perhaps in the approximate direction of Harterhow.

'When I was over there – last Thursday – I was checking about – and someone had laid roses on the grave.'

DS Leyton is wide-eyed.

'What – like a bunch, Guv?'

Skelgill shakes his head.

'Wild roses – a stem snapped off a bush. But there's none growing nearby – you get them in the lane, trailing over the walls.'

'So they were brought for a purpose?'

Skelgill shrugs.

'You'd be hard pressed to find the spot – the forensic team had raked everything back into place.'

DS Jones now chips in.

'Could it have been one of them, Guv?'

'Aye – though no one's admitting to it.' Skelgill has evidently asked the question.

'It is the fashion these days – for people to leave tributes – even though they don't necessarily know the person.'

Skelgill nods.

'Something and nothing, eh?'

His response might be sarcastic – but in fact his tone is mild and suggests that is exactly what he thinks. After all, they had announced the finding of human remains on Harterhow at the press conference on the Wednesday – and had spoken to Messrs Coot and Fox the day before that; ample time for someone to decide to pay a visit to the locality.

'*Rose*, then, Guv.'

It is DS Leyton that breaks the contemplative silence and brings them back to earth. His manner implies they have reached an unspoken consensus; and somehow in taking this one small step, *Rose* – hitherto a collection of decaying bones and hair, and more resilient dental work and jewellery – assumes a tangible persona. Then there is the prospect that they might see her 'in the flesh'. Skelgill turns to DS Jones.

'Aye – give it a shot.'

DS Jones is quick to rein in her obvious delight.

'Great, Guv – I've got the contacts – I'll get it moving straight away. I understand it can be done quite quickly.'

DS Leyton still appears a little dumbfounded, and takes a gulp of coffee as if it were a medicinal brandy. He lowers his mug to display a nose tipped with foam.

'Brainwave, Emma.'

DS Jones smiles; again with a degree of diffidence. Not being one to steal another's thunder she finds herself on the horns of a dilemma, for the "brainwave" – as her colleague generously puts it – in fact has its origins in the head of the precocious local reporter, Kendall Minto; it is the "clever idea" that he had expressly wished to "bounce off" her and in part, at least, explained his enthusiastic pursuit. Moreover, by nature candid, DS Jones finds this situation doubly taxing: if Skelgill were to know its source he would surely veto the plan.

Skelgill however seems to have entered a brown study. He has drained his mug and stares into it as if some intrigue is painted in the ebbing tide marks. Of course, while he has his team working in a methodical, linear fashion, assembling the facts and drawing logical conclusions, his own mind does nothing of the sort. Indeed, his mind is not what matters – it is what lies beneath – and in a modest way he can be likened to the great poet A.E. Housman, whose stanzas famously came to him while he took his daily walks (fortified by the odd pint of ale), and who was most irritated when he arrived home to find a poem incomplete, requiring him to finish it himself! By analogy, Skelgill is still mid-walk. Plainly he feels rumblings, informed by his experience to date, and confirmed by an irrational resistance to certain unarguable facts.

He starts – and looks up – his subordinates await his pronouncement.

'Leyton – have a deek – see if they've got any of those Eccles cakes left.'

13. LIVERPOOL – Thursday

'That's three full days since you were on the telly, Guv.'

'Happen she's not British *or* Irish, Leyton.' Skelgill groans and shifts position; he has the passenger seat of DS Leyton's car tilted back, so that he is half reclining. He stretches his legs as much as the limited space in the footwell will allow. 'Is this seat stuck, or what?'

DS Leyton glances briefly away from the road ahead.

'I reckon you've got it at the max, Guv – you must have long legs.'

'Aye, they run in the family, Leyton.'

'*Hah* – I thought that was noses, Guv!'

'Very funny.'

On this occasion Skelgill appears to take his sergeant's rejoinder with a pinch of salt, indeed his spirits are high by recent standards, no doubt buoyed by the hearty breakfast consumed prior to departure from their rendezvous at Tebay services. Thence, they have travelled deep into Lancashire, and will shortly take the M58, the dedicated motorway that serves the port city of Liverpool from the north. While DS Leyton flaunts the terrestrial speed limit, Skelgill seems to have resigned himself to accept that this case will move at its own pace, and that there are few metaphorical stops he can pull out in order to force its pace. Moreover – while he may be frustrated – it seems the powers that be are satisfied with the progress of the investigation, for the 'Iron Lady' has largely refrained from her habitual sabre rattling. Several promising leads have emanated from *CrimeTime*. DS Jones, her star in the ascendant, at this very minute is overseeing the facial reconstruction, an initiative for which no little praise has been heaped upon her from above. And Skelgill and DS Leyton hurtle like a dusty comet towards Liverpool because Spencer Fazakerley has been identified.

*

'Look, Guv – there's Aintree – that's where they hold the Grand National – most famous horserace in the world. Rule Britannia!'

Skelgill has been haphazardly reading his weekly fishing newspaper, trying to piece together the stories partly consumed by his dog. He puts it aside and glances up. DS Leyton sounds inordinately proud of the great equine institution, which appears somewhat underwhelming to Skelgill, given its fame.

'It looks deserted.'

'It's the flat season, Guv – Aintree's a National Hunt course – hurdles and steeplechases.'

Skelgill stares pensively.

'What's the difference – between hurdles and steeplechases, I mean?'

DS Leyton is unaccustomed to such a reversal of roles – normally it is Skelgill that pontificates upon the merits of some obscure river they have stopped to inspect, or replays the nagging conundrum of how can sea trout and brown trout possibly be the same species?

'Well, Guv – in a hurdles race the jumps are only three foot six – they're flexible brushwood panels, and the horses can more or less knock them back – you don't get many fallers. Good hurdlers jump low to maintain their speed. In a steeplechase the jumps are actual wooden fences dressed to look like flippin' great hedges, some with ditches or water – Becher's Brook's got a seven-foot drop. It's like in the old days when they'd gallop from one village church to another and meet natural obstacles.'

Skelgill is no aficionado of the turf, but this notion appeals to him.

'So a steeplechase is the original race, cross-country?'

'I suppose so, Guv – but they've been using courses for a good old time – the National's coming up for two hundred years.'

Skelgill glowers as they pass a mammoth billboard advertising an online gambling sponsor.

'Do you bet on it?'

'Nah – it's a mug's game – the National's a lottery, Guv. Hah!' He notices his own pun. 'It's a handicap, for starters – plus there's forty runners and it's four miles long – twice your standard distance – and the going can be brutal. How do you find any form in that?'

Skelgill has no idea – *really* no idea what DS Leyton is talking about – but there is a paradox that perhaps intrigues him – there will be a winner, and it will win for a reason. But DS Leyton is also musing along similar lines.

'Except for Red Rum, of course, Guv. Never been a horse like it. Three times champion, runner-up the other twice it ran. My old Nan used to tell of how she dreamt the Thames was flooding the Isle of Dogs – and it was streaming all clay-coloured down the walls of her bedroom – except it turned into red wine. Next day was Red Rum's first outing in the National. She wagered a pony at twenties and won a monkey!'

Skelgill makes an exasperated gasp.

'Whatever language you're speaking, Leyton – I still reckon with the right information you could pick the winner.'

Now DS Leyton purses his fleshy lips.

'Thing is, Guv – what you can't account for is the interference from all the other horses – on paper your selection might be a shoo-in – then some novice brings it down at the first.'

Skelgill nods – he is contemplating the analogy – that there is an unblemished truth which underlies the story of 'Rose' – but the more widely they investigate the greater the risk that it becomes battered and bruised by overlapping and competing realities – dangerous loose horses, one of which may be 'Spencer Fazakerley'.

*

'So you can confirm it's him?'
'Deffo, Inspector.'
'And his full name is Derek Emlyn Alun Dudley?'
'He was named after Liverpool footballers, like.'

'And you're Mrs Teresa Dudley – you're married?'

The woman nods.

'Coming up fourteen years.'

She indicates a framed wedding portrait upon the mantelpiece – she is short, barely five feet, and there is no mistaking the tall, gaunt groom, 'Spencer Fazakerley' – properly Derek Dudley – towering alongside her with arms folded like some dour Dickensian funeral director. He is not greatly altered from their more recent photograph. For her part, she has acquired bleached blonde hair and a few pounds, but she has regular, attractive features and pale blue eyes that give as good as they get to her interrogators. The sitting room is unexceptional, and representative of another twenty million like it across England; a large TV set the focal point, and various black boxes and channel changers and wireless controllers tidied beneath. Their own technology has guided the detectives to the suburban semi in Spencer Avenue, to where the local police bearing June Collins' snapshot had been directed by neighbours, for the identification to be confirmed by Teresa Dudley herself. Skelgill gulps appreciatively at his mug of sweet milky tea. DS Leyton sits beside him on the sofa, pencil and notebook poised. An artificial lavender fragrance hangs in the air, of the 'scatter and vacuum' variety.

'When did you last see him?'

'Last October – towards the end of the month – the boys were gutted on Bonfire Night when he never got back.'

With her strong Scouse accent she pronounces the word "back" as the Scots do "loch", ending with a lenited *"kh"* sound that infiltrates many consonants on Merseyside, and which to the uninitiated might be perceived as a harbinger of imminent expectoration.

'You haven't reported him missing.'

'I have.' She sounds surprised – and not at all pressured by the implied accusation. 'I went to the local bizzies not long after, like.'

That she uses the Liverpool slang for the police seems to add credence to her assertion, and both Skelgill and DS Leyton are rocked back on their heels, to the extent that is possible whilst occupying a sofa. They stare at one another – DS Leyton bewildered, Skelgill looking for someone to blame. Then – *duh*! – it dawns on them simultaneously: their inquiries have proved fruitless because they have been seeking a non-existent 'Spencer Fazakerley' – the man she reported missing is Derek Dudley. Skelgill turns back to the woman.

'He's a lo–' Skelgill is halfway through the word "lorry" (or perhaps "long-distance") when a small aftershock strikes him. He begins again. 'What does he do for a living?'

'He's a builder.' Again, Teresa Dudley appears perplexed, that the police do not know this.

'A builder.' Skelgill buys himself a few moments by repeating her answer. A little voice in his head is chanting the words "red herring" and he has to fight a rising anger – directed at his organisation, it must be noted. He contrives to produce a follow-up question, though hardly an incisive one.

'What kind of builder?'

'Small jobs – loft extensions, conservatories, walls knocked through, like.'

The woman seems unruffled.

'What – a bricklayer, or something?'

'No.' She has the Scouse way of pronouncing the "o" as the word *owe*, the sound contained in her nose. 'He supervises the work – books the subbies – brickie, chippy, spark. Derek always says, why buy a dog and bark yourself?'

Skelgill is regarding her thoughtfully. She knows the building trade vernacular for the various sub-contractors. And she refers to Derek Dudley in the present tense.

'You mean like a project manager?'

The woman nods.

'That's right.'

'Does he have an office?'

'Upstairs, in the box room, like.'

Now Skelgill nods.

'Perhaps you wouldn't mind if we had a look before we go?'

'Be my guest.'

Skelgill regards her closely. She's tough – then that's how they make them round here, you wouldn't want to pick a fight with a Liverpudlian – especially not a working-class woman with truth on her side, as one major police force knows to its cost. Her skin is smooth, but there are worry lines at the corners of her eyes; the pale blue irises are cold, but he sees the indomitable fire burning within. He has reached a point where diplomacy is called for, and this is not his strong suit.

'Madam –'

'Teresa.' She is quick to interject. Skelgill complies.

'Teresa – I'd be right in saying that Derek worked away on a regular basis?'

'Every week – most of his jobs are in the Lake District – people getting their holiday homes and guesthouses modernised and extended, like.'

'Where would he stay?'

'B&B – it's cheaper than a hotel – and there's usually one nearby – sometimes it's the same place as the job.'

'He told you this?'

'That's right.'

'You didn't make his reservations?'

She shakes her head. There is a hardening of the muscles of her jaw, and Skelgill detects that his line of travel presents her with some discomfort.

'He takes care of his own arrangements – I've got my hands full with my work – and looking after the lads.'

Skelgill glances distractedly at the computer games console and controls.

'What ages are they?'

'Ten and twelve.'

'You work part-time?'

'Iceland.'

It is a moment before he remembers *Iceland* is a store chain, frozen food, he guesses. She sees his hesitation and provides what might be an answer to his puzzlement.

'Checkout operator. I can fit the shifts around the lads' school times. I'm on ten till two today.'

She glances at her wristwatch, but then continues to look at it for longer than is necessary. Perhaps it was a present from Derek Dudley.

'We needn't keep you – now we know where to find you.'

The woman nods. Her lips are compressed as if she is bracing herself, perhaps to avoid becoming emotional – or perhaps just not to speak. Skelgill is conscious that he has allowed the conversation to drift laterally, when he ought to be forging ahead, asking whether she thinks her husband might have been having a liaison of a romantic nature. Yet neither has she posed what seems to him the glaring question, why are Cumbria police investigating, and not the Merseyside force? It is possible of course that she has no inkling of what Derek Dudley was up to – that she has not questioned why he was digging in country garden filled with delphiniums. Perhaps she assumed he was working at a property he was renovating. And maybe everything seems straightforward – she has reported her husband missing, here are the police on the case. Skelgill doggedly skirts around the central issue.

'And you're managing – money-wise?'

She lifts a hand to her throat and fingers the gold St Christopher she wears on a short chain. She has told them she is 43 – the same age as June Collins, as it happens – but Skelgill cannot help making the comparison; these hands have seen a harsher life, of mops and buckets and budget bleach, and none of your pampering creams and lotions and potions.

'We get by.' She holds his gaze with a steely determination. Then she adds a rider, as if to correct any misapprehension she may have caused. 'You could always use more, like – the lads grow out of their clobber while your back's turned.'

Skelgill nods and makes a face that might vaguely convey his understanding. He reverts to the practical matter of her husband's disappearance.

'You've not heard from Derek – not even a text message – since he last went away to work in October?'

'No.'

'And that's out of character?'

'He didn't get in touch while he was gone – but that was rarely more than a week, like.'

'To be out of contact for a longer period – is that something he's done before?'

She shakes her head.

'Never. He always comes home.'

*

'This tunnel's a relief, Guv – you know me and boats.'

'Come again, Leyton?'

'I've been bricking it all morning, Guv – thinking we'd be taking the Mersey ferry – *The Liver Birds* – *Gerry & The Pacemakers* – an' all that?'

Skelgill appears baffled – despite that his thoughts have been occupied by a related, if somewhat esoteric, aspect of their subterranean surroundings – the notion of the many fish that must swim above them, and the challenges of approaching angling from below, rather than the more conventional approach, from above.

'I reckon that's just for foot passengers, Leyton.'

DS Leyton turns out his bottom lip; ironically he gives the impression of secretly regretting that they are not using the iconic surface transport.

'That's some accent she's got, Guv.'

Now Skelgill glances sharply at his sergeant – it is enough to convey the unspoken sentiment, referencing pots and kettles – but then again, he has an accent of his own, and – when he chooses – an impenetrable local dialect to go with it, so he skates on thin ice.

'Easy enough to follow – the main thing is, she doesn't seem to be covering up for Derek Dudley.'

DS Leyton briefly cocks his head on one side.

'I thought she was a bit tight-lipped when you mentioned money, Guv.'

Skelgill blinks deliberately a couple of times. They have emerged into bright sunlight on the Birkenhead side of the river. He pulls down the visor.

'People always are, Leyton. And if Dudley's left a nice little stash, why would she admit it?'

'Right enough he'd be dealing in cash, Guv – black economy and all that – no income tax, no VAT.'

'No money back, no guarantee.'

They glance briefly at one another – Skelgill is po-faced, but DS Leyton smirks.

'You decided not to mention June Collins, Guv.'

Skelgill shrugs – perhaps a little evasively.

'Happen I didn't want to be the one to break the news Dudley was leading a double life.'

There is a little silence, interrupted by DS Leyton's satnav, which exhorts them to make a U-turn. He swings lustily into a roundabout, pinning a grimacing Skelgill to the inside of the door.

'Maybe triple, Guv.'

It seems Skelgill has considered this possibility.

'He'll be running short of names.'

'I was thinking "Emlyn Alun", Guv – those middle names make a decent enough moniker. I used to have a sergeant down the Smoke called Dave Allen, laugh a minute, he was.'

Skelgill makes a scoffing sound.

'You've been doing too many crosswords, Leyton.'

'No fear – that's DS Jones's department.'

Skelgill falls silent. The mention of her name perhaps kindles a train of thought. Upon leaving Teresa Dudley they had contacted the Liverpool police – sure enough she had reported her husband absent in November, and missing person checks had been conducted. Since there was no reason to suspect foul play, only the basic protocol had been followed; Derek Dudley was sitting on file, on some back burner, with a quarter of a million others. Skelgill's idea is that they may be able to trace him from one of the jobs he has performed – logically, the most recent – by interrogating the dozen or so lever-arch folders they have taken into custody from his box-room office. At first glance, Teresa Dudley's assertion that her spouse is a housebuilder appears to stack up. But Skelgill does not relish the prospect of trawling through the indecipherable paperwork. DS Leyton is evidently thinking along similar lines.

'I reckon she'd find Lord Lucan, if they put her onto it, Guv.'

He refers to DS Jones's capability to devour and digest written evidence. But Skelgill, somewhat irrationally, seems to bridle at this suggestion.

'I'd settle for finding *Rose*, Leyton.'

DS Leyton nods obligingly.

'Derek Dudley would do for starters, Guv. Reckon we ought to put together more of a profile on him?'

Now Skelgill's expression is distinctly scathing.

'Leyton – we're trying to eliminate him from our inquiries, not write his biography.'

DS Leyton looks crestfallen – but at this moment the satnav interjects with news that their destination is ahead on the left, and in Skelgill's reaction to this information DS Leyton recognises a stiffening of his superior's resolve, and a renewed focus that is borne out by his words.

'I'm more interested in what this lot might tell us.'

*

She's early for a Thursday. Marvin checks his notebook. Yes, Thursdays she's normally afternoons. *Suzie.* Well, Suzanne, he knows for sure – he's seen her name on an opened envelope left on the dashboard of her car. Address, too. Suzanne Symington, big house at Thornthwaite. But surely she's Suzie when the lights are low? It's more intimate. Just like her stretches. They all wear these tight yoga pants nowadays – even some of the female dog walkers in the park beside the lake. Do they go to exercise class afterwards – or do they just like to pretend they keep fit? He's seen some of them at the leisure centre at Penrith, through the plate glass, it's one-way after dark, and they all admire their reflections.

Suzie's a regular – here on Harterhow and at the gym. And now she's going through her familiar routine. Marvin lowers his binoculars. The best bit is just coming. He pulls his camera from a pocket of his gilet. Remarkable the power of the zoom. Quite artistic, the close-ups you can achieve: the female anatomy at fifty yards. The sleek fabric is like a second skin. Rarely much worn beneath. May as well take a few shots – *might get something better than before.*

*

'It was more of a buy-in than a buy-out, Inspector.'

'How does that differ, sir?'

'Well – same principle as an MBO – you pay for the business with the intention to take over and run it yourselves – except you're from the outside, rather than having been existing employees.'

Skelgill rubs the stubble on his chin and wonders whether it is one or two or more days old. The action must make him appear suspicious of the answer – and after all, they are the police – for the younger man opposite he and DS Leyton volunteers supplementary information.

'It's quite likely Marvin would have described it as a management buy-out – it's common parlance, and people more easily get the idea.'

Skelgill nods.

'So what was the attraction?'

Now the man glances about somewhat guilelessly – like a homeowner trying to remember just what it was that appealed to them about the property, all those years back. They have come to a converted red-brick warehouse, hoisted three floors in an original clanking goods elevator, to a meeting room overlooking the Mersey. The large space is bright and airy; there are long picture windows, comfortable modern sofas, a pool table, a beer fridge, a traditional pub jukebox and a gigantic wall-mounted flat-screen TV that plays a muted music channel. The man himself – introduced as one of three owner-Directors – sports a trendy asymmetrically shaved haircut, a finely knitted navy merino sweater and drainpipe jeans and fashionable leather trainers.

'The business was a good fit with our own. We were exclusively web design – it's given us an advertising arm – now we can offer the whole package, from origination through to execution.'

Skelgill appears unmoved by the mild jargon.

'Couldn't you have done that yourselves?'

The man responds with a thoughtful sequence of nods, their amplitude descending – as if to demonstrate that he thinks this is a wise question.

'In some circumstances, undoubtedly, Inspector. But the local market was already crowded. MMA – that's Marvin Morgan Associates – was an established player – it would have been a slow road to growth to compete against them. And there was a further strategic reason – their biggest client, and ours – was and still is the Local Authority. It's not easy to get on the government roster, but once you do there's a long-term source of regular income. We'd be dealing with the same clients – and because they already knew us well, they endorsed the takeover and committed to continue to work with us on the advertising side – better for them, a one-stop shop and they didn't need to go through the whole due diligence process.' He draws his hands carefully back over the crown of his head, as if subconsciously checking all facets of the hairdo are in place. 'In one fell swoop it eliminated the biggest risk of buying a marketing agency – that the clients all jump ship and you're left with a rusting hulk.'

Turning his head Skelgill gazes across the grey Mersey, as if he is seeking floating evidence of this metaphor. But right now craft are few and far between, and his gaze drifts to the Liverpool skyline, where the twin towers of the Royal Liver Building, once perhaps more salient, are absorbed into a disharmonious modern cityscape that grates upon his countryman's eye.

'So how well did you know Mr Morgan, sir?'

The man tilts his head to one side and briefly closes his eyes.

'Not especially well – of course, his reputation went before him – everyone in advertising on Merseyside knew of MMA – won every award going, twice over – but Marvin's was the generation before ours. He made his name back in the Eighties and Nineties when direct marketing was all the rage. We're basically a digital agency, born of this century.'

'So he was keen to get out, would you say, sir?'

'I guess he felt he'd served his time. He'd achieved the status of industry grandee. And there's no denying that the age profile in advertising is skewed towards the younger end of the spectrum. I remember Marvin talking about striking off into the sunset – that he'd got a little bolthole up in the Lakes.' His voice momentarily trails off. 'I guess that's where you guys come in?'

The question is intended to be conversational rather than prying – though the man must be wondering what is their purpose – beyond what they said in their bland introduction about conducting a background check on Marvin Morgan – there being nothing for *them* to worry about. However, Skelgill is not about to dispense gratuitous detail where none is needed.

'It's what – five years since you took over, sir?' The Director nods and inhales to reply, but Skelgill continues quickly. 'Is there anyone here who *did* work with Mr Morgan?'

The man now begins to shake his head – but then he clicks his fingers, and frowns in self-reproach.

'I was just thinking of Creative and Client Services. There's Loz – of course – in Accounts.'

'Loz?'

'Lorraine Debitson – she was Marvin's admin assistant – we kept her on – she just works mornings.'

'Is she here now, sir?'

'I haven't seen her myself – but we lock her away in a little garret – like Rapunzel.'

*

Skelgill has in mind how Rapunzel might look – though he would struggle to recall when such an image became burned upon his memory. But, in any event, Lorraine Debitson is not it. Her hair is short and grizzled and cut in the style of a female judge who is habitually required to wear a wig. She is of average height, but decidedly thin, and rather arthritic in her movements for a woman of only 50; Skelgill watches with a little alarm as she stalks across the meeting room to shake his hand, before starchily accepting a seat as directed. He is alone with her, DS Leyton having been chaperoned by the young Director to a spare office from where he may make some essential telephone calls. The woman does not willingly meet his gaze, and Skelgill is left wondering if this is just her regular manner, or whether some history underscores the caginess. Either way, he is provoked into a moment of devilment.

'Madam, if I said to you I believe Mr Morgan may have committed a serious crime – what would you expect that to be?'

Now she does glance at him sharply. In her eyes is the look of a frightened animal, deprived of a means of escape. Is this a reflex – self-preservation – or loyalty to her former employer? And yet, though Skelgill's opening question is leading to the point of being out of order, she surprises him with a straight answer.

'Fraud.'

Skelgill regards at her intently. He wants to know if this reply reflects some belief or basis in fact, and is not just a convenient retort. But she has averted her eyes, to render any reading of her feelings more difficult. He notes, however, that her Merseyside accent, which might naturally produce a questioning intonation, is decidedly flat. She says "fraud" less as a suggestion and more as a statement. Interesting, too, is that she decisively plumps for this white-collar genre of crime – when a more predictable reaction might be to throw up her hands in dismay at the very idea that her erstwhile boss is a criminal. Skelgill waits a short while before responding.

'How long have you worked here?'

'Fifteen years.'

Skelgill nods.

'So that's what – five years since the management buy-out – and ten years before that, when it was called MMA?'

'That's right.'

'And the new business is doing well?'

She nods, a little apprehensively now.

'As far as I know.'

Skelgill assumes an ironic – though affable – tone of voice.

'Aren't you the accountant?'

'Bookkeeper.'

'And there's a difference?'

She seems more comfortable with this line of questioning.

'Profitability is above my salary grade. I just process the admin – make sure we pay bills on time, that our invoices are paid – allocate expenses to the correct jobs – complete the quarterly VAT returns. One of the Directors uses my reports to produce the management accounts for the Board. We have a firm of Chartered Accountants that conducts the audit and prepares the statutory accounts.'

Skelgill spreads his palms in an appeal to her superior knowledge.

'So what would be an obvious fraud?'

'I should say the CAs are the best people to ask.'

Skelgill leans forward and rests an arm across one knee. 'But if you were going to... let's say, write a crime novel – and there was a crooked employee?'

The semblance of a smile turns up the corners of her thin-lipped mouth. Skelgill wonders if she is what a typical reader of whodunits looks like. Certainly the idea of unpicking a devious plot might appeal to her orderly and perhaps righteous mind.

'Well – VAT is the commonest type of fraud. You charge VAT to your clients and then don't declare it on your return. That's 20% instant extra profit. But it would be easy to detect.'

'Why?'

'Because you have to send invoices that detail the tax to your customers. The VAT inspector would gain access to them and want to know why you haven't remitted the appropriate balance after deducting your own VAT outgoings.'

'But the VAT's your job – so we can rule that one out.'

Her body language hints at a further small incremental warming to him.

'Then perhaps more likely would be to charge a customer for a service you didn't provide.'

'Wouldn't they notice?'

Skelgill's expression is blatantly ingenuous, and now she grins.

'You might be surprised, Inspector, if the number of times we've been paid twice for the same invoice is anything to go by. But that isn't what I mean. I'm talking about when they *do* notice – that they are party to the deception.'

'An insider?'

She nods.

'That's why big organisations need robust internal auditing procedures. When employees are entrusted to spend large sums of company money, you need to know that someone hasn't passed an artificially inflated invoice and received a kickback from the supplier.'

'Would you spot that – here?'

Quite guilelessly she shakes her head.

'I have no idea whether the invoices I process are correctly priced. We sell advertising campaigns – and no two are ever the same – from a few thousand pounds up into the millions. The Client Services teams price up the work.'

'Any reason to believe it has occurred – in the past?'

'No – no reason.'

Skelgill rises from his seat and ambles across to the windows. The room is at one corner of the building, facing east over the Mersey and its other windows looking north towards a seven-story residential apartment block. There is a paramilitary-style rubber-armoured telescope on a tripod, pointing across the water. Skelgill digs his hands into his pockets and casually lowers his left eye onto the eyepiece, which is angled at 45 degrees for the comfort of the user. The optical device is trained upon the area of the Pier Head, the huddle of grand old Edwardian buildings known as *The Three Graces* (though this classical allusion can only be a demonstration of Scouse humour). Still gazing through the scope, he speaks.

'He's a bit of a twitcher, your ex-boss.'

He stands upright and flexes his spine, exerting pressure with his knuckles into the small of his back. Now he returns gingerly to the arrangement of crescent-shaped sofas that encircle a round coffee table. Lorraine Debitson appears somewhat reluctant to comment; she sits stiffly, with her hands clasped upon the knees of her crinoline trouser suit. Skelgill resumes his position but still does not speak; eventually the silent treatment tells and she volunteers some information.

'He left the telescope to the new merged company. He used this room as his office as well as for meetings. A lot of visitors liked to look through it. Some of the clients from the council would tease him that they could see right into their building – and that Mr Morgan must be spying on them.'

Skelgill nods. He has just experienced the phenomenon – the magnetism of a telescope, its promise of a window upon some secret world.

'And what did he say to that?'

'Oh – he just joked about it. He kept a bird list taped on the window – of the different species he spotted each month. One or two of them were quite interested in that.'

Skelgill raises a questioning eyebrow. 'Is there much to see out there?'

'I believe the Mersey estuary is important for birds in winter. I think it was called a *Shelduck* that Mr Morgan would tell people about – that there are more here than anywhere else in Britain.'

'Must be a lot of shells.'

Skelgill's remark is patently fatuous, and the older woman regards him good-naturedly, as a schoolmistress might a former pupil.

'I suppose there must, Inspector.'

Now Skelgill appears to be at a loss for what to ask next. He casts about rather aimlessly, and then claps his hands and rubs them together. It is more a gesture of finishing the interview – but if Lorraine Debitson begins to relax her guard she is disappointed, for he finds a new angle.

'What was Mr Morgan like as a boss? He was a good bit older than you – that can sometimes be awkward – for an attractive woman in your position.'

In her reaction there is something of the snail that suddenly retracts its tentacles – but when it determines that the threat is not existential, the little eyes on stalks reappear. Perhaps Skelgill's flattery engenders an unaccustomed frisson that prevails over her former allegiances. Still, her response is somewhat oblique.

'The age difference – I think it's about seven years – that's nothing to speak of.'

Skelgill appears content with this analysis.

'Aye.'

'He was unmarried.'

It is a counter-intuitive remark. Is she trying to tell him there is another reason why Marvin Morgan would not have had her in his sights? Skelgill shrugs casually.

'Happen being single just suits some folk. More time for your hobbies – the likes of birdwatching.'

Lorraine Debitson folds her arms, her lips compressed. She looks like she may be trying to make up her mind about whether to open up. Again, Skelgill simply waits; he rarely suffers labour pains during a pregnant pause.

'He did work very long hours. I would sometimes see the lights on in here – when I was passing on the bus home from Liverpool – late in the evenings and at weekends.'

Skelgill can sense there is something she wants to say, but is perhaps reluctant to make a direct accusation. He provides a possible option.

'Could he have been involved with another member of staff? Working late so he could be here alone with them? Pulling rank, even?'

'Honestly, Inspector, I'm sure his conduct was very proper in that regard. I should say he set a good example – against any kind of exploitation. No, it's not that.'

She seems determined on this point – yet the implied alternative in her final phrase invites interrogation.

'So there was something?'

She makes a little cough and strikes again the dignified pose with arms stretched before her and hands clasped upon her knees.

'I suppose – it is of a similar nature – a personal issue.'

'Aye?'

'Well, just that – on occasion when I used to get in – I was always first in the mornings – I liked to have the mail organised and on everyone's desk before they arrived – and – well – it was the telescope, actually.'

Skelgill does not speak but bows his head in encouragement. She indicates with a raised hand towards the north-facing windows.

'It would be pointing across at the block of flats.'

*

'Sorry those calls took a bit longer than I expected, Guv.'

'You didn't miss much.'

'Typical accountant, eh?'

'Apparently she's a bookkeeper.'

DS Leyton postpones any response. He has become preoccupied with navigating the surging cataract that is Switch Island. Growling under his breath, he exchanges profanities with fellow motorists, they blithely unaware either that he is a policeman or that he cut his teeth on London's mean streets, and has little grasp of the concept of giving way.

'They're all the same to me, Guv.'

Skelgill does not reply, and DS Leyton falls silent; indeed his features drain of determination now that he has attained the calm waters of the motorway. He yawns profusely – but then this seems to shock him back into an appreciation that he ought to be more attentive to his superior.

'Did she shine any light on Marvin Morgan, Guv?'

'Maybe.' Skelgill is staring penetratingly ahead, his eyes narrowed. They are rapidly overhauling a bright maroon HGV with the words "Bargain Booze" painted in great letters on its rear end. As they overtake, he reads the advertising slogan liveried upon the flank, *"Making Life Richer... For The Pourer"*. He grimaces – it might be a distressed smile elicited by the corny strapline – but perhaps the garishly decorated vehicle neatly conflates the two-pronged conundrum that occupies his thoughts: Derek Dudley and his non-existent occupation as a lorry driver; Marvin Morgan and his extant proclivity for surveillance. 'Aye, happen she did.'

There is such a long pause between the two parts of Skelgill's answer that DS Leyton seems to have forgotten what they were talking about.

'Right, Guv.'

But now Skelgill is no more forthcoming, and DS Leyton, making a series of faces as if some little battle for precedence is going on among his thoughts, finally volunteers a new starter conversation.

'Well – there's good news and bad news, Guv.'

Skelgill folds his arms. In his book, this ostensibly even-handed cliché only ever spells doom – a token spoonful of good news to sweeten the bitter pill of the bad.

'Aye?'

'DS Jones reckons we'll have a picture of *Rose* by Monday morning. She says she's seen what they can do and it's going to look like a real photo. She was asking whether you want her to organise a press conference?'

Skelgill is not enthused. At the mention of such, a cascade of images crosses his mind's eye: DS Jones under the maternal wing of the Chief; the cynical pack of hacks – Kendall Minto's boyish features bobbing in the sea of faces; his own discomfort, tongue-tied when a cutting riposte is called for. It is half a minute before he responds.

'I'll think about it.' He rubs vigorously at one eye as if he is trying to subdue a nervous tic. 'What's the bad news?'

'Oh – well, Guv – it's not like it's a disaster – just the *CrimeTime* leads – no joy so far and they're dropping off one by one. There's still a few to go at.' He sighs. 'If only it were a geezer in that grave in the woods – we'd know it were Derek Dudley.'

Skelgill begins gnawing at a recalcitrant thumbnail, a habitual clue to growing frustration. After a while he spits an imaginary splinter and slumps back in his seat.

'What makes you say that, Leyton?'

DS Leyton blinks several times, seemingly surprised that he is called upon to justify his logic. He sticks out his bottom lip as a launchpad for his thoughts.

'He's vanished off the face of the planet, Guv. His mobile was a prepay type – not used since the beginning of November. We know he walked the dog in those woods. He disappeared about the right time – going by your idea about the storm. And if either of those women had discovered what tricks he was up to with the other – *wallop* – who knows?'

Skelgill now makes his sergeant suffer another long silence. Eventually, between gritted teeth, he utters a quiet pronouncement.

'It's time we grabbed this case by the scruff of the neck, Leyton.'

'Righto, Guv.'

DS Leyton's tone – rich with manufactured enthusiasm – tells he has absolutely no idea what his superior has in mind. Moreover, his body language reveals a degree of trepidation that is not without foundation.

'How are you fixed tonight?'

DS Leyton looks suddenly downcast. He swallows. It takes him a moment to summon a response.

'Thing is, Guv – the missus has been a bit under the weather lately. She had a check-up first thing this morning, down at the Doc's – he wants her to go in overnight to the hospital – so they can run a few tests – monitor her vital signs – whatever. It means I'd have to pick up the nippers from school, and get 'em fed and bathed and put to bed. It's tricky finding a sitter at short notice – plus they want danger money.'

Skelgill appears more disapproving than sympathetic.

'Friday's probably better, anyway.'

14. NIGHT OWL – Friday

A killer might keep returning to the scene to make sure the body has not been discovered. Once it has been found, their approach may change. They might be irresistibly drawn – but then they have the excuse of publicity. They might be compelled to see what the police are doing. They may think that by going there and acting casually they can actually make themselves seem less like a suspect. However a member of the public, who simply frequents the same vicinity for innocent reason, might exhibit exactly the same behaviour.

*

It's Suzie. After dark – and that's not a dog in the car!

Marvin Morgan feels the thump of his heart as he stretches for a better view – the sleek hot-hatch with the *SUZ* registration plate. Rather inconveniently she has parked midway between his stances. Is this the best angle – with a view into the back, or should he move along and try from the front? Stay put – they're less likely to look out of the rear window. There's a faint greenish glow from the sound system display. Seems like they've reclined the seats. It's a cold night – they must want the heater on – the purr of the engine was audible as he approached. Better get moving – before the windows mist up – *hah!*

He slithers cautiously to his knees. Not that they'll hear him – not over the sound of the music and the engine. But he likes the way his soft shooting coat does not even make a rustle. He snaps open his folding step-stool – always comes in handy for extra reach – and pushes it against the foot of the wall. Then he shrugs off his rucksack and delves for his equipment. His camera is fitted with the night-vision scope – just need to feed the object lens through the elasticated aperture in the home-made hood – can't have his eager face lit up like a transfixed teenager watching illicit videos.

He pulls the black cloth over his head; now he has to feel his way. Brace with one hand against the cold stone of the wall; step up gingerly. Slide the elbows forward over the flat slab; make sure everything is steady. Now he's poised like a Victorian photographer – they enjoyed a peep show back in the day!

Should he record first? Or just try for a couple of stills? Start with live action – he can always cut in – or take a screenshot from the video later.

A waxing gibbous moon is sailing above the mountains in the south – its reflection is flaring off the curved glass of the windows. Wait – something is taking shape – they seem to be embracing – and fully clothed – but that won't stop them – not if Suzie's wearing that little miniskirt she goes home in after the gym. That must be where's she's come from – perhaps it's one of the instructors? Whoever it is, he seems to be raising a blanket to cover them.

Marvin closes his eyes. Imagine what it's like. The adrenaline. The suffocation. The abandonment. He feels it! He's floating! Upwards – his feet leave the step – and backwards – he hits the ground – he's winded – a blow upon the turf to the back of his head – strong arms have him pinioned – the hood is ripped away – there are stars – and shadowy faces – and harsh voices – they're saying "police" and "arrest" and "caution" – imperfect perceptions that fade into oblivion.

*

'Think he's okay, Guv? He still seemed a bit groggy when they took him away.'

'Nowt a night in the cells won't cure.'

DS Leyton makes a face of affected concern.

'We put him down a bit quick, Guv – he kind of floated out of my grip for a second.'

'Aye – young Dodd's a strong lad, Leyton – farming stock from Matterdale.'

Ambulance headlights now illuminate DS Leyton's face and cause him to squint. The vehicle, in which the uniformed constable and a paramedic accompany a handcuffed Marvin

Morgan, is too large to turn safely in the narrow lane, and reverses steadily out of sight, its blue light eerily strobing surrounding trees. DS Leyton has ditched his regular lounge suit and city shoes in favour of a more robust outfit, jeans and a leather jacket, better cast for concealment and ambush. DS Jones, on the other hand, stands beside Skelgill with a woollen blanket draped about her bare shoulders, and is beginning to shiver. Skelgill flaps a hand towards the car, the borrowed decoy from which they tumbled upon receiving the signal that their colleagues had moved in to apprehend Marvin Morgan.

'Better get this motor back to the owner.'

'Want me to take it, Guv?'

Skelgill glances thoughtfully at DS Jones. Darkness has enfolded them now, the ambulance must have turned, and is being followed by a squad car, their headlamp beams bumping and twisting into the night. Only the moonlight remains; does he imagine the flush in her cheeks; her breathing still fast and shallow?

'Go with Leyton – get warm. I'll drop it off – the lady lives just beside *The Queens Head* – Woody's normally there for last orders – I've got a rod of his in the garage that I've fixed for him – he owes me a lift.'

DS Leyton nods – though DS Jones looks rather forlorn.

'What about searching the cottage, Guv?'

Skelgill jangles keys in his pocket.

'It can wait till the morning. Leyton – you got the rest of his gear?'

DS Leyton makes a quarter turn at the waist to reveal that he has a rucksack slung on one shoulder.

'Reckon he brought everything in this bag, Guv – just need to grab that little aluminium stepladder. I asked Dodd to come back early doors – have a scout round – just in case he's flung something else we didn't see.'

Skelgill is progressively edging towards the hatchback. He seems eager to depart, and climbs in. Not bothering to raise the back of the driver's seat, he makes a lurching three-point turn, each time approaching perilously close to the opposing walls of the lane. He lowers the electric window and looks briefly to his subordinates. He grins a little crazily, baring his teeth.

'Reet, I'll sithee.'

*

Marvin Morgan's cottage stands shadowy in the moonlight that filters through surrounding trees. Skelgill stops the car a few yards short and steps out into the coolness of the night. The pungent scent of honeysuckle hangs heavy in the still air. A moth brushes past his face on its way to the stars. As he reaches the porch an overhead security light comes on. He pulls the bunch of keys from his pocket; there are five, two mortise keys and three smaller ones. He contemplates them for a moment, before selecting – correctly – one of the mortise keys and unlocking the front door. He opens it just wide enough to slip through sideways.

Roughly three minutes later he emerges. He is empty handed but for a length of cord – but as he steps away from the door its purpose becomes clear – for attached to the end is Marvin Morgan's dog, the chocolate doodle – which trots eagerly beside him, anticipating a walk. However, when Skelgill opens the passenger door of the car, with equanimity it adjusts its priorities and jumps in. Good deed half done, Skelgill pauses to think. Will Suzanne Symington still be up at this hour? Will she be alone and wary of his knock? And how will she react to his entreaty for bed and breakfast? (Of the canine variety, of course.)

15. HOW COTTAGE – Saturday

'How did you know he'd be playing at Peeping Tom, Guv?'

'If I'm honest, Jones – it was a shot in the dark.' Skelgill swivels to face his colleague. 'But let's just say I've been doing a bit of peeping of my own.'

He does not expand, and sighs and slumps back into Marvin Morgan's comfortable sprung chair; DS Jones is balanced beside him on the ash stool. They have been interrogating the former's laptop – not, it must be said, with any significant results. There are hundreds of photographs of various forms of local wildlife – but this is no more than they have already witnessed. DS Jones, competent when it comes to modern technology, is confounded. There is an internet browser – but no indication of an email account – or any history that would lead to one of the big providers – just a link to his blog saved as a bookmark. And there are no archived files of any kind. On the face of it, Marvin Morgan uses the laptop exclusively for storing his photographs, editing, and uploading onto his blog.

DS Jones looks about, at the trophies and books arranged with precision around the cosy study. Skelgill leans an elbow on the arm of the chair, and supports the side of his head on his palm. He regards her casually as she apparently mulls over their predicament. She is quite strikingly dressed this morning, lithe-limbed in a short skirt in soft clingy material and a close-fitting top, and there is surely more make-up than her usual discreet ration – it had prompted him to joke whether she had an interview – a rather clumsy backhanded compliment, she had assumed. Now she bites one side of her bottom lip in a gesture of mild frustration.

'I never got an inkling that he might be so inclined, Guv.'

'What – he didn't ask you to pose for him?'

She flashes a diffident glance at Skelgill and quickly looks away; however her rejoinder sounds intentionally coy.

'Maybe, Guv.'

'I can understand that.'

Skelgill's retort is swift, and he keeps a straight face – and now DS Jones frowns with affected annoyance – but at this moment a forensic officer peremptorily interjects – he arrives to inform them he has identified two of the three smaller keys – padlocks on the garage and tool shed – but that one remains unaccounted for. The loft has been inspected but there is nothing of note. He leaves and a moment's silence prevails. When DS Jones is first to speak, it seems she is keen to return to the subject of last night.

'Since we had a blanket, does that go down as an undercover operation, Guv?'

She suppresses a half-laugh, and Skelgill grins.

'Keep it quiet – else everyone will want a turn.'

DS Jones looks at Skelgill with a strange light in her eyes – but now his gaze is fixed resolutely on the laptop, for the screensaver has triggered and images of Harterhow are beginning to dissolve one into another. She offers a prompt.

'Do you think he got any film of us? It will have to be admitted as evidence.'

Skelgill runs his hands through his hair. Unlike his sergeant his appearance is somewhat unkempt, and he looks like he had a late night with concomitant payback this morning. But before he can reply, his mobile telephone, lying on the desk in front of him, shrills. The caller ID is displayed as "Leyton".

'Happen we're about to find out.' He picks up. 'Aye?'

'Guv – you got a minute?' The sergeant's voice is wheezy.

'Where are you, Leyton?'

'Just legged it along to your office, Guv – thought I'd get privacy in here.'

'Smart's probably got my line tapped.'

Though Skelgill's mood is light, and he makes this joke, for once DS Leyton does not take time to humour him; instead he presses on with his point.

'I've just being going through all the material on Marvin Morgan's camera, Guv.'

'And?'

'The Chief wants to see it.'

'We've all got our little vices, Leyton.'

'Thing is, Guv –' DS Leyton pauses to catch his breath – and perhaps also to realign his tactics in the face of Skelgill's facetious manner. 'There's some film from last night – fair enough – you can read the car registration plate, and see people moving inside the car – and that's all – so the video's okay – just the job.'

Now DS Leyton stops – as if he doesn't want to relate what comes next.

'Guv – you were joking about the line being bugged?'

'Course I was, Leyton, you donnat.'

'Well, Guv – what it is – the still photographs – what's left on the memory card – they date back about three weeks. Mostly birds and wild flowers and whatnot – and there's some of that Suzanne Symington, doing her exercises – a bit spicy, if truth be told – but there's also a couple of you, Guv – along the same lines.'

'Aye.'

Skelgill sounds neither surprised nor concerned. He says no more – it is plain DS Leyton is reluctant to elaborate, but his boss's taciturnity leaves him no option. His voice momentarily becomes more distant – as if he has risen to check outside the door.

'Cut to the chase, Guv – there's one of you and DS Jones – *kissing*.' He hisses this last word, and when Skelgill still does not comment, he continues. 'And another – just you – it looks like you're – well, Guv, you know – having a gypsy's in the bushes?'

'These things happen, Leyton.'

DS Leyton makes a queer sounding groan of exasperation.

'Guv – I see where you're coming from – you know how to ride out these things – but what about DS Jones? A picture like that – on duty – it's not like it's the Christmas party – it could go against her with the Chief – affect her career, even.'

Quite whether Skelgill discerns that DS Leyton is tactfully suggesting that while his trajectory is probably permanently stalled, this does not apply to DS Jones, it is hard to judge – but he glances searchingly at his female colleague, who is diligently working through dates of photographs on the laptop and taking occasional notes; she shows no sign of eavesdropping. Casually he switches the phone to his other ear, furthest from her.

'What are you suggesting, Leyton?'

Now DS Leyton has a small coughing fit – perhaps asthma brought on by his exertions and the stress of the moment.

'You know me, Guv – all fingers and thumbs – *Mr Clumsy* my old woodwork teacher used to call me. Nearly had me hand off in the circular saw half a dozen times.' He gives a nervous laugh, and his self-deprecating tone intensifies. 'Cor blimey – I could be looking through a fancy camera like this – trying to get the hang of it – next thing I've deleted a couple of photos without even knowing I've done it. No one would be the wiser.'

Skelgill seems to freeze. He inhales and holds in the breath, causing DS Jones to look up from her work. His teeth are bared and his grey-green eyes glazed – but when his facial muscles do begin to move it is to form the tiniest smile, and he nods almost imperceptibly.

'Just leave it, Leyton – I'll deal with the Chief.'

*

'Not a whole lot there, Guv.'

'We know he's a clever bloke.'

Skelgill stares pensively down upon How Cottage, with its grey slate pitched roof and various extended dormers, and overhanging eaves typical of so many Lakeland properties. While the minute and thus far unproductive search continues within, he has brought DS Jones partway up the hillside, the northern flank of Harterhow – hauling his rucksack that contains his Kelly kettle, and settling down in a spot that catches the morning sun as it strikes over the south eastern shoulder of the small domed hill. DS Jones blows steam off her enamel mug – the powdered milk employed by Skelgill means it is far too hot, almost too hot to handle, though Skelgill is undeterred, and slurps noisily at regular intervals.

'Had you hoped for something in particular – in the cottage?'

Skelgill shrugs; his answer is oblique.

'I reckon the ball's in your court, lass.'

DS Jones turns her head to look at him.

'You mean *Rose?*'

'Aye.' Skelgill sniffs and rubs a cuff across his nose; his gaze remains fixed on the building below. 'We need to connect her – and fast.'

DS Jones nods. She realises now that Skelgill has for some time suspected Marvin Morgan – for reasons about which he has not been entirely forthcoming – and this explains his less-than-enthusiastic view of his subordinates' interest in the likes of Derek Dudley, aka Spencer Fazakerley. But also she understands the tenuous basis of their arrest of Marvin Morgan. The evidence – at least as far as linking him to the body in the woods is concerned – is entirely circumstantial. That Marvin Morgan has a predilection for prurience is no proof of murder – and provides inadequate grounds for detaining him any longer than the lesser charge allows. Yet her boss must be convinced, for he has made an early move by his standards.

'Not that he'll flee the country if we bail him, Guv.'

Skelgill nods, but his features remain grim.

'We've shown our hand. Once he's free – any evidence we've not found – *pff.*'

Skelgill expels a jet of air through compressed lips to illustrate the disappearing effect.

DS Jones looks at him earnestly.

'Guv – are you thinking he's got more photographs? It would be easy to conceal a memory stick – or you can just hide material online.'

Skelgill is silent. He nods slowly.

'Aye – photos, videos and other stuff maybe. Look at those trophies. His blog. He's retired and he's even kept all his advertising books.' Again he pauses; he is comparing his own accumulations of maps and fishing tackle and unnecessary outdoor paraphernalia of all kinds. 'He's a collector.'

DS Jones gazes at the cottage below; her dark eyes become narrow and small lines crease her brow.

'If he is, Guv – then I don't think he'll destroy his collection.'

*

'Mr Morgan, you understand you have been arrested under caution for suspected non-consensual voyeurism under the Sexual Offences Act 2003?'

Marvin Morgan, who has chosen not to have a lawyer present, shakes his head. It is not a repudiation of Skelgill's question, but a gesture clearly meant to indicate that the parties are at cross-purposes.

'This can all be explained, Inspector.'

Skelgill is sitting in a straight-backed plastic chair with his arms folded. DS Leyton is beside him. They have polystyrene cups of machine tea and across the table Marvin Morgan has one of water. The interview room is just a regular office on the second floor of police headquarters. The detectives have their backs to large windows that give on to partly wooded farmland to the south of Penrith, which in turn admit the morning sun and cause Marvin Morgan to squint. He wears the same outfit of outdoor shirt and trousers in which he was apprehended, but has managed to look presentable, albeit unshaven. Indeed, he appears composed and possessed of a surprisingly good-natured disposition. Skelgill drains his cup and pulls a face of distaste.

'Then perhaps, sir, you might start by explaining what you were doing last night on Harterhow?'

Marvin Morgan nods obligingly and leans forward; he places his elbows on the table and intertwines his fingers. He looks from Skelgill to DS Leyton, and then turns his gaze back upon Skelgill.

'Inspector, I have been trying to film a Long-eared Owl for several weeks. It is a scarce species in Cumbria and a pair has a territory in that area. Naturally, like most owls they are nocturnal – elusive and very shy – so you have to go at night – and effectively stake them out.'

Such radical evasiveness wrongfoots Skelgill – hackles raised, emotion impedes a swift response. He requires a minute to gather his thoughts.

'Why did you film the car – and its occupants?'

Now Marvin Morgan leans back and presents his palms for inspection – it is a gesture of repentance.

'Inspector – my apologies to those concerned if that occurred by accident – you saw my portable hide? It's a bit of a Heath Robinson affair, based on the focusing hood that early photographers used. Unfortunately when I am setting up it's almost impossible to see what I'm doing – I often end up with some opening footage of my feet or the sky – or something that's wildly out of focus. Until I get sorted out and into a settled position.'

Skelgill is grim faced.

'Why would you try to film an owl when there's an engine running a couple of yards in front of you?'

'I assumed the car was about to leave, Inspector – as you say, the motor was idling.'

Skelgill pauses. He inhales and exhales ponderously, as if it is with some reluctance that he commands his will to live.

'You've been there before at night.'

It is a statement rather than a question – Skelgill knows Marvin Morgan cannot deny this – he has already referred to his familiarity with the supposed owl's habits.

'I have, yes. Occasionally I take the dog out late that way, it's handy to keep close to the wall so you don't lose your bearings – that's when I first noticed the owl – it has a particularly distinctive *cooing* call. Perhaps your officers heard it? It's most unlike the hoot of the Tawny Owl.'

Skelgill treats the question as rhetorical.

'So you know that folk park their cars down there at the end of the lane – after dark.'

Marvin Morgan takes a drink of water. Skelgill watches his hand lift the cup, but there is no sign of a tremor; however his thick eyebrows kink at their junction.

'I can't say that I've seen anyone at that time of night, Inspector – the occasional dog walker during the day, certainly.'

Skelgill is patently irked by what he considers persistent evasiveness. He opts to change tack.

'Mr Morgan – how do you explain the still photographs that were on your camera – close-up shots of a woman exercising – and of myself and Detective Sergeant Jones – plainly taken without the subjects' knowledge?'

Now Marvin Morgan nods and manufactures a look that rather too convincingly combines regret and sheepish guilt.

'Yes – of course – I confess it is remiss of me not to have deleted these images you mention.'

'So you admit to taking them?'

'Well – strictly speaking, *I* didn't take them.'

'Would you like to explain that, sir?'

'With pleasure, Inspector. As I'm sure you're aware, these modern cameras have advanced technology – such as a motion sensor and autofocus – and can be programmed for close-ups. You see – from time to time roe deer visit that clearing to graze – but they are very alert and excessively shy. I think you've seen the one that's on my blog – taken by my camera, concealed and left to its own devices, so to speak.'

Skelgill does not intend to reveal just how much he has discovered about Marvin Morgan's clandestine habits.

'Where else do you keep your photographs – videos?'

'Those I don't delete I transfer to my laptop, Inspector – you have seen my collection, both you and your colleague whom you mention.'

Skelgill makes a reluctant grunt that suggests he is prepared to give Marvin Morgan the benefit of the doubt.

'There's no second computer, memory sticks – online archive?'

Marvin Morgan frowns in a rather exaggerated manner.

'I can't think why I would want to duplicate my equipment – or my nature blog.'

'What if your laptop were stolen?'

Now Marvin Morgan makes a conciliatory gesture with the palm of one hand.

'Ah – well – I do have a plug-in drive. About once a month I back-up my hard disk – but it is essentially the same content.'

Skelgill does not react. The police have found the said device – it was kept on a bookshelf in Marvin Morgan's study – not easily to hand for a casual burglar – but neither hidden in such a way that would make it look suspicious to the authorities. The search – now complete – has not revealed anything else – and has encompassed the outbuildings and his car. But – as DS Jones has pointed out – a memory stick is easily concealed. Skelgill has concluded that he himself would seal it in a watertight bag and climb a tree that he regularly passed and put it down a hole. In a wood the size of Harterhow it would be like searching for a needle in a haystack. A stick in a forest.

Skelgill glares pointedly at DS Leyton, and then again at Marvin Morgan. He begins to rise. 'That's all for now, sir – we'll be back with you later.'

DS Leyton concludes the formalities for recording purposes. As they cross to the exit Marvin Morgan calls to them, a plaintive note in his voice.

'Inspector?'

'Aye?'

'I would do the same – I mean, in your shoes – I appreciate you have a murder to solve and this looks a tad suspicious.' He folds his hands upon the desk and grins assuagingly. 'But I can assure you I am an innocent member of the public going about my legitimate business.'

*

'He's taking it too much on the chin for my liking, Guv.'

Skelgill glares at his subordinate. DS Leyton's observation is couched in doubting tones, and – while on the face of it he suggests that Marvin Morgan is putting on an act – a pessimistic interpretation could be that he suspects such protestations of innocence are genuine, however contrived they may seem. Skelgill opts to respond to the metaphor rather than the ambiguous sentiment.

'Wish I had the excuse to lamp him on the chin, Leyton. Lying creep.'

Of course, this is a sanitised version of what Skelgill actually says. DS Leyton grins dutifully: after all, the man has photographed his boss relieving himself, and it would be only natural to exact some revenge. However, before he can comment, a raucous explosion of locker-room laughter reverberates about the canteen. In a far corner DI Alec Smart is holding court amidst a fawning clique of lower-ranked officers. He glances across and catches Skelgill and DS Leyton gazing on; he winks triumphantly – look how the fools eat out of his hand! Skelgill and DS Leyton turn away, unsmiling, but he has scored his little point. The incident appears to exacerbate DS Leyton's gloomy outlook.

'Guv, Morgan didn't want a solicitor – he's not even trying to argue the legal point. He must know there's no law against photographing people in public places.'

'Aye – but videoing someone at night in their car without their knowledge or permission – he can't deny that – we've got witnesses and the tape.'

DS Leyton seems compelled to pour cold water upon Skelgill's optimism.

'Maybe we should have left him to film a bit longer, Guv. What if you can hear that flippin' Long-legged Owl tooting away in the background? He'd probably convince a jury that's what he was really up to. He's got plenty of form as a twitcher.'

'Eared.'

'Come again, Guv?'

'Long-*eared* Owl, Leyton – not legged. There's Long-eared and Short-eared. I spoke to the Prof – he reckons there are a few pairs in the Lakes. Both types. And it's hooting, not tooting.'

DS Leyton ruminates for a moment.

'Must admit – I never knew birds even had actual ears – still, I suppose there'd be no point 'em tooting if they didn't.'

Skelgill looks at DS Leyton with resignation.

'Let's hope it's irrelevant, Leyton. We only need to convince the magistrate to let us hold him long enough.' But Skelgill can't suppress an involuntary sigh. 'Roll on Monday.'

'The photo of *Rose*?'

'Aye.'

'Reckon it'll really make a difference, Guv?'

Skelgill shrugs.

'It's our best hope – the search of the cottage has been a dead loss.'

DS Leyton still looks down in the dumps.

'Thing is, Guv – you'd think those rings would have done the trick – and at least there's no mistaking them – I mean, how do we know this reconstruction is going to be accurate?'

But Skelgill's attention has been wrenched away – for he has spotted a stout member of the catering staff barrelling towards their table, bearing a loaded tray.

'Thoo'll be fair brossen efter this.'

That the dinner lady has a twinkle in her eye reflects her familiarity with Skelgill's prodigious appetite, and in her local dialect she warns of over-eating. In turn he repays her with an uncharacteristic helping of charm.

'Annie, folk hereabouts couldn't sleep safe in their beds if it weren't for you.' He casts an imperious arm about the cafeteria. 'This great army of coppers marches on its stomach.'

The woman flashes a gap-toothed grin – however, as she manoeuvres herself away she tips her head towards DI Smart and his motley crew.

'Not a lot of marching ower yonder – sitting ont' backsides bletherin', more like.'

Skelgill shrugs helplessly, knife and fork already poised over the crowded plate. He tucks in, and for once DS Leyton requires little encouragement to follow suit. Indeed, his application to the task draws Skelgill's notice.

'You not getting fed at home, Leyton?'

DS Leyton looks rather ill at ease.

'Missed breakfast, Guv – had to get the nippers ready for their Saturday-morning clubs – running riot they were – then I remembered I had to get that rucksack of Morgan's booked in and examined – the camera an' all.'

This explanation evidently reminds him of his coded conversation with Skelgill concerning the photographs – for he retreats behind the cover of a forkful of food. Skelgill, in any event, is engrossed with the same.

'Hear you've nicked your pervert, Skel. Nice one.'

The two detectives raise their heads in unison. DI Alec Smart has sauntered unobserved to stand behind DS Leyton. He has his fists balled in his trouser pockets, and a scheming glint in his weasely eyes. Skelgill continues chewing, prolonging the moment when he must respond. DS Leyton hunches his shoulders and regards his superior with a pained expression.

'Just a matter of time before you indict him on the homicide rap, eh, pardner?'

DI Smart brings out imaginary six-shooters and simulates an American accent; he looks pleased with his efforts. Skelgill has no desire to play along.

'Something like that, aye.'

DI Smart affects surprise.

'I thought it was all over, bar the shouting?'

'There's still a few loose ends to tie up.'

Skelgill aches to sound confident, but is wary of gilding the lily; if he has to eat his words, DI Smart will exact the maximum pleasure in reminding him. And now DI Smart reveals something of his real purpose in coming across.

'Been running round Liverpool like headless chickens? I promised the Chief I'd drop off a file – got a review meeting with her at one.' He glances at his ostentatious wristwatch and then casually kicks a heel against the tiled floor. 'Might be a few things in there you ought to know.'

Skelgill is conscious that DI Smart's acolytes have fallen silent and must be trying to eavesdrop on the exchange. And it seems his artful colleague still harbours ambitions to put his own spin on the case.

'Anything I ought to know, Smart – you ought to tell me.'

DI Smart affects an affront; he reverts to his American accent.

'Gotta protect my sources – play by the rules, buddy.'

Ordinarily, instructing Skelgill to play by the rules is rather akin to asking a dog given two sausages to save one for later – but in this instance 'the rules' refers to DI Smart's own devious brand of detection, a strategy that relies upon a shadowy network of spivs, spies and second-rate supergrasses, employed in lieu of actual legwork, one that finds the cocksure Mancunian glued for hours to his mobile phone; hanging about in supermarket car parks and outside telephone kiosks; or making clandestine rendezvous in and seedy clubs and dingy bars.

Skelgill is still searching for a suitable rejoinder when DI Smart delivers his coup de grace.

'Word is there's one or two tasty photographs been taken into custody?'

He taps the side of his nose with a forefinger and leaves the question hanging, and begins to back away. DS Leyton's expression becomes one of alarm – that Skelgill might think he has something to do with the leak. But Skelgill is glaring at the smirking DI Smart.

'Aye – we'll see about that.'

That this remark has no substance – and that Skelgill fails to land a glove on DI Smart – might be noticed, for as DI Smart returns to his coterie there is another burst of hilarity, and furtive glances are cast in Skelgill's direction. Skelgill pretends to ignore the attention, setting about his plate, and now DI Smart's crew gets up and leaves as one. After a minute or so of silence, DS Leyton speaks – evidently keen to make sure no suspicion attaches to him.

'How does he get to know stuff, Guv?'

Skelgill makes a vague growling sound.

'Happen he's guessing half the time.'

DS Leyton nods dutifully, but he remains disconcerted.

'Reckon the Chief tips him off, Guv?'

Skelgill is finishing a last giant forkful of fried food; he pushes away his plate, and rises and then reaches to swig down the dregs of his tea. He smacks his lips and wipes his mouth with a cuff.

'I'll go and ask her, Leyton.'

16. PRESS CONFERENCE II – Monday

'So why are you calling her *Rose* if that's not her real name?'

'Happen it is her real name.'

The Chief and – it must be said – DS Jones, too, glance sharply at an exasperated Skelgill as he supplies this surly retort to the journalist. With the Chief in the chair, Skelgill has insisted upon a prominent role – though it is DS Jones who has introduced to the press conference the digitised reconstruction of how the murder victim may have looked. As a matter of fact Skelgill himself is not happy with police PR department's campaign – *"Recognise Rose?"* – a supposedly catchy slogan to capture the public's imagination; but he is not about to criticise his own in front of the hyena pack that is the media. Instead he is irked that, as he sees it, the reporter is splitting hairs. A profession he ranks somewhere between ticket touts and loan sharks – he detests the ethos which seeks to find fault where none is due, to undermine honest graft and self confidence (and which he holds responsible for singlehandedly demolishing the chances of an England team ever again winning the World Cup).

'Someone start a book on it!'

This is a chirrup from elsewhere in the crowd, and immediately other hacks rise to the challenge.

'7/2 it's Rose Gardener!'

'4/1 says Rose Bush!'

'Evens it's Rosie Lea!'

Sniggers expand into guffaws as the would-be wordsmiths put more witty combinations forward. A certain amount of controlled hilarity is tolerated by the authorities – it is not a live broadcast and they rely on these journalists for a good outcome – but when "Rose From The Dead" is proposed, the hacks, like an unruly class of schoolboys sense the steely eye of the headmistress – one who wields sanctions ranging from instant expulsion to future exclusion. Realising they ought not abuse her beneficence, a silence permeates the group and innocent faces are presented for further edification.

Into this hiatus – perhaps having waited his moment – chime the clear tones of Kendall Minto.

'The local man arrested near the site of the grave on Friday night – is he a suspect for the murder of *Rose*?'

All heads turn to the back of the room, where the young reporter evidently prefers to station himself. Even the police look alarmed. Skelgill, however, is staring at DS Jones – but her eyes too are fixed upon Minto, and she shows no sign of culpability, only fascination. Then the spotlight gradually reverts to Skelgill. They expect an explanation. Skelgill glances at the Chief, but she is stern-faced and gives him no clue as to which answer will find him in the least hot water. He gulps from a glass and clears his throat.

'A 57-year-old male was arrested under caution for an unrelated offence. He is assisting with enquiries.'

Now the mob scents blood – a hail of quick-fire questions has him cornered and confused.

'Is he the killer, Inspector?'

'Has he been charged?'

'What's the charge if it's not murder, Inspector?'

'What's his name?'

'Is it a local man, Inspector?'

'Does he have a record?'

'How long have you been watching him?'

'Did he tell you she's called *Rose*?'

'Is it the husband, Inspector Skelgill?'

The police, of course, are not obliged to publicise details of those whom they apprehend. And neither has Marvin Morgan exercised his right to inform someone of his arrest – saying there is no one *to* inform, and insisting that in any event the misunderstanding will soon be cleared up. Therefore, it is only if he is actually charged before a magistrate that his predicament will become known. And yet the public – or, at least, one of their representatives (and now a roomful) – already seems to know. It is at rare moments like this that Skelgill grudgingly appreciates the firm qualities of the Chief, for with imperious disregard for the congregation she brings to an end the press conference before its main purpose is subverted, and briskly leads out her officers. Furious hacks turn their frustration upon Kendall Minto, rounding upon the young whippersnapper to demand a slice of his scoop.

*

'So that's your little school pal put the cat among the pigeons.'

DS Jones shifts uneasily in her seat. They have retreated to Skelgill's office, where they have met up with DS Leyton.

'I don't know where he gets his information from, Guv.' She looks Skelgill in the eye – and with a hint of defiance. 'But I'm sure I could persuade him to tell me.'

It is hard to determine the exact nature of Skelgill's ire, but it perhaps becomes a little clearer as he reacts to DS Jones's rejoinder.

'Forget it, Jones.' He glances away, and for a moment aimlessly pushes around some papers that have appeared on his desk during his absence. 'It's a sideshow – pound to a penny it's Smart up to his tricks. Anything to trip us up.'

DS Jones regards Skelgill from beneath long lashes; a knowing grin teases the corners of her mouth. Then, decisively, she hands out colour photographs of *Rose*. Perhaps for the first time they each properly consider the image. And it is striking – half an hour earlier it silenced a cynical audience when it was flashed up on the big screen. Of course, there is brown hair and the prominent white front teeth – this much they knew anyway from the physical remains – but most captivating is the particular juxtaposition of well-formed brows, angular cheekbones, small ears, a snub nose, and slightly hooded blue eyes, contained in a face that is unusually broad. Interestingly, the hair has been drawn back from the head, as though in a ponytail. It demonstrates the creators' confidence – why hide behind a hairdo when you know the precise physiognomy? It is a countenance that exudes vitality. *Rose* she may not be, but real she is.

DS Jones is first to speak.

'That daft knockabout, Guv – over her name?'

'Aye?'

'It gave me an idea.'

'A daft idea?'

She smiles patiently.

'It started like that. When someone said *Rosie Lea* I thought of a cup of tea.' She glances at DS Leyton – as a native exponent of Cockney rhyming slang he confirms with a nod. 'And then I suddenly thought of a fortune teller – you know, with the tea leaves?'

She stops and now Skelgill is looking at her like he knows there *is* a daft idea coming. He inhales to make some protest – but hurriedly she pre-empts him.

'I don't mean that we should consult a fortune teller – or even that she was one.' Now she holds her copy of the photograph up for inspection. 'But what if she were a traveller? It could explain the Irish connection – and also why we've had no success in tracking her down. If the person who knows her identity is on the road – they could easily have missed the news coverage.'

DS Leyton now makes a rather sullen contribution.

'There's Appleby.'

Both Skelgill and DS Jones regard him acutely. What DS Leyton refers to is the biggest annual gathering of gypsies and travellers in the British Isles, the week-long Appleby Horse Fair, which takes place every June – only twenty minutes' drive from where they sit.

Again they ponder in silence. And perhaps they share a common if unrealistically bucolic image: a handsome gypsy cob that clip-clops along a leafy lane, in tow a traditional bow top caravan; at the reins, pulling contentedly at a pipe, the reclining incumbent, blissfully ignorant of the image of *Rose* that at this very minute envelops him, if only he could access the invisible electronic ether.

'I read there's 15,000 gypsies and travellers come to Appleby, Guv.'

Skelgill blinks and then looks at DS Leyton as though he is surprised to find him there. However, he has registered his sergeant's rider.

'Aye – but they all know one another, Leyton.'

DS Leyton looks doubtful. It is a common tactic, that his boss employs hyperbole to win a minor argument. For his pessimism is justified to the extent that this disparate community convenes once a year with no form of registration, many of no fixed address, and most preferring to remain anonymous to outsiders. Come the end of the fair, they scatter to the four winds, some to spend the rest of the summer on the road, others travelling where tradition and casual work dictate. Had *Rose* been discovered at the beginning of June instead of July, then the police would have been able to circulate her image at the great gypsy jamboree. As it stands, only bonds of kinship now connect the diaspora. DS Jones, however, has a suggestion.

'Guv – I stood in at one of the meetings of the Horse Fair liaison committee. I think there's a chance they'll be able to contact the *Shera Rom* – the head gypsy. I could have a word with the secretary?'

Skelgill turns out his bottom lip.

'Might be worth a shot.'

'A long shot, Guv.'

Skelgill ignores DS Leyton. He checks his wristwatch and turns towards DS Jones, but in fact he surveys the weather beyond the window. It is bright and showery, more like a day in April, and one that would lend itself to fishing, with a cool flush of fresh water percolating through the lakes. He stands and from a peg improvised from a size 9-aught treble hook he reaches down his jacket, and shakes it to verify that his car keys are in a pocket.

'Leyton – be on standby to field any leads that come in about the photo – Jones, you follow up your daft idea.'

DS Jones gives a purposeful nod, a twinkle in her eye; DS Leyton looks a little disgruntled.

'What about you, Guv?'

Avoiding eye contact with either of his subordinates Skelgill stalks over to the door.

'I've got to see a man about a dog. Woman, actually.'

*

'Inspector – such a pleasant surprise – won't you come in for tea?'

Another dressing gown, satiny and revealing – Leyton was right. Skelgill glances about as if he is checking for spectators. Is that the old lady's curtain twitching next door?

'I thought I'd just take Morse. And these boots are a state.'

June Collins steps back as if to draw in Skelgill, but the Lakeland Terrier darts out and begins to perform tight circles around Skelgill's legs. It seems to settle the argument. June Collins pouts and makes an adjustment to the belt of her kimono, and then wraps her long pink talons around the edge of the door.

'When you drop him back, then.' Her tone is insistent. 'I'll have something nice and hot ready – my first guests won't be here until seven.'

Skelgill nods rather curtly.

'Aye – I wouldn't mind a quick chat – just something that's come up in our investigations into – Spencer.' Skelgill almost says "Derek", but a sixth sense saves him from showing his hand.

June Collins looks a touch dismayed. She does not respond directly, but squints past Skelgill to his car parked beyond her small front garden.

'You don't have *your* dog, Inspector?'

Skelgill is down on one knee, in the process of looping a length of blue baler twine through Morse's collar.

'My neighbour – she's in the doggy day-care business. Comes in handy. Plus mine's big pals with hers – Sammy.'

*

Morse knows his way. No sooner has Skelgill lifted the tailgate than the terrier, a liquid blur of black and tan, pours out and slips under the stile; immediately Skelgill can hear the frantic crackling of dry bracken as a rabbit hunt ensues. He locks his car and then pauses to wonder if he should pull a tarp over all the gear in the back. But on reflection one look at the great melange of tackle would have the average sneak thief recoiling with a migraine. His is the only car, and he has parked it in the same position as the police decoy on Friday night. He stoops to peer through the interior and up to the top of the wall, at the two photographic stances where Marvin Morgan replaced the upright coping stones with flat rocks. A passer-by would not think twice about them, if they even noticed; in the dark the arrangement would be undetectable.

Skelgill now turns to consider the scene across the lane. Beyond the opposite wall is a small cluster of old Scots pines, characterised by their orange upper limbs, their dense bottle-green crowns providing thick cover. Is that where a Long-eared Owl might reside? Beneath, the rough pasture slopes away, a continuation of Harterhow, bristling with common rush and marsh thistle; a couple of dozen black-faced Swaledales are finding some pickings, the grass refreshed by the latest rain shower. Accordingly Skelgill inspects the sky. The weather is coming up from the south west; the temperature is ideal for walking and he decides to take a chance without a waterproof.

He pauses at the gate to read a small sign that denotes what to do in the event of a fire. "Don't start one," would be Skelgill's advice. The gate itself is in reasonable repair; a couple of the spleats and one of the braces have been replaced with newer wood; however the old posts have seen better days – they look like railway sleepers, slick with diesel oil. The chain and padlock are also fairly shipshape; for a moment he considers the idea of Marvin Morgan's unmatched key – but the lock is another brand altogether.

When he passes near to the site of the grave he finds Morse already there, snuffling about. There are no new tributes, however. He calls the dog and it seems willing enough to move on; they strike uphill and shortly break the cover of the oak wood and emerge into the clearing. Skelgill gives an ironic chuckle – at least he knows Marvin Morgan is not watching him. For a fleeting second he experiences a crazy urge to moon in the direction of the 'hide' – but what if there is another camera, one they have not found?

Trousers thus untroubled, he crosses the clearing and barges backwards through the prickly foliage at the margin of the pinewood. But rather than follow the faint path that crests Harterhow on its way to Marvin Morgan's cottage, he follows his nose – or, rather, Morse's nose – for the dog gambols ahead of him, traversing the steep wooded hillside with some purpose in mind. Despite the cross-slope, the going is easy underfoot; next to concrete these plantations are a naturalist's worst nightmare, inadequate light penetrates and nothing can grow; a fine network of tree roots sucks up what moisture is in the ground.

Skelgill takes his time. He is not sure what he wants to think about, but figures it might happen anyway. The dense forest cocoons him in its eerie brown light – greener if he cranes his neck to look up – a kind of sensory deprivation. He fancies that a shower is passing – but no raindrops reach down here. There are occasional signs of deer – they leave their calling cards in neat clusters – and odd cones stripped and discarded by red squirrels; but songbirds seem to have deserted Harterhow, though he knows they must be skulking about, shepherding their fledglings, trying to avoid the attention of the hawks that have their own chicks to fatten.

Morse is digging.

Skelgill sees the dog a good way ahead, its front legs a blur of motion, mulch spraying out from between the back. Skelgill is just thinking that they are on a path – although sometimes it is simply the way the fallen needles settle, like ripples of sand on a beach, a pattern formed by a less mindful force. The terrier is worrying some object beside a small pile of rocks. As Skelgill nears it successfully detaches the thing and pulls it away. Skelgill instantly recognises a skull.

But it is the skull of a badger or fox.

'Argh – come away, lad!'

He collars the dog and makes it drop the skull – it is narrow with two long curved fangs – surely a fox. Then a glint of silver from the dark exposed earth catches his eye.

'Stay.'

But "stay" is no good – he fishes out the baler twine and attaches the terrier to a branch beyond reach of its latest excavation. He produces a lock-knife and winkles out the shiny object. It is a metal disc and he realises it is attached to something else – he gives it a sharp yank and a strip of leather pulls free of the loose soil. It is a dog's collar. He rubs the disc clean between finger and thumb. It is engraved. It says, "Rebus."

Skelgill rises and takes a couple of steps backwards. It is a grave. The dog has clearly been buried here. That's what the rocks are for – to prevent foxes and badgers from doing exactly what Morse has just done – and perhaps to mark the spot. But time and tide has degraded the structure and Morse knew where to come.

Of course – most likely Derek Dudley buried the dog. And – actually – why not? Plenty of people do this with their pets. Take them to a place they liked to be. Somewhere that the owner would regularly pass – a way to remember them. A boyhood rat of his own is buried on Haystacks.

Skelgill restores the skull to its intended resting place and kicks mulch back over the bones (he pockets the collar and disc, however), and then kneels and pulls the rocks back into position. When he is satisfied with his handiwork he rises and inspects his hands: there is fine black peat beneath his nails – but there is often fine black peat beneath his nails. He looks about; the terrier seems resigned to its fate and sits obediently. Beyond the dog there is a definite line of wear in the woodland floor, angling slightly downhill. Perhaps he was right about this being a path. He releases the dog; and as if to corroborate his theory it bounds away, taking the same course. Skelgill follows.

In spite of the absence of landmarks the lie of the land tells Skelgill they are heading in a north easterly direction, towards Portinscale. And it is no surprise to him that, after leaving the boundary of Harterhow reserve (via subtle wall-steps that might easily escape the notice of passers-by), the path begins to converge with the minor road that extends past the village – but not before it makes a sharp right turn, butting up against the dense hedgerow that surrounds the secluded property inhabited by Archibald Coot and Lester Fox.

Morse, of course, pays no heed to the law of trespass (in common with Skelgill, some would say), and slips through the thick barrier, no doubt using a fox's trail – an invitation that is plain to him but invisible to the human eye. Skelgill calls and whistles and snaps his fingers, but to no avail. From time to time he can hear the creature panting excitedly and he begins to envisage the excavation of a precious vegetable patch. He could follow the path to the lane, and then double back up the driveway – but he spies a more expedient solution in the shape of an overhanging beech. He scales it with little trouble.

Dropping down into the garden he pauses to wipe green algae from his beige hiking pants, but only succeeds in making the smears worse. Surveying the scene he sees the roof of the cottage some fifty yards off, the lower part of the building concealed by well-trimmed topiary. There is no vegetable plot, and in fact the decorative theme sweeps past him, with low hedges of clipped box dividing off a winding gravel path from beds that burst with Mediterranean herbs such as rosemary and lavender; a weeping willow overhangs an ornamental lily pond, its fountain a copy of the *Manneken-Pis*, functioning as nature intended. Surrounded by woodland, the effect is of a peaceful oasis, and as the sun emerges from behind a cloud it turns up the volume of the bumblebees that harvest nectar from the lavender.

Then Skelgill spies – or rather hears – Morse. He spins 180 degrees to face – behind a partial screen of bamboo – a small single-storey outbuilding, of considerable age, built in the vernacular style, with no windows and just a solid door at the front – perhaps an ancient byre that became enclosed within the property. While many such buildings can be seen about the Lake District, leaning precariously in farmyards or crumbling in field corners, built on outcrops from the nearest available stone, this particular one is in excellent repair. The roof, though in traditional slate, is new, and the pointing recently restored. The door is varnished oak, and Morse has his nose applied to the gap at the bottom, and takes long loud sniffs.

'Come away, lad.'

For the second time this afternoon Skelgill issues this instruction, but he does not expect the dog to comply and strides towards it, pulling the twine from his pocket. As he reaches down the creature tries to evade him, and dislodges a short plank of wood propped against the wall beside the door. It falls with its other side uppermost, and Skelgill sees that in fact it is a hand-painted signboard with eyehooks and a chain to hang it. He turns his head to read the words: "Welcome to Harterhow Visitor Centre." He pauses, bent over the object, his brow knitted. He is just restoring it to its original position when there comes a rustling in the bamboo behind him. He wheels around.

Alarmed, white knuckles wrapped about the handle of a grass rake, stands a trembling Archibald Coot.

'Ooh – ooh! Mr – er – *Inspector*?'

Skelgill draws himself upright.

'Aye – Mr Coot.'

Skelgill now pulls the terrier between then by lifting the makeshift leash to shoulder height with an arm outstretched.

'This dog got into your garden.'

Archibald Coot looks like he thinks Skelgill might set the creature on him. He takes a step backwards and glances nervously over his shoulder. Or perhaps he fears his housemate will arrive at any second to admonish him.

'But – but – the side gate is kept locked.'

Skelgill makes a clicking sound with his tongue and gives a casual tip of the head.

'He's a fox terrier – there's no stopping them. He'd have your onions up before you could say Jack Robinson. Lucky I caught him.'

That there are no onions, and that — presumably — Archibald Coot is more concerned about how Skelgill got into the garden does not seem to trouble Skelgill — and he is not about to admit to his means of ingress. Archibald Coot shifts his weight from one foot to the other. With an unsteady hand he wipes perspiration from his pale bald crown, and then he makes a half-hearted gesture with the rake.

'I was just tidying up some leaves — I came to put this back in the — the tool shed.'

On the face of it this might be an attempt to suggest that he doesn't understand how the inspector apparently ghosted past him — but Skelgill is more consumed by the obvious discontinuity in the man's description. But any further question he might pose is pre-empted by the ring of his mobile phone. Archibald Coot starts with fright. Skelgill, however, knows the ringtone.

'Jones.'

'Guv — we've found her.'

'Who?'

'*Rose* — we've identified her.'

Skelgill inhales and holds back the breath. He glances at Archibald Coot and then at the outbuilding, and then at the Lakeland Terrier.

'I'm just, er —'

But DS Jones is insistent.

'Guv — I think you should come — DI Smart is on the prowl.'

17. 'ROSE' – Tuesday

'You look worried, Guv.'

'What?' Skelgill casts a quick sideways glance at DS Jones, his eyes screwed into tight pinholes. 'My sunglasses are in my fishing jacket. Knew I'd left something – just couldn't think what.'

'You're welcome to mine, Guv.'

Skelgill makes a rather ungrateful scoffing noise – which could generously be interpreted as a reaction to the prospect of donning the unashamedly feminine designer shades. In any event, DS Jones, behind the dark lenses, seems unfazed. Skelgill faces the road ahead, determined to see out the ordeal – signs for Scotch Corner are beginning to flash by and they'll be turning south shortly. A 6am rendezvous at Penrith means they have met little traffic on the eastbound A66, but the rising sun has provided a challenge. Their destination is Seamer Horse Fair, near Scarborough – a trip of around two-and-a-half hours.

It is a breakthrough that cannot be ignored. Yesterday, as Skelgill was pottering about in Harterhow Woods, DS Jones – with her 'daft idea' – took one giant leap. Having consulted the secretary of the Appleby Horse Fair liaison committee she made contact with the *Shera Rom*. While the head gypsy was unable to shed any light on the identity of *Rose*, he did inform DS Jones that there was such a thing as the Irish Travellers' Association – curators of a heavily subscribed social media page. Within an hour of the reconstructed image of *Rose* thus being posted online, three people had independently named her as Miriam O'Donoghue, an Irish traveller originally from Tuam in County Galway. And one had supplied the information upon which Skelgill and DS Jones now act: that she was last known to be travelling with a Romany gypsy from England, William King.

Skelgill now experiences a small conflict of instincts. Ahead of them in a broad layby a white catering trailer defiantly flies a tattered St George's cross. ("This may be Scotch Corner, but you're in Yorkshire, mate.") Already the aroma of frying has permeated Skelgill's car. He sees the queue of hungry truckers.

175

Though it pains him – for his stomach responds with a groaning plea and a concomitant spasm – his urge to press on wins the day. His right foot is unwavering. They speed past.

And therein lies the little germ of truth that DS Jones has exposed through her concern for Skelgill's frame of mind. With Marvin Morgan in custody – but not for much longer – this journey to England's east coast, every minute taking them a mile further from the epicentre of the case, symbolises Skelgill's growing unease: though he would not wish to admit it, there could be another explanation altogether.

But there is a silver lining. Word has it that William King – a stalwart stallholder of the gypsy fairs – as befits his name, is renowned as purveyor of some of the finest burgers in the land.

*

'Ar – that's 'er – that's Miriam.'

William King nods – his chestnut brown eyes glisten as he grips the photograph with grease-stained fingers. Perhaps a semblance of regret causes his lips to become increasingly compressed; but it is difficult to judge entirely his reaction to the news that *Rose* is dead.

Short and wiry, and somewhat cheerless, he is not Skelgill's idea of the touted 'Burger King' – as suggested by a sign near the entrance to the camping field – whence Skelgill's car had been trailed by a glowering pack of swarthy children armed with sticks and stones and a Shetland pony. Indeed, his expectation was of an amply proportioned, ruddy faced and welcoming character, a living advertisement for the output of his mobile fast-food emporium. Moreover, his accent – when they might have expected a Romani brogue that can sound more like Hindi – is deepest East Midlands, with its lazy vowels and dropped aitches: "Ar kernt 'elp it, me duck – it's 'ow I were bought up." (There is no *brought*.)

'Where d'yer get the photer? She din't like 'aving 'er photer took. She were superstitious.'

DS Jones glances animatedly at Skelgill – the reconstruction is *that* good – the man thinks it's a real photograph.

They sit in a cramped camper van, its slept-in air stale with the stink of unwashed laundry. Skelgill and DS Jones occupy one side of a fixed table and William King the other. There is no sign of a television or laptop or even a transistor radio. Much of the space is filled with haphazardly stacked cartons, wholesale SKUs of ketchup and tins of onions and packets of salt, and boxes marked as packaging for takeaway food. Attached to this vehicle is a trailer, serving hatch closed, liveried with the words 'BURGERS' and 'KING' in red capitals and juxtaposed such that they surely flaunt the laws of passing off. At just after 9am it is too early for the proprietor to be firing up his broilers, thus breakfast has not yet been mooted (if indeed the offer will be forthcoming) – though they have strong milky teas in polystyrene cups with unsatisfactory lids.

Skelgill takes a gulp and ignores the direct question, and reverts with one of his own.

'When did you last see her?'

'It were Appleby – last year.'

'In June – at the Horse Fair?'

'That's right – she went off to visit her son – never came back.'

Skelgill and DS Jones exchange glances.

'What's her son's name?'

'She called him Forrester – that's all I know.'

'Is that a surname?'

'I assumed it were – from his father. She wouldn't talk about the bloke – nor the son, come to that.'

'Do you know the address she went to?'

William King shakes his head.

'He were s'posed to meet her off the bus toward Keswick – he weren't on the road, though – I believe he had a house.'

The man has an unconvincing manner, he looks away each time he answers a question, and then furtively returns his gaze to the interviewer to check the results of his reply – as though he is accustomed to being evasive in the face of authority, and that to be candid conflicts with an entrenched habit.

'Did she tell you how long she intended to stay?'

'I thought it were just a couple of days – but – she went while I were working on the stall.'

'Aye?'

'She took all her stuff – in a big suitcase – one of the lads told me afterwards – she'd asked him for a lift down to The Sands on his two-seater gig.'

Skelgill folds his arms.

'Are you able to give us the name of that person?'

For the first time William King looks suddenly alarmed – as if he has just realised that he is a possible suspect and must act fast to clear his name. He nods urgently, and inhales deeply as though he is in need of a cigarette.

'It were Frankie Boswell's youngest – they're here at Seamer. They do buggy rides for visitors.'

Skelgill glances at DS Jones who nods as she writes to confirm that she has the note. Skelgill turns back to William King.

'When did you last hear from her?'

'I ain't heard from her.' Once more he glances away and then back – but now pathos infects his expression – as it sinks in that neither will he. 'The last time I spoke to her were the night a'fore.'

'So you don't know if she arrived in Keswick?'

William King shakes his head solemnly. Skelgill remains silent, watching the man, as if he is intentionally cranking up the tension.

'Mr King – why didn't you report her missing?'

Now he looks doubly evasive – and casts about the camper as if a suitable answer will be found by reference to some item of its contents.

'I had no claim on her – we'd only been going together a couple a'year.'

Skelgill extends the silent treatment, and after half a minute it produces a small result.

'An' I din't want no trouble for her.'

'What do you mean, trouble, Mr King?'

His countenance is pained – clearly it goes against the grain to say what is on the tip of his tongue – but self-preservation is winning the day.

'She took half a week's takings.'

'How much was that?'

The oblique default is back in action.

'I hadn't counted it.'

Though this seems unlikely it is a detail that does not concern Skelgill – he understands that the loss of the money – far from being a reason to report the woman's disappearance – would be a reason *not* to do so – since it would surely invite an investigation into William King's finances – non-existent books, cash and the black economy likely being the order of the day. The man is too valuable a witness (if not a suspect) for Skelgill to let a small detail like this become an obstacle to progress.

'Enough to make you think she'd left you for good, eh?'

He looks sharply at Skelgill, with surprise in his eyes – that the Inspector has taken this pragmatic line; perhaps also the insight. He nods.

'Reckon so.'

Skelgill pauses for a moment's thought.

'Where did you go after Appleby – last year?'

'Same as this year. Appleby to Epsom – for the Derby – then Cambridge, Henley-in-Arden – then came back up here.'

'How long are you on the road?'

'April to the end of October – Water Orton's the last horse fair of the year, down in Warwickshire – then it's only 25 miles home.'

'Which is?'

'Burbage.'

Skelgill looks in need of enlightenment.

'Aston Firs, beside the M69 in Leicestershire – it's a permanent traveller site. I grew up there – went to the village school – some o' the time.'

Skelgill glances at DS Jones, she is diligently taking notes – but in a shorthand that he can't read.

'So Miriam O'Donoghue lived with you there, as well?'

'That's right, Inspector.'

'She didn't go back after Appleby?'

'Definitely not – the van weren't touched – and I'd have heard if she'd been seen.'

Skelgill nods – this is something that will be easy enough to corroborate.

'You said you'd only been together for two years?'

'I met her at the Stow Fair – she did my reading.'

'Your *reading*?' Skelgill for a moment assumes this is some matter of illiteracy.

'Tarot – *Gypsy Rose*, she called herself.' His response is introspective – perhaps recalling that first meeting – and he seems entirely unaware that both officers stiffen at his words. He shakes his head and glances up. 'There weren't much of a living in it.'

Skelgill recovers quickly.

'So she had a stall at the fairs – doing tarot readings?'

The man nods.

'It were a tent.'

'I assume she didn't take that with her.'

Now William King shifts uneasily in his seat.

'I sold it – after a couple of months, like.' He waves a hand about appealingly. 'It took up a lot of space, you know?'

Skelgill does not appear judgemental.

'Did she mention that she might be meeting anyone else – other than her son?'

The man shakes his head, his expression blank.

'What about folk she may have had connections with in the area – Keswick, Penrith, Appleby?'

The response is the same – though after a pause William King adds a proviso.

'She told me she hadn't seen her son for above fifteen year. She must have found out from another traveller that he were living up in the Lakes.'

'Prior to when you met her – at Stow-on-the-Wold – where had she been?'

'She said Ireland – that she'd not long started coming over for the English fairs.'

Skelgill nods. The early indications from their Gardaí contacts would confirm this suggestion. It appears Miriam O'Donoghue had lived alone near Galway for some time.

'What about Liverpool – did she ever mention she knew anyone there – or who came from the area – Merseyside?'

Another shake of the head.

'Like I say, she din't make a habit of talking about herself. I got the impression she'd had a bad time and din't want to be reminded of it.'

Skelgill thinks for a moment and then turns to his colleague.

'Jones – the rings.'

DS Jones slips a photograph from her file and slides it across the scored laminate table. It is one taken of the rings worn on her hands held side by side, to show their positions. William King considers them for a moment, and then jabs a soiled index finger at the image.

'They've got that the wrong way round – the Claddagh ring – I gave her that – she wore it pointing in – towards her heart.'

The detectives know enough to understand that he means the convention of showing she was in a relationship. Skelgill grimaces, but decides to spare the man the knowledge that the picture represents exactly how the rings were found upon the fingers of the dead woman. Meanwhile William King is shaking his head ruefully.

'I wondered if she'd come back to me at Appleby this year – come back and see me, at least.'

*

DS Jones makes a small exclamation of triumph. She is interrogating her mobile phone.

'Last year's horse fair at Water Orton ran from 22nd to 27th of October, Guv – if William King was there, that would put him two hundred miles from Harterhow on the night of the storm.'

'There'll be no shortage of witnesses. Whatever you'd say about him – he makes a decent burger.' Skelgill is still sporadically sucking at his teeth as drives. 'Even beats that van our lot closed down beside the A66 above Keswick.'

DS Jones grins – Skelgill had made short work of his "King Size" burger and, to her relief, half of hers. But while she is ebullient he has been morose, and now he renews his grip on the steering wheel and stares grimly ahead. Paradoxically, this decisive breakthrough seems to trouble him in inverse proportion to his colleague's burgeoning optimism. It is a minute before he makes his next utterance.

'Forrester – so-called.'

He articulates the words as though they are a snatch of an argument that is going on within his own head. DS Jones looks sharply at him.

'Do you not believe him, Guv?'

Skelgill shakes his head – but then contradicts the action.

'Aye – I believe him – like he believed her. But that doesn't mean she told him the truth. The only thing we know for sure is that she did go to Keswick, or thereabouts.'

DS Jones is frowning.

'The problem is, Guv – if Forrester doesn't exist –'

She stops and there is a moment's silence until Skelgill speaks.

'Aye. It'll make looking for Derek Dudley seem like shooting fish in a barrel.'

Now a longer silence prevails – but DS Jones's mind is plainly turning over.

'She met *someone*, Guv.'

'Aye. Someone who knew Harterhow.'

The exchange reaches something of a stalemate. DS Jones seems reluctant to speculate further. She has wired ahead, and already wheels are in motion to begin tracing anyone by the name of Forrester (and Forrest and other variants). Skelgill might play devil's advocate – or simply be stubbornly anchored to deep preconceptions – but this new line of enquiry that she has driven forward offers real hope. They are homing in upon a textbook suspect: one who knew Miriam O'Donoghue; one with whom she apparently made contact shortly before her death; and one whose estrangement might underlie the motive for murder. However, she is discomfited to be at odds with her superior, and makes an attempt at conversation.

'Heck of a coincidence about the name *Rose*, though, Guv.'

'Was it?'

*

They couldn't have found anything at How Cottage. If they had done, they'd have been down on him like a ton of bricks by now. He just has to sit it out – the wronged-but-amenable-victim-of-mistaken-identity act seems to be working. Just need to wait until they run out of time. He's intentionally not asked them when they can hold him until – but it can't be much longer. Anyway – how can they charge him for a crime he didn't commit? That's what they really want to do – but even that dimwit of a local inspector, Skelgill, must realise there's not a shred of evidence – how can there be! As for the photographs – there's no law against it. Though he should have deleted them off the memory card when he copied them over. That was a lapse – he must change the default to auto-delete. Luckily he'd not taken many lately – what with the body being found – he'd kept away quite a bit himself. Only the video of the two people in the car is contestable – but is it really worthwhile the police trying to prosecute him for that? There's nothing to see.

Yes – it has been a valuable exercise – a dry run – arrested and questioned – on safe ground – but if you weren't you can imagine now how it would feel. It needs willpower, mental stamina. And the logistical side – precautions taken at the cottage have stood up to professional scrutiny. Marvin Morgan nods and grins – yes, he's coming through with flying colours. Now, what next to think about to pass the time? *How about an evening with Emma?*

18. FORRESTER – Wednesday

When Skelgill makes notes it is a clear sign that he is stumped. The written word is no ally of his; at best they have shared an uneasy truce, learning not to meddle with one another. At his desk this morning it should be no surprise to the onlooker, therefore, that when he takes out a pad it is not a paragraph he writes, or a string of bullet points or a table of facts, but a strange doodle – it resembles a childishly sketched outline of a ghost. There are two eyes, offset and angled up to the right, and a mouth shaping the sound *"oo"*. But now the doodle acquires a wiggling flagellum top and bottom – a bacterium? Next, other lines (some continuous, some dashed) and shapes and hatched areas begin to surround it. It is only when Skelgill begins to add letters – K, P, MM, C&F, JC among others – that the meaning becomes clear. It is a map. The 'ghost' (or 'bacterium') is in fact a faithful facsimile of the shoreline of Derwentwater – the eyes and mouth its islands and the flagella the River Derwent entering and leaving the lake. "K" is for Keswick and "P" for Portinscale, and other letters represent the properties of Marvin Morgan, Messrs Coot and Fox, June Collins and so on. Crosses mark the location of the grave of *Rose* (and of the dog, Rebus) and the summit cairn, and various lines the perimeter wall and the network of paths he has divined on Harterhow.

After a while he begins to chew the end of his pen, staring at the map. But his eyes, rather than dart about joining the dots, seem glazed as if some kind of *Magic Eye* image will materialise if he waits long enough. However, the trance seems to break of its own accord and he begins to draw fish. A pike stalks a shoal of what might be roach. A trout rises for a disproportionately large daddy longlegs. A stick fisherman (Skelgill?) leans into a leaping salmon.

Somewhat capriciously he discards his pen and pushes back his chair and stalks to the window – but he only looks out for a second before returning to pick up the telephone on his desk. He dials a short code.

'Leyton – how's it going?'

This is not an inquiry about the sergeant's wellbeing but a demand for news.

'Just about finished, Guv – no sign of a Forrester.'

DS Leyton sounds despondent. Having arrived late he missed the opportunity to venture out with DS Jones in search of Forresters in the flesh, several of whom have already been identified; they must be visited if only for elimination purposes. In his stead she is accompanied by one of her DCs, a burly if surly former rugby league prop that she can rely upon in the event of a rumble. DS Leyton, meanwhile, has been assigned to the task of slogging through the list of contractors' invoices supplied by the local council.

'What about the repair to the gate at Harterhow – who did that?'

DS Leyton makes a strange strangulated sound that might be a protest at this typically impossible question.

'When was it, Guv?'

'How should I know, Leyton – within the last twelve months.'

Now there comes a pause; Skelgill can hear the turning of pages, the regular wheezy breathing of his sergeant, occasional tutting and perhaps oaths mouthed in silence.

'There's nothing about a gate, Guv.'

*

'There he is – get your skates on, Leyton, he's climbing back on his quad.'

Skelgill now abandons his colleague and swarms over the wall into the rough pasture on the downhill side of the Harterhow parking area. His object is Stanley Gill, an ancient hill farmer of moderate acquaintance, whose wife has directed them here. Skelgill lets loose a piercing whistle – simultaneously the heads of a pair of Border Collies perched on the pillion twist to look his way – the old man follows their line of sight and sees

Skelgill, who raises a palm and begins to jog towards the little shepherding outfit.

DS Leyton pulls up panting a minute later, having been delayed by the combined difficulty of scaling the wall, an inspection of damaged trousers, and unsuitable footwear. Skelgill and the farmer have exchanged pleasantries. Rarely a lengthy process – this being Cumbria, where men tend to be of few words, and farmers even fewer, "Hoo's t'gaan" just about summing it up – they are already engaged in a similarly pithy conversation. DS Leyton notices that the dogs are giving him the evil eye – their main pleasure being the nipping of sheep and strangers – and he sidles closer to Skelgill improve his odds. Meanwhile, evidently having thought at length about a question posed by Skelgill, the farmer fixes a rheumy gaze upon the spot whence they have come.

'Yon yat? On t'other side? Aye – it were brocken – t'gale weren't it?'

Skelgill's eyes narrow.

'The storm – in October?'

'Aye – last backend. Knocked yon girt pine ower an' all. Yowes were reet flaiten.'

He gestures with a gnarled hand towards the clump of Scots pines halfway to the wall. Skelgill sees what the farmer means – one of the trees has been snapped clean off – and of course now he realises he has seen this before – it is among Marvin Morgan's photographs of havoc wreaked by the tempest.

'So what fell on the gate? There's no trees near enough.'

The farmer shrugs.

'Mebbe some daft ha'porth int' car – there's plenty a' folk wouldn't let storm put 'em off.' He winks at Skelgill to confirm his salacious meaning. 'But I divvent ken who done it.'

'Stanley – it's who fixed it I'm trying to find out.'

'Aye that were Norman Church frae Braythet – leastways it were one o' his trucks – saw it mesen the next morn.'

Now Skelgill is suddenly animated.

'Did you see who?'

'I din't deek – I were too busy chessin t'yowes.'

'Norman Church.'

Skelgill is already backing away. He thanks the farmer, who seems not in the least perturbed by Skelgill's abrupt termination of the conversation, and fires up his quad bike. DS Leyton has to scurry to keep up with his superior, and looks in constant danger of tangling his feet in a clump of rush and tumbling headlong.

'What did we find out, Guv?'

Skelgill grins over his shoulder and picks up the pace.

'He were chessen t'yowes – they were reet flaiten.'

*

'Looks like someone's here, Guv.'

'Aye – with any luck it'll be Norm.'

Skelgill slides to a crunching halt on the gravel of the builder's yard, close to a grey *Portakabin*. The journey to the small village of Braithwaite ("Braythet", as the farmer put it) has taken just fifteen minutes through winding back-lanes, progress that was slowed by scores of young pheasants recently released for a couple of months' R&R before being blasted to smithereens when the shooting season begins; those that make it past the roadkill stage, that is. The compound is bordered by a tall wire security fence, and holds various neat stacks of bricks and blocks, and scaffolding planks and poles, and pyramidal heaps of sand and stones, and there is covered racking containing various types of sawn timber. A single liveried pick-up is parked in one corner, its tailgate down ready to accept some such materials. The sounds of Skelgill's somewhat rude arrival prompt a scowling figure to appear in the open doorway of the hut. The man – a weathered-looking character in his fifties, with a closely shaven head and wearing a cement-smeared ensemble of t-shirt, cargo trousers and rigger boots – glares suspiciously, but upon recognising the car he gives a rather sardonic grin and produces for display a kettle that he is holding, before disappearing from sight.

This time Skelgill introduces DS Leyton, and they are invited for a "mash" – since Norman Church is just about to have elevenses. Skelgill knows the older man well enough. They share a common interest in fishing – and real ale – and a few minutes are spent bemoaning the unsuitability of the prevailing weather (a standard conversation among anglers, whatever the weather) and various techniques that are currently proving unsuccessful. But once they are seated with large mugs of sweet builder's tea around a makeshift table – a door laid upon a pair of sawhorses – Skelgill gets down to business.

'It's a bit of a long shot – but you'll know about the body in the woods at Harterhow?'

The man nods, and for the first time there appears a hint of alarm in his thus far easy going demeanour.

'Aye – a woman, weren't it?'

Skelgill nods; his expression is conspiratorial.

'We've identified her – she's not from around here.' He sinks back in his chair, and gives the impression that this is good news for them all. 'But that's making our job tricky.' (The man nods over his tea.) 'There's a witness we'd like to trace.'

Skelgill now explains what the farmer has told them, that a 'Norman Church' vehicle was present for the repair of the gate. But the proprietor is looking confounded. He rises, shaking his head, and clumps over to the far end of the cabin, where a broad shelf serves as a desk. He takes down a lever-arch file from above, and begins flicking through the contents. After a minute or so he turns, the downward curve of his mouth foretelling of a negative outcome.

'There were no such job, Skelly lad.'

'You do work for the council.'

'Aye – it's our biggest contract.'

'Could you have done it as part of another job – just included it without bothering about the admin?'

'Aye – we could – but yours truly would have to have known about it – and the time and materials would still need booked out and invoiced.'

Skelgill dunks a digestive biscuit and expertly swallows it whole before it can disintegrate.

'Do you recall anything? The morning after that storm.'

The man digs his shovel-like hands into his pockets and stares at the protruding steel toecaps of his scuffed rigger boots. Then he looks back at the detectives.

'Aye – I remember that morning, right enough. We were all over at Cockermouth – flippin' great tree fell on a school building and we had to make it safe.'

'All of you?'

Skelgill's question sounds like he is repeating the obvious, but Norman Church understands he wants a staff breakdown – and this makes him realise there is an anomaly.

'Aye – except – *no* – what were his name? – Jimmy Forrester – that were it.'

Anyone familiar with Skelgill would see he is not reacting normally, for hormones have kicked in that would be more use were he about to spring into some kind of fray. He is perfectly still, and conscious of DS Leyton's eyes trained upon him.

'I take it from that he's not working for you now?'

Norman Church does not seem to notice the heightened tension in the air. He pulls a disparaging face. 'Started turning up late – and the worse for wear – reekin' of booze. Can't have someone like that in our line – too dangerous – never mind the reliability. Take that morning with the tree – he'd got saws and axes we could have done with in the pick-up he were using. Let him go in the New Year. Thought it were a bit harsh to do it a'fore Christmas.'

Skelgill has waited patiently (though "saws and axes" had him visibly twitching).

'Where was he living, Norm?'

The man shrugs and screws up his lined features as he interrogates his memory.

'Reckon one the lads said he'd got a caravan – parked up at Threlkeld – beyond them garages up by t' beck.'

Skelgill glances at DS Leyton and gives a tip of the head towards the door – but DS Leyton is already rising and delving in his jacket for his mobile phone. Norman Church looks a little startled.

'Is he your man?'

'He's got the right name. It would be a bit of a coincidence.'

But now the builder seems perplexed.

'If it were him working at Harterhow he must have been doing a foreigner.'

Now it is Skelgill's turn to look doubtful.

'If it were a job for the farmer I could see it – but to repair a gate for the council, Norm? Who's paying cash-in-hand for that?'

The man shakes his head pensively.

'No – you're right, Skelly – it don't make sense.'

'How long did he work for you?'

'Must have been in the spring I started him – he just rocked up looking for casual labour – no questions asked. Thing is – he were quite useful – could turn his hand to most jobs when he could be bothered coming to work.'

'You've not got any details?'

Skelgill's tone is pre-loaded with a lack of expectation, and Norman Church looks relieved that the question is so phrased.

'Not that I can put my hand on right now – like I say – I didn't have him ont' books as an employee – call him a self-employed contractor. Tax and whatnot were his business.'

Skelgill grimaces; he is not about to reproach one of his own for grinding out a hard-earned living. And now DS Leyton appears in the doorway.

'That's DS Jones on the way, Guv – she reckons they're only five minutes from Threlkeld. I said we'd be there in ten.'

Skelgill finishes his tea and gives a gesture of cheers with the mug. He rises and strides to join DS Leyton at the door.

'You in *The Queen's* tonight, Norm?'

'It's darts night, Skelly lad.'

Skelgill raises a finger.

'I'll buy you a pint.'

*

'This can't be right, Guv?'

'Have faith, Leyton. Any road that leads to water, I've been up it.'

DS Leyton makes a resigned face and then flinches as Skelgill accelerates along the narrow potholed track. They are hemmed in by stone walls against which butt up shanty-like sheds and outbuildings; basically they are driving between two rows of rather neglected back gardens. Up ahead the track appears to take a sharp left turn after a perpendicular row of run-down garages. Skelgill has shaved a couple of minutes off DS Leyton's predicted ten, and maybe they are first here.

'You sure this is a – *LOOK OUT, GUV!*'

What happens now is not precisely what will be recorded in the official police account of the apprehending of James Forrester (although Skelgill if pressed would no doubt argue there are times when the end justifies the means). DS Leyton's vocal ejaculation refers to the alarming sight that materialises before them: around the end garage hurtles a piebald pony; its bareback jockey a man in his thirties, stripped naked from the waist up, shoeless and unshaven, wild-eyed and grimacing, long lank brown hair trailing in his own slipstream. He sees Skelgill's car and drives the animal on towards it, suddenly veering to the passenger side, meaning to squeeze past by means of a recessed gateway – Skelgill anticipates and slews his car to block the manoeuvre – but the rider reacts and reins the horse to the left – for a gap has now been created on the driver's side – but Skelgill is equal to the tactic and instinctively he flings open the door of the car and braces it with his right foot. The pony might be fleet on the flat but he is no jumper – and abruptly he refuses this hurdle. The rider flies out of sight.

As Skelgill and a shaken DS Leyton tumble from the vehicle, from around the bend bounces DS Jones's car, the detective constable beside her, their pale faces peering anxiously through the windscreen. They pull up short and join their colleagues at the double. Skelgill indicates to the surly burly DC to keep going, jerking a thumb over his shoulder – instructive moaning sounds emanate from beyond a low wall.

DS Jones is breathless.

'He was in bed, Guv – the caravan was unlocked – but he dived out of a window – it must be him, Guv – else why would he run?'

'Guess he were flaite.'

*

'Fractured wrist and two cracked ribs, Guv – otherwise nothing serious – no head injuries. They want to keep him in overnight as a precaution – but we can interview him in the morning.'

DS Jones lays her mobile phone on her notepad on the edge of Skelgill's desk. Her words are a message relayed concerning the condition of James Forrester.

Skelgill scowls unsympathetically.

'Should think himself lucky he didn't face-plant in a cold frame. What did they do with the horse?'

'There's a small livery in the village – they were happy to take care of it for the time being.'

Skelgill nods vaguely; he looks haggard. He has just come from a long meeting with the Chief; the apparent success of their operation is not reflected in his demeanour. DS Jones regards him empathetically.

'Like me to fetch you a tea, Guv?'

Skelgill does not respond for a moment – and then stares at her with scant enthusiasm, as though he has not properly understood the question. However, she persists.

'I don't mean the machine – I'll pop down to the canteen.'

'Aye – why not?'

His tone is flat and once alone he sits in brooding silence. After a minute or so a text illuminates DS Jones's mobile. He leans across and turns the handset around. The sender's ID comes up as "KM" and the content simply *"Moet?"* with a champagne bottle emoji beside it. Skelgill glowers at the screen until the backlight automatically switches off. Is "KM" Kendall Minto? But any further speculation is curtailed – for he hears footsteps approaching along the corridor. He slumps back in his chair. In fact it is DS Leyton that now enters. He looks harassed and is checking his watch.

'I reckon that's all the admin I can get done tonight, Guv – the CPS have shut up shop.'

Skelgill is plainly distracted and gazes out of the window; a shimmering column of gnats that dance in the rays of the evening sun holds his attention. DS Leyton has to prompt him.

'Alright if I do one, Guv?'

'What?' Skelgill looks surprised. 'Aye – whatever, Leyton.'

But now his sergeant lingers – as if this permission is insincere. But actually there is a message he must convey.

'Thing is, Guv – I've just been politely reminded – we can't hold Marvin Morgan any longer than midnight – unless we shake the leg of a magistrate and request another extension.'

Skelgill appears indifferent to this item of news, though he folds his arms.

'Let him go, Leyton.'

DS Leyton nods out of habit – but he is surprised by his superior's apparent lack of concern.

'I'll sort it on my way out, Guv.'

Skelgill does not reply and DS Leyton takes the opportunity to leave – but now Skelgill calls after him.

'Tell him I'll bring his dog round tomorrow.'

DS Leyton raises an affirmative thumb as he disappears – but it is evident he now crosses paths with the returning DS Jones, for there is a friendly exchange of goodnights and DS Leyton adds a parting word of congratulation. DS Jones says something about DS Leyton's wife – but her voice is hushed and

Skelgill does not catch the gist of it. A moment later she enters and carefully places the mug before Skelgill – she has nothing for herself – and resumes her seat. It is a couple of seconds before he acknowledges her kind act – he utters a belated "Cheers" – but now she becomes distracted: when she lifts her pad and phone together onto her lap and out of habit jabs a finger to check for activity she realises the handset has been inverted in her absence. Casually she drops the phone and pad into the slimline satchel that rests against the leg of her chair.

'Do you want to clear out and get a quick drink, Guv – make a plan for the morning?'

Skelgill has been watching her – but he still seems only half engaged with events around him. However, this offer seems to stir his consciousness.

'What?'

'When we've finished here – a drink, Guv? Beer.'

Skelgill makes a pained expression. He has not yet touched his tea and now looks at it forlornly. Then he waves a hand aimlessly into space.

'I need to keep an appointment – a darts match.'

'Oh, right.'

DS Jones looks a little downcast. Perhaps she is not convinced by his explanation – Skelgill as a member of a darts team is a new one on her – or it could just be that she is disappointed by his lackadaisical response to the past couple of days' developments. Ordinarily such rapid progress on a case would merit some alcoholic lubrication to keep the wheels turning and foster collective morale. Ordinarily, however, it is Skelgill that is in the driving seat.

He lifts the mug and sighs; it is the precursor to a solemn pronouncement.

'Any road – we've got a busy day tomorrow. You should get your beauty sleep.'

19. THRELKELD – Thursday

Skelgill scowls upon the scene.

It is a scintillating July morning and promises to be the hottest day of the year. Beneath a powder-blue sky the gentle green lower slopes of Blencathra rear up into vertiginous cliffs of shattered mudstone, challenging Skelgill to an immediate duel. In contrast, at his back lies the chocolate box vista of St John's in the Vale, with its trout-stream and the promise of hard-fighting brownies. For an outdoorsman such as he, some days his job is hard to stomach. Never mind that he is hung over. Never mind, even, that they have their man.

Skelgill has slunk away from James Forrester's caravan. It is parked at the end of the row of garages, tucked out of sight from the two terraces of back-to-back cottages. The immediate vicinity has been sealed off and guarded overnight until a proper forensic unit could be assembled. Now it is a hive of activity. But if the team are workers then he is a drone, aloof, tetchy – a lone task to perform when called upon, a self-destructive destiny. Right now he hovers apparently aimlessly in a kind of rickyard that marks the end of the lane. There is an open-fronted shed that has obviously served as a makeshift stable for the pony; its corrugated iron roof is half caved in, but there is a manger with some sparse hay, and a rusted drinking bucket. Beside the byre is an abandoned trailer, of the sort normally towed by a motor vehicle, but adapted with shafts for horse-drawn use; both tyres are flat, their rubber perished. Between a log pile and a dung heap is a jumble of corroded household appliances – ranging from a fridge with its door missing to the perforated drum of a tumble dryer; it looks like James Forrester at one time dabbled in scrap – but not so recently. More topical however is an improvised brazier, an industrial-scale oil drum with holes punched in its wall – 'more topical' because a wisp of smoke rises from within.

Seeing this Skelgill seems to recover his sense of purpose – for he picks up the bucket and strides across to the nearby brook. He stands astride two rocks; a Grey Wagtail flits about a patch of shingle a dozen feet upstream, but determines he is no threat and continues to dart at mayflies. He dunks the bucket and hauls it to the brazier and methodically pours half its contents over the smouldering fire. When the hissing subsides with the sole of his left boot he shoves the brazier off its supporting ring of cracked house bricks. It topples with a dull clang and he has to grab it to stop it rolling away. Now he upends the thing and delivers to the base a couple of solid thumps with the side of his fist. Finally he pushes the drum aside to reveal a volcano-like cone of grey ash and charred debris, faintly steaming. He returns to the beck to wash his hands as best he can. Just as he is selecting a loose stick from a tangle of flotsam, a cry reaches his ears – a note of triumph in the familiar voice.

'Guv – Guv – you gotta look at this!'

He turns to see DS Leyton approaching, his shambling gait hindered by a pair of clear polythene evidence bags that he grasps, one in each hand. He reaches Skelgill and takes a succession of wheezy gasps.

'Have a butcher's, Guv.' He raises the bag with the bulkier contents. It is a thick wad of used pounds sterling banknotes. 'Gotta be fifteen grand there, or I'm a monkey's uncle!'

Skelgill narrows his eyes, though it may just be a reaction to the morning sun, against which DS Leyton holds his prize.

'What's in the other one?'

'Whole bunch of cheques – look like they're half-inched – not made payable to him – unless he's got a shedload of aliases.'

'Let's see.'

Skelgill snatches the bag. He is about to break protocol by opening it – but the clear polythene reveals all: the topmost cheque is made payable to "William King". It might be a relatively common name, but this simply cannot be happenstance.

'Bingo.'

'Come again, Guv?'

He displays the bag.

'There's only one way this could have got here.'

'Guv – that's the burger bloke! So *Rose* must have brought it – Miriam O'Donoghue.'

Skelgill nods.

'Looks like half a week's takings wasn't all she filched, Leyton.'

DS Leyton grimaces, and weighs the bag of cash ostentatiously.

'I reckon it were a lot more than half a week's takings, Guv – if she turned up with this above a year ago – how much of it has he spent?'

Skelgill looks pensive.

'Maybe he didn't start spending until after Christmas.'

'He certainly wouldn't have been fussed about getting the sack from your mate, Guv.'

Skelgill raises a hand to his temple – as if this reference to Norman Church has brought about a little resurgence of his headache.

'You'd better tell Jones.'

DS Leyton nods in a businesslike manner.

'She said she'd tried to call you early doors, Guv. She thought she should hold off interviewing Forrester – in case we found exactly something like this in the caravan. I said I'd ring her about eleven with an update.'

Skelgill passes the cheques to his colleague. DS Leyton now notices the small scene of destruction wrought by Skelgill, the overturned oil drum and the heap of damp ash.

'What's going down here, Guv?'

'You tell me, Leyton.'

Now Skelgill begins to poke with his stick. Though a rake would be better he is an old hand with fires, and deftly begins to spread out the blackened debris. As is the way with braziers, there is an accumulation of layers of residue, incompletely combusted, not just slag and cinders, but strands of charred material and bent wire and melted plastic. Almost immediately he spies something and swoops to retrieve it.

'What is it, Guv?'

Skelgill dunks the item into the remaining couple of inches of water in the bucket. Then he holds it up for inspection. It is a scorched and slightly distorted piece of metal, rather like a hinge.

'Looks like the locking clasp of a suitcase to me, Leyton.'

There is a moment's silence; then the penny drops with DS Leyton.

'Cor blimey, Guv – are you thinking he torched all her gear?'

Skelgill is looking rather imperious. Nonchalantly he drops the clasp back onto the pile of ashes.

'Better get someone up here who knows what they're doing. Never mind the cheques – everything we might need for a conviction could be lying there.'

DS Leyton is looking jubilant.

'Wilco, Guv – reckon we've cracked this one, eh?'

'I wouldn't say that, Leyton.' Skelgill is grim-faced and quick to answer. He stares in silence at the amorphous mass of debris like he is willing it to reveal its secrets – though his next words suggest his thoughts have drifted elsewhere. 'Too many loose ends.'

DS Leyton regards him with concern.

'But, Guv – if you're thinking about that Liverpool malarkey – like you said – shake someone's closet and it'll probably rattle – you find strange behaviour – but no actual crimes committed – nothing serious, anyway – not even the Morgan geezer, really. And Derek Dudley – it's not our problem – he's listed as missing on Merseyside's books.'

Skelgill does not immediately reply; however he has made up his mind about something, and begins to walk in the direction of the caravan, beyond which his car is parked.

'Take over here, Leyton. We'll catch up the three of us later. Maybe back at the ranch.'

'What're you gonna do, Guv?'

Skelgill now trots out his current pet phrase about a human and a canine.

*

That Skelgill, for once, really does have to see a man about a dog – usually a conveniently oblique non-reply – means that a humiliating climb-down must shortly ensue. He cannot be relishing it. But first he has to collect the Labradoodle from its temporary billet at Thornthwaite. En route, however, he makes a detour to Keswick. He takes the A591 Windermere turn, and diverts into town alongside the River Greta, craning to snatch views where he can; the water is unseasonably low and martins swoop for hatching flies above becalmed pools. He parks in a large supermarket lot – does not trouble to buy the requisite ticket – and emerges from the store a couple of minutes later with a one-pound box of *Milk Tray* tucked under his arm. A thank-you to Suzanne Symington for services rendered? But it would be an ill-considered choice of gift, remembering the woman's dedication to fitness and physique. A further crack appears in this hypothesis as Skelgill ignores his car and strides towards the town centre. Indeed, barely a minute later he skips up three steps into the unprepossessing portal of the council offices. Flashing his credentials at reception he asks to see "Cheryl in Planning". And no, he does not have an appointment.

There is a connection between Skelgill's headache and his presence now at the council. Intending last night to fulfil his promise of a pint for Norman Church, he soon became subsumed into the buying of rounds amongst the latter's four-man darts team. In such circumstances it is often difficult to determine just when everyone has done their duty, and once five is inadvertently passed, ten is required to restore the status quo. However, the upside was that it enabled Skelgill to pick his associate's brains without seeming so obviously mercenary. Norman Church, like any builder worth his salt, is well versed in the machinations of the local council's planning process. Indeed, he has gone one step better, in acquiring an administrative 'mole' in the shape of his sister-in-law (Cheryl). And Cheryl does not look like the sort of person who would turn down a box of milk chocolates.

Having parted with his offering – well received, as anticipated – and accepting a mug of hot tea to which he has added an inestimable quantity of sugar (no disapproving frown from Cheryl on that front), Skelgill explains his purpose. He understands from his good friend Norman that all renovations and improvements to properties in the National Park, including changes of use – however minor – should be registered and certified, in order that the traditional fabric and integral beauty of the region is maintained. Developments failing to do so risk being reversed by law. Cheryl nods obligingly, part-distracted as she is by a choice between *Hazelnut Swirl* and *Strawberry Temptation*. (Still – there's always the second layer.) Skelgill goes on to list the addresses that interest him, and the dates that he has in mind. This appears to be at least a three-chocolate question, as Cheryl gets busy at her computer terminal. Skelgill is content to relax and sip his tea, declining frequent offers to indulge in the diminishing confectionery. In fact four chocolates later he has his answer, and within a couple of minutes is back at his car, stuffing into the black hole of his glove box with many others the parking fine that has been affixed to his windscreen.

*

'Another dog? You'll be getting a job with the RSPCA at this rate, Inspector – are you sure you won't come in? You promised last time and then you had to rush off.'

'Aye, well – happen something pretty urgent came up. You know what police work can be like.'

'And now look at poor Morse – he's so disappointed.'

The terrier is watching them through a window, from a perch on the back of a sofa.

'I'll take him again soon.'

June Collins pouts disapproval. For once she is not between ablutions or some other such aspect of her beauty regime, and Skelgill has found her rather clumsily cutting roses in her small front garden. Her outfit, however, is a skimpy white housecoat that makes her look like a hospital nurse, although pink fluffy carpet slippers and yellow rubber gloves rather detract from the effect.

'Well, you could help me – I need three more.'

She presents him with the secateurs that she has been wielding. Skelgill acquiesces. He examines the bunch she cradles against her bosom, as if to assess what it is he needs to look for.

'All red?'

'Yes please – with long stems.'

She rather crowds him as he performs the operation, and it seems to prompt him to state the purpose of his passing visit. He closes his eyes momentarily – a little double take to remind himself to refer to Derek Dudley as 'Spencer'.

'My sergeant mentioned that Spencer didn't leave behind any documents.'

June Collins' expression is set at its most ingenuous, her mascaraed lashes fluttering helplessly – though Skelgill suspects she would be reacting this way whatever his question.

'Did he have a desk or whatever – some kind of filing system – or a computer and printer?'

Now June Collins shakes her head decisively.

'There was nothing, Inspector – nothing at all. I never saw him with any papers the whole time he was here. Come inside, I can show you.'

Skelgill notices a deep burgundy tint revealed by the sunlight in her glossy raven hair, and her movement causes the mixed fragrance of the roses and her own musky perfume to envelop him. It is a pleasant combination to which he experiences a small urge to yield. He wavers for a second, but then he presses upon her the secateurs and the three roses he has cut.

'If there's nothing – I can't see it, madam – now, can I?'

He steps away and wipes his fingers across one another several times. June Collins looks rather forsaken – but she recognises his determination.

'Well, Inspector – you will come back for Morse? Otherwise he'll start to get jealous.'

*

It's Inspector Skelgill – what a brass neck! He's brought back the dog in person. Can't imagine he's going to apologise – he's too full of himself. He's probably convinced himself they've still got something on him – that little bit of blurred video – but it'll never stick. He's basically stupid. So let's have a little bit of fun at his expense. Set the wheels in motion. Carefully close everything up. He can wait a couple of minutes; it's a nice day outside.

*

'Mr Morgan – I was beginning to think you were out on the hill – I'm returning your dog – safely cared for.'

'Marvellous, Inspector – he looks in the pink – I must congratulate your veterinary service.'

Skelgill glances down at the Labradoodle; the dog does not appear particularly animated at being reunited with its master; perhaps it recognises its repatriation to a more austere regime than it has enjoyed over the past few days. However, Skelgill is not about to reveal that the very woman whose car he used to snare Marvin Morgan in the act of clandestine filming has looked after the animal.

'Aye – it was a top-notch B&B, you might say – much like your own used to be, I believe.'

Skelgill makes this statement offhandedly, as he stoops to free the dog from the lasso knot he has used on its collar. He is not looking at Marvin Morgan, therefore, when the man's rubbery lips stretch into a triumphalist crescent.

'Ah – you have done your research, Inspector – but of course I would expect nothing less of our excellent police force.'

Skelgill has shown no sign of conveying regret for the man's detention, yet he lingers – a state of affairs that appears to amuse Marvin Morgan, as though he believes it is just a matter of time, and that Skelgill is skirting around the edges of an excruciating apology. When he could plainly end the encounter by thanking the Inspector for returning his dog and simply retreating indoors, he makes a rather surprising offer.

'Would you like a guided tour?'

'I beg your pardon, sir?'

'My guest facilities – I am still open for business.'

Skelgill looks a little confounded. He gestures vaguely at the front of the cottage. 'I don't see a sign – nor at the end of your drive.'

'Ah, well, Inspector – it's all about the target audience.' Marvin Morgan looks pleased with himself. 'I fear my prices would rather embarrass the average walk-up customer. You see – How Cottage is to the ubiquitous guesthouse what the boutique hotel is to the big chains. Let me show you.'

He steps back and gestures for Skelgill to enter. Skelgill now shakes the twine free from the dog's collar – but it shows no great inclination to charge ahead of him.

'Up the staircase, Inspector – and follow the landing back round to the front – I'm right behind you.'

Skelgill has to duck his head to avoid low beams – roof trusses really, for the upper floor of the cottage is effectively a conversion of the attic space, with various gables and dormers that have been added down the years. The landing twists and turns until just two doors remain – on his right a narrow slatted affair that is obviously an airing cupboard, and in front a more substantial oak planked door with a wrought-iron thumb latch.

'Just go in, Inspector, please do.'

Skelgill bobs beneath the lintel and enters what is a deceptively spacious chamber, the window directly ahead, a four-poster bed to his left, various items of period furniture, vernacular in style but classy nonetheless, a full-length floor mirror, and in the corner on his right a polished glass shower unit equipped with a traditional Victorian riser, and beside that on the adjoining wall a washbasin with old-fashioned colonial fittings. The soft furnishings have been skilfully chosen to coordinate with the old dark wood of the beams and furniture, and the cream plaster of the walls, and create a fusion that is at once traditional and modern. Scented candles, though unlit, infuse the air with intense vapours, and patterned cushions and throws are strategically placed around the room. Though Skelgill is no aficionado, he recognises there is substance in Marvin Morgan's 'boutique hotel' boast.

'So you see, Inspector – it's a far cry from your common-or-garden backstreet B&B.'

Marvin Morgan is leaning proprietorially against the door jamb.

'How many rooms have you got, sir?'

'Oh – just the one – I promote to couples – you know, the 'Mr & Mrs Smiths' – they like the idea of not having someone sleeping just through the wall – and older, of course, that's a big market in the Lakes, the well-heeled empty nesters, to use the advertising jargon.'

'So how do they find you if you don't have a sign?'

Marvin Morgan gestures to a broad four-legged ottoman upholstered in striped coffee-and-beige fabric that stands at the foot of the bed; upon it lies a neatly arranged fan of glossy journals.

'I advertise in special interest magazines – country pursuits, fine dining, historical properties – that sort of thing.'

Skelgill on entering the room has automatically gravitated to the dormer window on the opposite side from the door, overlooking the front driveway. Now he puts a hand on the casement and presses his forehead to the glass, as though he is interested in some structural aspect.

'Your builder did a nice job of the place, sir.'

'It's mostly my own work, Inspector – I have always been interested in DIY. And I have the luxury of time, of course.'

Skelgill remains staring out of the window.

'Happen we didn't disrupt any of your customers' plans?'

This statement contains the first semblance of possible remorse from the side of the authorities – in the shape of Skelgill – and behind his back it prompts the return of Marvin Morgan's rather unsettling grin.

'In fact I don't take bookings in July and August, Inspector. As you know, the Lake District seethes during the school holidays – my typical customers tend to avoid these overcrowded periods – they prefer spring and autumn for walking, and cosy winter breaks. Even then I limit myself to just one or two nights a week – it's more of a hobby that brings in some pocket money – makes use of my tax-free allowance.'

Skelgill steps away from the window and casts about appreciatively, as if he can imagine availing himself of the facilities – but suddenly from below comes the bark of the dog – it is agitated and persistent.

'That's not like him – excuse me a second, Inspector.'

Marvin Morgan turns and stalks away, leaving Skelgill on his own in the bedroom. Skelgill takes a couple of deep breaths, as though he has been finding the encounter nerve wracking but has fought to conceal it. He moves towards the bed and regards it pensively, his hands in his pockets. Then he shrugs off whatever reverie has come upon him and crosses to the washbasin. There is a rectangular vanity mirror on the wall above it and Skelgill leans in to inspect his reflection. For a moment he appears to be trying to stare himself out – but then he notices an errant nasal hair and with a decisive jerk he plucks and discards it in a single motion.

The dog has been silenced, but since Marvin Morgan shows no sign of returning Skelgill leaves the room and wends his way downstairs; the dog is eating at its bowl and Marvin Morgan is washing his hands at the kitchen sink. He hears Skelgill's approach and speaks without turning.

'There must have been a fox in the back garden, Inspector – it's not like him to bark for food – these doodles are notoriously indifferent to their meals.'

Skelgill looks at the dog, which is making heavy weather of an undersized ration of unappetising dried pellets. Small wonder, when recycled cardboard is on the menu – although, on reflection, his dog would probably hoover it up, regardless.

Skelgill now makes his excuses; that he has a meeting to attend. Marvin Morgan wishes him good luck with his investigation. There is something in his tone that suggests he knows – or at least guesses – that there has been progress in some other direction – although no public announcement regarding the apprehending of James Forrester has yet been made. Skelgill is not about to enlighten him – but Marvin Morgan, rather than take offence, seems only amused by Skelgill's clumsy taciturnity.

'Perhaps see you out on the hill some time, Inspector.'

*

Hilarious! If he's not urinating in public he's picking his nose – the minute he was left alone in the room! And let's not forget the other photograph of him kissing his colleague. It is becoming quite a little collection – if he ever wanted to embarrass the dumb detective.

20. EVIDENCE MOUNTS

"Back at the ranch" turns out to be more ranch-like than the cliché intends – for, by mid afternoon, it *is* the hottest day of the year and Skelgill has decided that his stifling office is no place to work. Instead he has called a parley in the garden of a pub at Pooley Bridge, a short fifteen minutes' drive but a world apart from the industrial-estate ambience that surrounds the M6/A66 Penrith junction near their base. They have a rustic picnic bench fitted with a broad parasol, set a little away from the rest. They have cooling drinks – DS Jones tonic water with ice, DS Leyton a *Coke*, of the nutritional variety, and Skelgill a pint of orange squash, already half consumed. And they have an idyllic setting, with apple trees and – yes – ranch fencing and green fields with cattle grazing beyond and the blue waters of Ullswater lapping just far enough away such that Skelgill cannot be distracted by the rising of fish.

Yet, he *is* distracted, notwithstanding.

Such disquiet might be put down to the holidaymaking clientele with whom they share the beer garden – the raucous laughter of collectively inebriated parents, inured to screaming offspring that vie to subvert the health and safety precautions of the play area – but in fact Skelgill behaves as though he has screened out this uncouth brouhaha, like the distant rumble of a motorway, or the hum of a city at night; his distraction is of a more aloof, serene nature. Yet the meeting itself promises to spark the attention – for his subordinates have arrived armed with news aplenty.

The evidence, however, does not come from the lips of James Forrester who, in keeping with his futile equine escape bid, is effectively refusing to cooperate with the police. And it is on this point that DS Jones – who earlier conducted an initial interview with their suspect – is updating her colleagues.

'It's not that he won't talk at all. He's just denying that his mother was ever there – he insists he hasn't seen her since he left Ireland as a teenager.'

DS Leyton bridles at the man's claim.

'He's got no chance with that story, Guv – I did house-to-house calls on those cottages – three people recognised her from the photo reconstruction – one woman says she used to see her at the bus stop for Keswick – taking laundry – and the village shopkeeper reckons she was in regular – always paying cash, I should add.'

Skelgill's eyes narrow.

'When was she last seen?'

DS Leyton is nodding, anticipating this question.

'Course – people can't remember exactly, Guv – but they're all saying it must be well before Christmas. The shopkeeper asked Forrester where his mother was – says he told him she'd gone home to Ireland. What's more, Guv – Bonfire Night – seems Forrester had a whopping great blaze. Couple of the cottages – there's people with nippers – they were out the back letting off their fireworks – say they can remember seeing the glow from behind the garages. SOCO reckon there's remnants of clothing and buckles from women's shoes and a hairbrush amongst the fire debris – good chance we'll get intact DNA that would prove they belonged to her. Plus we can probably get descriptions of some items that William King may be able to identify – the make of the suitcase, for instance. There's melted cosmetics tubes and lipsticks – and, how about this – a charred pack of tarot cards – only got burnt round the edges. She weren't much of a fortune teller, Guv.'

If a joke is intended Skelgill appears to miss it; perhaps he is recalling his prediction that compelling evidence would rise from the unpromising heap of ashes. Now DS Jones interjects.

'Regarding DNA, Guv – the priority swab we submitted from Forrester has come up positive – there's no doubt that Miriam O'Donoghue is his mother. And now the Gardaí know where to look, they're saying it's just a matter of time before they track down the source of her dentistry – and with it all her personal details.'

Skelgill turns to DS Leyton.

'What about Forrester?'

'There's nothing in the caravan to confirm his official identity, Guv – no passport, no driving licence – not even any government papers – such as if he were signing on. Looks like he's been operating under the radar. One of the neighbours remembers there being a maggoty white *Transit* – when he first arrived – suppose he had to tow the caravan somehow. But that disappeared when he got use of the builder's wagon.'

Skelgill is nodding.

'What about the tools?'

'I collected the axes and saws that your mate Norman thinks Forrester had in his truck on the night of the storm – they're with forensics – the boffins are confident of getting a match between the blades and the damage to the skeleton. After you'd gone we discovered the lock on the end garage had been forced – haven't managed to trace the owner yet – but there's marks on the concrete that suggest he hid the body there – the lab are processing samples.'

'Did you speak to his workmates?'

'Seems he kept his own counsel, Guv – bit of a loner, even at work – but one interesting snippet. Young apprentice and Forrester had been dropped off to dig some trenches – they finished early and had to wait to be picked up. It was a Friday afternoon – not long before Forrester got the heave-ho – started to rain so they went in the local pub. In no time Forrester's had a skinful – he starts behaving really sinister, like – tells the geezer that he's "done something bad" and that "he'll burn in hell" – won't say any more than that – and the poor lad's too scared to ask him.'

Skelgill listens to this last item with his nose in his pint glass as he drains its contents. He exhales and rises, still holding the tankard.

'I'll get us some top-ups.'

This offer takes his subordinates by surprise; he is marching away before either of them can protest. A small boy boots a plastic football in his direction, and he makes a rather gawky left-footed attempt to pass it back; the ball balloons up in the air and curves away in the breeze, narrowly missing a crowded table of revellers. Someone teasingly shouts "Dinnae gi'e up the day job" – they are a bunch of Scots; their schools finish a fortnight before the English. He displays a hopeless shrug – and wishes he had a one-liner that would convey his feelings right now about the day job, if only he knew what they were. At the bar he is pensive; he watches patiently while a tall dark-haired girl with a slight Eastern European accent pours four pints of lager for a rather dour tattooed middle-aged man; she reminds him of a brown-eyed Scarlett Johansson and when she turns to him she has to ask him twice for his order, and when he starts she gives a little laugh that conjures in his mind the tinkling of a stream on a high mountainside. Her badge says 'Samanta' and a tiny red-and-white flag shows she speaks Polish; her voice is kind and he leaves her a tip that is almost the same as the cost of the round, and her eyes follow him quizzically as he scoops the three glasses together and carries them away.

'So what's the pitch to the Chief?'

Skelgill addresses this to no one in particular as he reaches to put down the little triad of drinks, but DS Jones understands the question is directed at her. She waits while he feeds his gangly legs between the seat and the table.

'Are you sitting comfortably?'

Skelgill does not look very comfortable, but he nods for her to continue.

'Miriam O'Donoghue left William King at Appleby last June. She intended the split to be permanent – since she took his savings – that may have been an afterthought, because she had already told him approximately where she was going. She stayed with her son James Forrester in the caravan at Threlkeld until her death in late October. He killed her – but I don't think he intended to – perhaps it was an argument over the money. He hid her body in one of the disused garages and dismembered it using tools from his job. He figured no one would be out on the night of the storm and that's when he took the remains to Harterhow. He must have damaged the gate when he was reversing the pick-up – and came back early the next morning to fix it – to avoid drawing attention to the spot. He used Bonfire

Night as cover to burn all of her belongings in the brazier. He gave her a kind of Christian burial – and I think it was he that put the roses on the grave.'

DS Leyton is listening open-mouthed – his breathing audible and wheezy. Of course, he knows the facts and suppositions, but to hear them woven into a succinct and yet comprehensive narrative imbues freshness such that he might be hearing it for the first time. Skelgill is singularly impassive. He drinks and then clears his throat.

'What about an accomplice?'

DS Jones takes a moment to react – and when she does she looks like he has asked her a question that she cannot process.

'Guv?'

Skelgill's expression is challenging.

'The day we found the body – or June Collins' dog did – you asked me what if there were two people.'

DS Jones is unprepared – true, she voiced the concern – but it was light-hearted speculation, at a time when they had nothing to go on. Now the mystery has unravelled so neatly they might have been handed the skeleton plot of a detective story.

Skelgill persists.

'What if William King's money wasn't stolen – what if it were a payment?'

'You're not serious, Guv.'

'What about Derek Dudley? He's playing along two women – at least two – then he disappears the same time as Miriam O'Donoghue is murdered.'

Now DS Jones remains silent.

'What about these creeps that live around Harterhow? We know about Morgan's nocturnal habits – and Coot and Fox are keeping something under their hats.'

DS Leyton – perhaps on his colleague's behalf – is looking troubled by Skelgill's salvo of *what ifs;* that he won't settle seems to be a feature of this case. He was unduly dismissive when his subordinates were keen to follow diverse leads early on; now – when it seems his instinct in that regard was correct – he is indifferent to the elegant solution that has been arrived at. Perhaps out of sheer frustration, therefore, DS Leyton reminds his superior of another variable.

'For that matter, Guv – June Collins – you know what the statistics say about the person who finds the body.'

But now there arrives a further twist of caprice – for Skelgill responds with a disparaging scowl. Whether this is an outright negation of the suggestion, it is hard to judge – but paradoxically the intervention seems to appease him and after a moment he turns more benevolently to DS Jones.

'What I'm saying, Jones – is the Chief's going to ask these questions – and she'll want answers before she parades herself in front of the media tonight.'

DS Jones has quickly recovered her poise; she seems not to resent Skelgill's little tirade.

'Guv – I have no doubt we've caught the prime suspect,' (Skelgill is actually nodding at this) 'And I think it would be right to investigate any connections we can find to James Forrester. When we speak in depth to neighbours and co-workers, and conduct a thorough background check on him, perhaps a link will emerge. Maybe in time *he* will reveal something.'

Now Skelgill's expression is more pragmatic.

'Here's a starter for ten. Forrester worked in the building trade, right? Derek Dudley was a builder that did domestic jobs in the Lakes. Marvin Morgan – and Coot and Fox – applied for change-of-use certificates that involved construction work on their properties.'

DS Jones is listening keenly.

'When was that, Guv?'

Skelgill folds his arms – ironically she has homed in on the flaw in his construct.

'Roughly five years ago – coinciding with them moving up here – or just after.'

Again DS Leyton is prompted to interject.

'But, Guv – that's a big gap in time. According the locals, Forrester didn't appear in Threlkeld until last May. You're talking three or more years unaccounted for.'

'Aye – so where was he before Threlkeld?'

Skelgill's sharp retort is plainly rhetorical: they all know that they don't have the answer, but that it is something they can find out – easily, if James Forrester will tell them; with some difficulty, if he will not.

DS Jones has been computing the probabilities. Now she makes an assessment.

'Guv – it's difficult to see why there would be a connection between Miriam O'Donoghue and the others locally whom you mention. Maybe tenuously – if say James Forrester had been in the area back then, and had done some labouring work for Derek Dudley – and that could also explain how he got to know about Harterhow reserve. But certainly what you said about William King – if his sob-story were all crocodile tears?'

DS Leyton, however, is still glowering. He suspects his superior's recalcitrance stems from his subsidiary role in solving the case, and is less inclined to be accommodating than his younger female colleague. Moreover, to his mind there is a fly in the ointment.

'But the cheques belonging to King – that doesn't make sense – not if King's in on the murder. Why would Forrester have them?'

Skelgill shrugs indifferently – he can think of an explanation but can't be bothered to iterate it – for it is not the specific pitfall that hampers him, but a widespread mire of incomprehension, a feeling that this perplexing miasma of an investigation is still shifting beneath the surface; it has not yet yielded up all its secrets. He checks his watch – the time is moving on and they will need to be back within the hour for a confab with the Chief prior to the press conference. He wipes his brow, for the afternoon heat is causing him to perspire, and the umbrella does not as well shade him as his colleagues. It seems, however, that the headache, which has pursued him through most of the day, has now been shaken off.

'Anyone fancy a proper drink before we shoot? Pint of shandy, Leyton?'

It is not like Skelgill to drink during official working hours, and DS Leyton glances rather suspiciously at his own glass, which is still two-thirds full, and then realises there is something moving in the meniscus.

'Aw, Guv – there's a flippin' wasp in my *Coke*.'

'It's too soon for wasps, Leyton – that's a hoverfly – just pick it out – go on – they're harmless.'

A reluctant DS Leyton observes his superior's orders. Gingerly he grasps the interloper between finger and thumb – and lets out a great yelp as the 'hoverfly' stings him – flinging it into the air as he recoils. As he frantically sucks at his thumb and makes concomitant moans, Skelgill watches, frowning.

'Happen they're out early this year.'

*

'Emma to take centre stage, eh, Skel – or are you hogging all the limelight?'

Skelgill notices that whenever DI Alec Smart attempts to wind him up, it is always in a public place, where a form of witness protection operates. Right now they cross paths in the foyer outside the gents' toilets (Skelgill leaving, DI Smart entering) – and Skelgill is in a hurry – but perhaps that is a good thing. As usual he bristles and his urge to sock the snide Mancunian threatens to override a reasoned response. But as he is walking away a line strikes him. He stops and turns.

'We're still waiting for your Manchester drugs connection to come good, Smart.'

DI Smart shrugs casually – as though it is just a matter of time. He raises a hand of farewell.

'Well – keep your flies done up, cock – else one of those ladies sitting either side of you will be getting the wrong idea.'

Smirking, DI Smart disappears into the restroom. Skelgill glances about – and then casually checks the front of his trousers.

*

215

The press conference is unremarkable – indeed an unsatisfactory anticlimax – which is often the way when a significant breakthrough is announced. Of course, the police want to reassure the public that the threat is over – and to demonstrate how well they are protecting them. And naturally the journalists salivate for scandal, the more sensational the better – who is he – where was he hiding – did he put up a fight – has he confessed – what is his terrible history – what else might he have done if he had not been apprehended? But the nature of the judicial process means that all the police are able to say is that a 34-year-old male has been arrested in connection with the death of Miriam O'Donoghue (*Rose*, now identified) and will be appearing in Carlisle Crown Court on Monday – charges as yet to be specified while key aspects of the investigation continue. Perhaps surprisingly there are few dissenting voices amongst the audience of reporters, although – perhaps *un*surprisingly – the most salient inquiry emanates from the familiar source of Kendall Minto. "What about an accomplice?" It could be that, as a native, the inaccessibility of the grave site has more obviously struck him as worthy of the question – or perhaps he has his own reasons for suspicion – or maybe he just wants to win the attention of DS Jones. For her part – no small thanks to Skelgill – she is well prepared. No – there is no reason to believe there was an accomplice, but the police are examining all aspects of this point until they can be certain there was not.

'Right – who wants a proper drink?'

Skelgill is rattling loose change in his trouser pocket. He has his back to his colleagues and is perusing the map of the Lake District on his office wall – it is a fine, warm evening and he appears to be trying to ascertain where might be the most suitable venue under such circumstances. At first neither sergeant replies – DS Leyton standing, looking rather hot and flustered, his jacket on, DS Jones seated, but perhaps poised to move. They glance at one another, and then DS Leyton does the honourable thing.

'I would, Guv – but I've just listened to a message from the doctor's receptionist. They've had to take the missus back down to the hospital – she took a bit of a turn while she was in for an appointment. The nippers are round with a neighbour – but she's just an old girl and they'll be running amok. I'd better scoot, Guv, if it's all the same.'

Skelgill nods without conveying any great emotion either way, and regards DS Jones expectantly. Now she exhibits the same signs of wavering as her colleague.

'I've got a fitness class that starts in about twenty minutes, Guv – I do it with a regular partner – you have to work in pairs for some of the routines – I really ought not let them down.' She brightens, however. 'I could meet you afterwards – maybe eight-thirty – for an hour?'

She does not elaborate on why this may be – but Skelgill makes an ambivalent face that could hide disappointment. He stalks across to the window and gazes out. The evening sun is casting long shadows of trees from west to east, picking out old stone buildings and walls with light and dark, and illuminating crows and pigeons, gilding their wingtips as they beat about their business.

'Aye – maybe. Think I'll get a stretch of the legs in first. It's too good a night to waste.'

He continues to stare out, and then when he turns he acts surprised that his colleagues are still there – despite that DS Jones is seated just beside him.

'Off you go, then – skedaddle.'

The pair slink away somewhat self-consciously, departing together for strength in numbers. Skelgill makes no immediate move to implement his plan to go for a walk, and after hanging about for a minute or so he wends his way through the building to DS Leyton's workstation. There are several officers still at their computers in the open-plan zone, but nobody pays him particular attention. Leaning precariously against the desk is the stack of folders taken from Derek Dudley's box room office. Despite DS Leyton's best intentions, the job of interrogating them has been successively postponed, by the furore surrounding the arrest of Marvin Morgan, and likewise James Forrester. Skelgill clears a space on the surface and opens the topmost file. Without disengaging the lever-arch mechanism he flicks cursorily through the contents. It takes him about fifteen seconds. Then he closes the folder and drops it carelessly on the floor behind him. The thud prompts a couple of heads to rise, but only momentarily. He repeats the procedure with each of the files – setting them out in what is in fact an untidy chronological sequence. This enables him to identify the most recent folder. He takes longer over this one, flicking through the docketed papers. But if he finds anything significant it cannot be complex – for he neither makes a note nor extracts any pages that he might perhaps photocopy. Abandoning the folders as variously strewn, he returns to his office, gathers up his personal effects, and departs.

21. HARTERHOW

It may be Skelgill's intention to kill two birds with one stone – combining his evening constitutional and his promise to the persistent June Collins – for has collected the landlady's hyperactive hound and headed for the hills, or at least a hill of sorts. Ordinarily he would prefer to be alone – bereft of responsibilities, at liberty to wander in body and mind – however the company of Morse seems to please him. If truth were told, compared to his own Bullboxer the Lakeland Terrier is more a dog after his own heart, quick, inquisitive, resourceful and impatient.

Of course, there could be a third 'bird' – else why has he gravitated to Harterhow? It has never figured high on his list of local walks, too confined an area to be of utility to a fellsman such as he, hemmed in as it is by oversubscribed attractions like Catbells, Derwentwater and the Newlands Valley. That it remains largely deserted – for its lack of a striking feature, such as a viewpoint, or waterfall, or notable summit, and being to all appearances private property – would not sway him, not when he can find ultimate sanctuary simply by launching his craft into the great millpond that is Bassenthwaite Lake, just three miles to the north. It would seem DS Leyton has hit the nail on the head – that, for once, the rattle of closeted skeletons that is part and parcel of almost any case has derailed Skelgill. To conflate idioms, it is the job of the detective to leave no stone unturned; when unpleasant revelations scuttle for cover a clear head is called for; as Skelgill often says, it is the detective's obligation not to become sidetracked.

Of course, there is a paradox; Skelgill is a man of impulse rather than rationale. Like the prospective homebuyer that knows instantly that they do (or don't) want the property they are inspecting, but not *why*, Skelgill trusts his instincts to inform him when a correct solution presents itself, when an investigation nears its endpoint. Thus far these same instincts – if not exactly having deserted him – have been playing a curious game of hide and seek. When his subordinates went looking one way, he was sure he was smarter, and went another. Now the chase has swung back past him, he seems condemned to blunder on in the opposite direction.

Is it by wishful thinking, therefore, that he returns to Harterhow? Are as-yet-unturned stones a figment of his imagination? Should he not simply accept that there was a logical pathway that ran through this case – as DS Jones sensibly did? She pushed for the idea of the facial reconstruction; she identified the traveller connection that proved to be the key to unlocking both the identity of *Rose* and the explanation of her subsequent demise. Ought he just be satisfied that he has made significant contributions – not least in clarifying the timing of the murder, and the swift tracing of James Forrester; and surely his actions have clipped the wings of Marvin Morgan, and caused him to curtail his clandestine hobby, that goes under the guise of nature photographer?

*

She's there. She's by far the best looker in the class. Face and physique. She has the poise of a ballet dancer and the grace of an athlete. Set the dash-cam rolling. Settle back and enjoy the show.

*

Skelgill screws up his features in a way that he rarely does in company. It is a fishing face, one he uses when he is trying to decide which fly will tempt the first trout of the season, when no pattern has yet had time to establish itself; or when he is about to cast a baited pike rig and is spoilt for choice of swims, all looking equally enticing from his vantage point in his boat. It is not a pretty face, shrew-like, with bared teeth and flared nostrils, though deliberative rather than anxious. While the dog has taken its regular route under the stile into the nature reserve Skelgill loiters, looking (shrewishly, perhaps) at the gate repaired by James Forrester. It is a neat job, the joints are concealed and only a contrast in the weathering of the wood reveals the foreign timber, which must have been reclaimed from a similar artefact. Skelgill toys with the notion of taking it in as evidence and whether – as a smile raises the corners of his mouth – out of devilment he should refer to it in his report in farmer Stanley Gill's local dialect, *yon yat*.

But for now he vaults the said yat and follows Morse; judging by its echoing yelps the dog has taken the narrow path that dips into the shadowy oak woods. The canopy is at its most verdant, the leaves having attained a bottle-green maturity; akin to those thrust by the far-reaching fingers of the autumn storm into the black peaty soil and the rude last rites of Miriam O'Donoghue. *Rose*. Skelgill pauses as he nears the spot – though it is some twenty yards off the path and he does not care to find it now. Did James Forrester – as DS Jones speculates – place the wild spray upon the unmarked grave? It was an act completed in the space of a day or so, between the forensic team clearing out and the morning of his photographed 'encounter' with his female colleague. It is over five miles as the crow flies from Threlkeld to Harterhow – would Forrester have taken such trouble? Would he, indeed, have risked approaching the site? To do so on horseback would have courted inordinate attention – though he may have been unaware that the body had been discovered – the first public announcement was only the day before. But if Forrester did not leave the roses, who did? Was it in fact one of the forensic team, who was then too embarrassed to admit it? An anonymous member of the public, acting in all innocence? Or someone else?

Skelgill moves on. The air beneath the trees is still and midges are massing; they home in on his breath. He is wearing a short-sleeved shirt, and has no other protection with him. He can hear the dog ahead – the undergrowth crackles with testosterone or whatever is the canine equivalent – but now a deeper note reaches his ears, the strangled bark of a roe deer. He calls to the dog, hissing its name in an urgent tone. It does the trick and it trots back expectantly – only for Skelgill to snare it with a length of baler twine looped through its collar.

Morse seems to understand they are hunting, and walks obediently at heel. Tracking the periodic grunts brings them to the edge of the wood; beyond, the large clearing stretches away up the slope. In the hazy dusk two roebucks are facing off. Skelgill watches as they enact their timeless ritual, their movements synchronised, each the mirror image of the other: they paw the turf with alternate hoofs and back away with heads turned coyly, only to spring into the tackle like footballers pouncing on a loose ball; the clatter of antlers. The dog, of course, cannot see over the waist-high undergrowth, and what little breeze there is comes from behind; he shows no sign of wanting to take off. Skelgill begins to edge through the bracken – how close can he get? It seems the battle is more important than any audience (indeed, where are the does – watching from the wings?) – for at twenty feet the deer are still hard at it, no quarter yet given. Skelgill thinks about filming with his phone – he is now easily within range. He grins sardonically – it would make a good post for Marvin Morgan's blog. Although – come to that – why not start one of his own? But on second thoughts, if he had a blog, it would need to be about fishing. The idea amuses him; he could do 'Catch of the Week' – that would silence the doubters in the pub.

By now Morse's patience has worn thin. He can hear the exertions of the elegant beasts, their choreographed prizefight, and finally lets out a warning yap. In unison the bucks turn and calmly trot away – an observer would never guess that a moment earlier they were locked in mortal combat. Skelgill waits a minute and then releases the dog – it darts to inspect the divots in the turf, but shows little inclination to continue in pursuit of their spoor. Skelgill takes a bearing off the dark fringe of the pinewood, and marches uphill towards Marvin Morgan's hidden viewpoint. He is thinking there is some veracity in the latter's claim about the rutting site.

Beneath the pines everything looks just as he last saw it – the ground is undisturbed and an inconspicuous cross of twigs he left behind is still in place. But Marvin Morgan has only had a day or so to have come here since his release, quite likely he has not. Now Skelgill ponders his options; where does instinct beckon? He can traverse to his right and pick up the path to Portinscale, or he can head up and over the hill, past the cairn. Either route will reach the perimeter wall and thence lead him back to his car, anticlockwise or clockwise respectively. He looks at Morse; the terrier is enlarging a rabbit hole; a fresh scent must emanate from within. If Skelgill takes the Portinscale path it will mean passing the grave of Rebus, with the risk that Morse will get there first and try once again to exhume his predecessor. Pragmatism must step in where intuition fails to lead; Skelgill turns uphill.

'Come on, lad – this way – *foxy* – see him off.'

*

Kendall Minto's heart beats a little faster than normal; he can smell his deodorant as damp patches form at the armpits of his crisply ironed shirt. It's not like him, he usually thrives on stress, reporting often brings him into situations where brazen self-confidence is called for. He glances again at the bunch of flowers in their cellophane wrapper on the passenger seat beside him. They look like they're beginning to wilt – the interior of the car is hotter beneath its black canvass canopy than he would have imagined. But he doesn't want to drop the hood – or turn on the engine to activate the a/c – the brand new red convertible is conspicuous enough as it is.

Here she comes. She looks like she's straight out of the shower; her hair is still damp – she's obviously in a hurry. She has changed into a close-fitting clingy tracksuit – she manages to look great whatever she wears. Should he honk – or just casually get out – her car is parked only a couple of spaces away.

But as Kendall Minto fumbles for the unfamiliar position of the door catch he witnesses his ambitions thwarted. A middle-aged man has appeared and now moves to intercept the girl and engage her with a greeting. The man has his back to him. Kendall Minto's eyes narrow; she looks a little uncomfortable – but she's trying not to show it. They are only half a dozen yards distant, at an angle to his left – but they probably can't tell he's here because of the glare of the evening sun that reflects from the curve of the tinted windshield. Cautiously he lowers the electric passenger window. He can hear snatches of conversation between the swish of cars that cruise to and fro seeking spaces. The man is speaking; he feels like he has heard the voice before, it is calm and persuasive.

'Old memory card... completely forgot I had it... vital missing link in your case... in two minds whether to delete the picture... compromising for me, you see... your boss might take an ill view... bit of a downer on me... I thought if you handled it... smooth the path... value your opinion...'

The girl is nodding. However, Kendall Minto recognises her expression as conflicted – a mixture of keen interest and suspicion; though she strives to conceal the latter; funny, how he knows her of old. Her response carries to him more clearly, since she faces in his direction.

'Where is it, Mr Morgan?'

So it's that Morgan character – of course. The man raises a hand to rub the top of his short-cropped head; it is a subconscious act of body language that suggests discomfiture. Kendall Minto holds his breath and strains to hear the response.

'Didn't like to bring it out with me... prefer to show you on my own equipment... sure you'll understand?'

She hesitates for a second or two.

'Okay – I'll follow you.'

Now the man makes an accommodating gesture, raising open palms.

'Honestly no need... couple of things I can explain on the way... back for a late-night shop... will drive right past... drop you off here.'

Kendall Minto watches keenly. A car slows down and obscures any further sound – but he can see her face as she tries to make up her mind. Clearly she thinks the matter is urgent; she looks like she's asking herself why shouldn't she travel with him. Then she says something and Marvin Morgan noticeably relaxes; he swings half around and points to what must be his car, four or five rows away, a silver SUV with heavily tinted windows that faces the glass-sided exercise studio. He begins to amble in that direction, glancing back a couple of times.

Her car is parked just across the designated roadway. Kendall Minto watches as she comes round to the rear and lifts the tailgate. Again he experiences a small pang of attraction as he regards her athletic form. She must have told Morgan that she'll put her kitbag away – and he sees her take her mobile from a zip pouch. But rather than go immediately she keeps her head bowed – out of sight of Morgan – and now she appears to be sending a hurried text – she types and then frowns as she watches the display – she seems to try again – then comes a cry of "Everything alright?" from across the car park – and she resigns herself to whatever is the failing of her phone and slips it into a belly pocket. She pulls down the tailgate, locks the car – stands for a moment as if to compose herself – and then purposefully weaves through the matrix of parked vehicles.

To reach the exit Marvin Morgan's car has to swing around past where Kendall Minto is parked. The reporter presses himself against the seat – but the SUV cruises by without either of them looking his way. He fastens his belt, engages the ignition, and sets off in pursuit.

*

Skelgill has attacked the steep gradient of Harterhow with gusto, picking a more challenging line to the summit than indicated by the faint path that leads from Marvin Morgan's hidey-hole. Sweat is matting his thick eyebrows and he rubs them simultaneously with the hairy backs of his hands; all in all, he is not his usual well-equipped self for being out of doors – it is the danger of casual dog walking – he should actually have come ready for the fells; he might even have brought his Kelly kettle and stopped for a mash by the cairn. He is conscious DS Jones has not yet contacted him – she's probably nattering with her pal – he thinks about phoning her – but his mobile is jammed into a tight pocket on his thigh, safe but tricky to extract. In any event – now his attention becomes diverted by familiar frantic yelps that filter down through the timbers – it sounds like Morse has cornered his vixen.

Skelgill is panting as – from his perspective – the old cairn heaves into sight. From its far side come the muffled sounds of canine agitation. He circles the rock pile – it must be eight feet high and twenty around its base – to discover the creature up to its rears in a cleft, where a stone has been dislodged, perhaps by vulpine vector. Instantly Skelgill sees that if he doesn't act now he might have some explaining to do to June Collins – and it's a heck of a long way to bring the fire brigade; embarrassing to boot for a man who should know better than let a fox terrier get within a furlong of an earth. Unceremoniously he grabs Morse by his hind legs and drags him out. The dog protests only to the extent that he determinedly tries to claw his way back down the hole – and he is a game little beggar and gives a good account of himself before Skelgill has him on the leash and secured to the nearest stump.

Skelgill turns to regard the cairn. The sun is setting and its last golden rays stretch through the pine trunks to strike the derelict landmark. The illumination is intense, and he notices a phenomenon comparable to the mended gate – an incongruity, a mismatch in the mottled pattern of the ancient lichens in the area around the cavity. It is as if there has been a partial collapse and the rocks replaced, some with their original faces now turned inwards. As he stares, curiosity becomes alarm – he feels the hairs prickle on his forearms; the tingle of electricity creeps up his spine. Unblinking, he steps forward. A pungent reek infiltrates the pine-scented ambience – but it is unlike the familiar sharp hot stink of fox. Among the scattered debris that Morse has ejected is an untidy web of small bones, browned, loosely attached by gristle and sinew. Skelgill grimaces – even to his untrained eye it is clear these are human carpals and phalanges – fingers in plain English. But what is more – to his *trained* eye there is a startling revelation – burnished by the soil and stained by water seepage – but nonetheless unmistakeable – amidst the bones is a cabochon ruby gold signet ring that he last saw in a photograph on Teresa Dudley's Liverpool mantelpiece.

For a moment Skelgill is immobile. Then he checks his watch – there is at least an hour's twilight, perhaps more if it remains cloudless. He rips his mobile phone from its pocket – but there is no signal. He sets his jaw, thwarted by technology. With urgency in his eyes he assesses his options, turning on his heel to successive points of the compass. To the north west lies Marvin Morgan's cottage. North east is Portinscale and the home of Messrs Coot and Fox. South west leads back to the gate. They are all three roughly equidistant. But Morse lets out a little whine – it reminds Skelgill of his practical obligations; he opts for his car. He unties the dog and sets off downhill at a run.

*

Kendall Minto has no difficulty in keeping up with the SUV. His new convertible punches well above its weight. He hangs back as they hasten west on the A66. If he overheard correctly, they're heading for Morgan's place, How Cottage, tucked away in the woods around the far side of Derwentwater. He could probably find it himself, having followed his erstwhile schoolmate ten days ago. He expects they'll turn off at Braithwaite, or maybe before that, and double back through Portinscale. But he figures it's best to keep them in sight, just in case they have a change of plan. Then he'll need to be more circumspect for the last stretch through the lanes – if the Morgan fellow is paying attention to his mirror, that is.

*

His powerful shooting brake spitting gravel, Skelgill reverses recklessly along the narrow wooded driveway and all the way up to the cottage. Thus facing the exit, he leaves the keys in the ignition: two small timesaving precautions. He approaches and hammers upon the front door; there is no response. A vintage Morris Minor in traditional porcelain green stands outside a planked wooden garage. He marches across to the car and gets down between the front wheels. He reaches up inside the engine compartment. There is a metallic clunk as the bonnet jumps an inch; he scrambles to his feet and raises the lid. It takes him only a couple of seconds to locate the distributor – good old-fashioned electrics. He unclips the distributor cap and removes and pockets the rotor arm. Call it an immobiliser. Then he drops the lid with a clang.

A six-foot gate bars the way between the corner of the cottage and the garage. It is locked, but it is sturdy, and easily bears his weight as he hauls himself up and flops over. From behind him, through the gap he has left in his car window, comes a plaintive protest from the Lakeland Terrier – perhaps it recalls the fun of its last visit. A narrow path bordered by tall bushes skirts the building; Skelgill recognises the sitting room as he passes the mullioned windows. At the rear there is no sign of occupancy. The kitchen is empty; he tries the door – it is unlocked. But he continues down the garden.

When he reaches the restored byre he notices a key in the lock; deftly he extracts it. From a vent just below the eaves on one side billows a jet of steam. The wooden sign is where he left it, propped against the front wall. He jerks open the door; a wave of arid heat envelops him.

The next impression is the aroma of eucalyptus; the interior is almost completely dark, but for the faint incandescence of a nightlight somewhere overhead. It takes Skelgill's eyes a couple of seconds to adjust – and his mind a couple more to process the sight that materialises. Two elderly men are sprawled naked on towels on slatted pine benches, one either side. They might have been asleep, or certainly insensible, for they are slow to react to his incursion. Lester Fox is first to sit up, gathering his towel around his midriff.

'What the –?'

Skelgill reaches in and grabs him by the wrist. He yanks the man to his feet and catapults him through the open doorway.

'You – out.'

As Lester Fox staggers backwards, fighting to keep his balance and at the same time preserve his modesty, his bearded features twist into an angry mask.

'The key! You fool, Coot!'

For a moment Skelgill stares disparagingly at the tall gangly man. Then he slams shut the door and locks it from the inside. He turns to face a trembling Archibald Coot. The plump, pale man is sweating profusely, but that may just be the heat of the sauna.

'I don't think you're that much of a fool, Mr Coot.'

*

Kendall Minto has his nose pressed up against the window of Marvin Morgan's study, so when a forearm wraps around his neck and threatens to choke him, and a rough hand covers his mouth, he is taken unawares and offers little resistance. Before he knows it he finds himself face down on the lawn, his own right arm uncomfortably high up his back.

'Keep quiet! What the hell are you doing here?'

The contradiction is not lost upon him – and he realises he recognises the local accent.

'Sh-she's – she's in there.'

'Who?'

'Y-your sergeant – Emma.'

Skelgill releases his grip on the younger man, and rises quickly. He offers a hand to pull the other to his feet.

'Where's her car?'

Skelgill has approached stealthily on foot. He found the red convertible half-hidden in the wooded lane at the bottom of the driveway. Kendall Minto shapes as if to brush at the grass stains on his knees, but then thinks the better of it. In as few words as he can summon – which is at least a journalistic skill he possesses – he relates the account of his eavesdropping in the car park of the leisure centre – leaving out both his motivation for being there in the first place, and for following in the second. However, the bouquet on the passenger seat of his car has not escaped Skelgill's notice.

'She would have texted me.' But then Skelgill remembers he has no signal. 'Damn it.'

'I think she tried to send a message just before she left with him.'

Skelgill strides across to the study window. The evening light is fading fast and the room is more or less in darkness. Kendall Minto's hushed voice comes from behind.

'The windows and doors are locked. I've been all round. There are candles lit in a dining room. The table is set for two. But there's no sign of anyone downstairs.'

'Follow me.'

Skelgill rounds to the front of the property, and Kendall Minto does as bidden. Skelgill backs away and cranes up at the dormer window directly above the little gabled portico. It is the guest room; a subdued glow emanates from within – perhaps the flicker of candlelight – and perhaps even a shadowy movement. Without warning he makes a sudden charge – but just when it seems he will launch a hopelessly optimistic assault upon the solid oak front door, he leaps and grasps the cast iron guttering.

'Quick – give us a bunk up, lad!'

Kendall Minto looks alarmed – but he seems to understand he is to get his shoulders under Skelgill's feet and raise him by standing upright. He drops to his knees on the gravel, inflicting further damage to his trendy drainpipes. But it does the trick and Skelgill thus propelled is able to heave himself onto the angled roof of the porch. Above him stretches a tiled slope, thick with dark moss, and then a narrow leaded ledge beneath the bedroom window.

'Inspector – what should I do?'

Now that his focus lies ahead Skelgill seems to have forgotten about his press-ganged assistant. His response is uttered through gritted teeth, without looking back.

'If you've got a signal – call 999.'

Under regular Cumbrian climatic conditions, the pitched roof that confronts him would be unassailable, its coating of greasy moss and algae the biological equivalent of anti-climb paint. But the largely dry spell has changed all that – the surface is brittle and crumbly and Skelgill is able to get sufficient purchase to reach the ledge. He feels gingerly for the windowsill and slowly rises to peer inside.

Thus far he has been circumspect in his actions, but what happens now involves a sudden escalation of passion. The room is softly lit. Slightly to the right, near the foot of the bed, stands Marvin Morgan – his expression is a curious conflation of anger and dismay – and at the same time imploring – and his dark monobrow is heavily kinked at its centre. He has his hands out in front of him and yet leans back, and the explanation for this unnatural posture can only be DS Jones. Facing him she half-crouches, her hair is dishevelled and her tracksuit top seems disarranged – her expression is one of trepidation, alarm – fear, even – but her eyes are blazing, a tigress at bay – and she wields double-handed a long square-based brass candlestick. Skelgill yanks open the window (the very one he looked out of only two days ago; oddly the catch is not fastened). He grabs the frame above his head and launches himself feet first into the room. His boots raise dust as he lands – both parties are rooted to the spot, startled by his dramatic entrance. He pitches forward and in a single smooth pirouetting action snatches the candlestick from DS Jones and swings it at head height with all his might.

*

'Inspector – you are so late – I almost phoned the police.'

'I am the police.'

June Collins makes an affected giggle.

'And Morse – he's okay? I thought perhaps he'd run off again?'

'He's in the car.'

Now the woman hesitates, trying to work out why this might be. Skelgill adds a rider.

'I didn't know if you'd have gone to bed.'

'Oh, no – I've waited up especially for you, Inspector.'

Skelgill does not appear to have a ready answer. As stars twinkle overhead a warm glow from within casts a halo around the slender figure of June Collins. She steps a little to one side, opening the front door wider. He notices she is not wearing carpet slippers, but high heels – and the lateral movement unbalances her. As she reaches to steady herself with her free hand her dressing gown slips open to reveal a glimpse of a satiny basque and not a great deal else. She smiles coyly.

'I think I may have something you want, Inspector.'

'Aye, I think you probably do – madam.'

22. POLICE HQ – Friday

'Alright, lass?'

Skelgill seems in a chipper mood as he bustles into his office bearing two store carrier bags. DS Jones stands up to greet him, but then sits down again when he takes his seat and stuffs the bags under his desk. He reaches for the mug of tea that his colleague has thoughtfully provided, and takes a gulp without testing it for heat.

'I'm fine thanks, Guv – how's your hand?'

Now Skelgill frowns – as if at first he does not know what she means – and then he glances cursorily at the knuckles of his left hand; they are bruised but nonetheless he demonstrates they are functional.

'Never mind me – that was a scary situation you got yourself into. That guy's a nutcase. And that's only Minto.'

DS Jones grins sheepishly – but she is clearly happy that Skelgill's reprimand is tempered with a joke, albeit somewhat barbed.

'Honestly, Guv – it was more Miss Havisham than Hannibal Lecter. And I had just come from a jujitsu class.'

Skelgill frowns over the top of his mug.

'Remind me – which jujitsu move uses a candlestick?'

DS Jones chuckles and shakes her head. She watches her superior for a moment, her eyes bright.

'How on earth did you know to smash the mirror, Guv?'

Skelgill manufactures a wry grin.

'I saw my reflection and acted on impulse.'

DS Jones laughs, her voice a rich liquid cascade. She lifts up a sheet of paper from the corner of Skelgill's desk.

'You wouldn't believe what they're finding, Guv.'

'I think I would, Jones.'

However, he nods for her to continue.

'The access to the secret room behind the mirror is through the airing cupboard on the landing. It's cleverly concealed – and lined with soundproofing and deep pile carpet so his guests wouldn't hear him creeping about. The previously unidentified key fits a steel cabinet – among other things it contained a second laptop packed with images – the history shows he was regularly accessing the dark web – it looks like he might have another blog – you can guess the content. There was also a manual logbook that dates back over a decade – there are entries from when he was working in Birkenhead. We think he used a system of codes to record what the people he watched were – er, well – doing to one another.'

She draws her last sentence to halt rather abruptly. Skelgill raises an eyebrow, inviting her to continue.

'We're in it, Guv. Recorded as level 2 the first time and level 3 the second – in the decoy car. A question mark against level 4.' Now she grins a little ruefully. 'It goes up to level 7.'

Skelgill makes a muffled exclamation – possibly an oath – or perhaps even an expression of disappointment.

'How about names?'

'It's just dates – and Mars and Venus symbols to indicate the gender of those present.'

'Are there a lot of sevens?' Skelgill's voice sounds detached.

'Apparently so, Guv.'

Skelgill draws a long breath and then exhales with a hiss.

'I wonder what he had in mind for you, Jones.'

DS Jones shifts a little uncomfortably in her seat – but her expression remains composed.

'Well for one thing, Guv – the camera behind the two-way mirror wasn't recording last night.' She folds her hands on her lap and leans forward. 'If I'm honest, Guv – I was probably a bit extreme in my reaction – I just wanted to let him know where he stood. I think from the way he was behaving he genuinely thought I would be his girlfriend – however deluded that seems. I know he lied about the photo to get me there – but I don't think he would have tried to harm me. He'd cooked a dinner. You probably didn't need to punch him.'

'Aye – I needed to punch him, alright.'

Their eyes meet; Skelgill's gaze is steely, and DS Jones responds with the tiniest smile. She sits upright and crosses her legs and takes hold of her uppermost knee; she wears a short-sleeved navy mini-dress and her bronzed limbs in the sunlight draw Skelgill's eye.

'I have him down as a unhinged, Guv – and you could call him a pervert – but not a serial killer, surely?'

Skelgill counters her assertion.

'Aye – try telling Derek Dudley that. Name a series that doesn't begin with number one.'

DS Jones nods pensively, and then gives a little affected shiver – an acknowledgement that Skelgill has a point. They each contemplate in silence for a few moments, until Skelgill rouses himself.

'No sign of Leyton?'

DS Jones shakes her head.

'He's been in, Guv – while you were out – he said he had to drop off his wife for a couple of tests this morning.' Now she pauses and bites her bottom lip. 'It's obviously a worrying time for him – especially with having young kids.'

Skelgill scowls but he nods in a manner that suggests some understanding.

'We need a round-up, the three of us – get our ducks in a row – I want to be spot on with the charges. Have we got June Collins here yet?'

'She's in an interview room – George phoned about twenty minutes ago.'

'Right – let's you and me go and talk to her. What about the clothes?'

'They're being priority tested as we speak – and Liverpool CID have arranged to show photographs to Teresa Dudley at her place of work this morning. DS Leyton was liaising. They're also investigating the city council, and anything they can discover about June Collins' business.'

'Happen she'll tell us herself.'

*

'Madam – first of all I'd like to ask you about Mr Archibald Coot.'

June Collins looks scared and conflicted, unsure of what line to take, and discomfited by Skelgill's opening remark, which is not a question as such, but which clearly presses for an answer – especially as he now sits in expectant silence.

'I don't really – I don't really know him.'

'Madam – when we interviewed Mr Coot late last night he provided a very plausible account of how he and his associate Lester Fox met Marvin Morgan, and later the man you knew as Spencer Fazakerley – and that they convened at your premises in Liverpool. Actually you are acquainted with them all, correct?'

June Collins lowers her eyes.

'It wasn't exactly a beauty parlour you ran – as you suggested to Sergeant Leyton when he first spoke to you.'

'It was entirely above board – I worked alone, you understand?'

'But you were not unknown to the authorities.'

June Collins now puts up a spirited defence, beginning with a vigorous fluttering of her eyelashes.

'A wide range of beauty treatments were available.'

'But probably not of great interest to the majority of your customers.'

Her demeanour becomes outrageously prim.

'I couldn't help that the sauna was always most popular.'

Skelgill raises his eyebrows. So popular that Coot and Fox built their own.

'What did you know about their plans to move to the Lake District?'

'Nothing.'

Her denial on this point is more subdued, and as such sounds convincing.

'Nothing at all?'

She shakes her head.

'Why should I have done, Inspector? It wasn't for me to pry into my clients' private lives.'

It is with knitted brows that Skelgill considers this proposition – something of an oxymoron given her role in what surely *were* their private lives.

'Marvin Morgan had a second home here. Archibald Coot and Lester Fox then purchased a cottage nearby. Fair enough – that's got nothing to do with you. Except that not very long after, you moved into the area. Within the year – let's call him Spencer – arrives on the scene. You can see why it might seem – irregular?'

'But it was Spencer that told me the guesthouse was for sale – at a bargain price. He said he'd been lodging there and that it was a good little business.'

'You had a good little business in Liverpool.'

She looks at Skelgill imploringly.

'I felt it was time for a change, Inspector.'

'You told Sergeant Leyton that Spencer came to stay in Keswick – and that's how you got to know him.'

It takes June Collins a moment to fashion a reply. Her long hair is gradually encroaching upon her face, and she seems content to operate from behind its partial veil.

'It *is* how I got to know him – that's when we – when we became a couple and he moved in.'

Skelgill regards her pensively; it is a forthright admission. Thus far, her version broadly tallies with what they have learned from Archibald Coot.

'Did you have any idea that his real name was Derek Dudley?'

Now she draws back her raven locks with long painted talons.

'Not until you told me last night – honestly, Inspector.'

'Nor that he was married, with a family in Liverpool – the Fazakerley district?'

June Collins pouts – Skelgill realises it is a gesture of despair – her large bright blue eyes flood with tears and she regards him defiantly – then she turns to DS Jones, in an appeal for sisterly understanding. DS Jones obliges with a brief smile of compassion. In the event, June Collins does not reply to

Skelgill's inquiry – it seems she is genuinely choked – and he waits a few moments, for his next question delves deeper.

'What did you think had become of Spencer when he didn't return?'

'I just thought he'd left me. We weren't getting on so well. He was impatient and bad tempered. And when he'd gone I realised – there was nothing to keep him here – he didn't own anything – there were no relatives – no family – no friends.'

'How about Marvin Morgan? And Archibald Coot and Lester Fox?'

'Spencer didn't like them coming round to our – to *my* place.'

'And after Spencer disappeared – did you see them?'

She shakes her head. This appears to be the full extent of her answer.

'Until Lester Fox arrived with a case containing Spencer's clothes?'

She nods, her countenance still disconsolate.

'He told me that Spencer had been going to their sauna – that he'd kept a spare set of clothes there – but they couldn't keep them forever. He said I should just put them in Spencer's wardrobe – and not mention it to anyone – he said Spencer wouldn't want it known he went there.'

Skelgill runs the fingers of both hands through his hair. 'You didn't happen to recognise it as the outfit he was wearing when you last saw him?' His tone is casual and it sounds like a throwaway remark.

'I never looked – after all that time I'd shut Spencer out of my mind. I just put the bag in the cupboard and it's been there ever since – until you took it last night.'

Skelgill rests his elbows on the desk and leans forward, intertwining his fingers. The muscle memory of his features does not extend to sympathy, but he does now exhibit a modicum of concern.

'June – when your dog unearthed the bones – you thought that was Spencer.'

His statement draws a sudden look of astonishment from June Collins – as if she is flabbergasted that he can read her mind. However she fights a little rearguard action.

'Anyone would be shocked finding that. A human skull – even you would be, Inspector.'

Skelgill makes a small concession to her argument with a tilt of his head.

'But afterwards – when Lester Fox brought the clothes – you had your suspicions.'

She lowers her eyes and gives a half-hearted shrug.

'June – were you intimidated?'

If she senses Skelgill is leading her, for her own benefit (else why is he now using her name?) she perhaps wisely does not show it. But she gladly takes the cue.

'They were all a bit creepy – frightening – even Spencer could be at times.'

Skelgill nods slowly. He is silent for a few moments.

'You put the wild roses on the grave.'

The supposition comes out of the blue – and indeed Skelgill's intonation suggests he utters aloud his thoughts, as much as questions her. He slumps back in his seat and gazes contemplatively at the ceiling. Suddenly it seems so obvious.

'It must have been a relief when we announced it was a female.' He does not wait for a response to this assertion, but sits up in a manner that suggests he is ready to conclude the interview. 'Madam – is there anything else you'd like to tell us – or ask?'

'Will I be charged?'

June Collins' alacrity in responding catches him off guard. He glances at DS Jones before turning back to her.

'It's not for us to decide. Happen you've not done a lot wrong – if you've told us the truth, that is. We shan't keep you here much longer today.'

*

DS Leyton is waiting for Skelgill and DS Jones in Skelgill's office. He looks pale and drawn but nonetheless jumps to attention as they enter – he brandishes a sheaf of notes.

'The wires are going crazy, Guv. It's all coming together.'

'Such as?'

Skelgill indicates they should be seated – though for once he perches on the edge of his desk, ignoring the various reports and documents that crumple beneath his backside.

'They've finished excavating the cairn – the skeleton is more or less complete – a tall male in his mid forties. Dr Herdwick reckons the cause of death is undoubtedly a massive blow to the head – the skull is completely smashed in. They've got a boulder they think was used as the weapon – it's clearly bloodstained – it's in for DNA testing – they're hoping it may have the assailant's DNA on it, too.'

Skelgill is nodding. DS Leyton continues.

'We've already got DNA results on the clothing from the suitcase – it matches the remains – now it's being cross-referenced with samples from Liverpool. Teresa Dudley has identified the signet ring and a belt and some of the garments. But here's the main thing – the clothing also has traces of DNA from Lester Fox – *and Marvin Morgan.*'

Skelgill is grim faced.

'Bring on the boulder.'

'It shouldn't be long, Guv – they're pulling out all the stops. But it fits the story you got from Coot – that Morgan whacked him and Fox helped him to hide the body.'

Skelgill holds up his palms in a quietening gesture.

'That's just my interpretation at this stage, Leyton. What Coot actually said was that Fox told him Morgan had found Derek Dudley – that he'd met with an accident – and they concealed the body for fear of becoming suspects. Otherwise Coot was kept in the dark.'

DS Jones now draws a parallel with the first corpse.

'It was odd that they went to the trouble of stripping the body – but left the ring.'

Skelgill casts a brief glance at his own ringless fingers.

'Aye – but it was probably done in the dark. It would be easy enough to miss a ring. Morgan ambushed him when he was on his way to collect. The path took him right past the cairn. Ideal spot – no transportation – ready made burial site – and hardly anyone ever goes there.'

'You said *collect*, Guv?'

DS Leyton is looking perplexed. He has not yet had the benefit of a full debrief of the blubbering confessions of Archibald Coot.

'Derek Dudley was blackmailing them. Coot has admitted it. Dudley would take the dog for a walk – that was his cover, at least some of the time – and drop in on one of their cottages for his weekly wad of cash.'

Skelgill watches DS Leyton while his sergeant absorbs the information.

'They pulled some sort of scam, Leyton. Morgan's firm was a supplier to Liverpool council – we already knew that. As his former bookkeeper helpfully pointed out – in the advertising game all you need is a bent client and a bent supplier. Morgan used to take Coot and Fox to June Collins' little place – corporate entertainment.' He gives a sarcastic laugh. 'They get to know Derek Dudley – a regular customer – operating under his alias as Spencer Fazakerley. One day they're sitting round in her sauna discussing their pipe dreams – retiring to the Lakes – and Dudley sees his chance. He offers to launder the cash through his business, help out with the building work. So Morgan generates inflated invoices, Coot processes them and Fox signs them off; Morgan pays Dudley who organises the cottage purchase. Morgan gets a smart little upgrade to his existing property. Dudley gets the work – and, when the penny drops – and maybe it did from the very start – a nice little earner. Call it a pension scheme. Then he charms June Collins into moving north – starts leading his double life good and proper. What more could a man want?'

DS Leyton is nodding in mild wonderment.

'What made Coot spill the beans, Guv?'

'I put it to him, Leyton.' Skelgill now pauses and stands up and digs his hands into his pockets. He gazes beyond DS Jones and out of the window. It is another fine summer's day. His thoughts have backtracked and he resumes his explanation from an earlier point. 'From the minute I met him I knew he was hiding something – both of them were. But I came round to thinking that was all about the barn conversion – which he's also admitted to. They applied for a grant to upgrade a non-existent visitor centre for Friends of Harterhow – even had a sign made for the photograph in the application. They pretended the local magistrate Veronica Crampston MBE was their treasurer – to lend credibility. In fact she'd moved down south and knew nothing about it. They got away with it and used the money to fit out the barn as a sauna.'

It is an audacious ploy – and plainly would not be expected of two ostensibly respectable elderly men; but DS Leyton is eager to understand Archibald Coot's motivation to confess.

'You said you put it to him, Guv? You mean like a plea bargain?'

'Aye – in a manner of speaking.' Skelgill affects a grin. 'He didn't take a lot of persuading – I reckon he's been under the cosh from Fox – and the pair of them from Morgan – at least since they did away with Derek Dudley. Coot's the weak link in the chain – he wasn't involved in the murder or the disposal of the body, so he's banking on saving his skin by grassing up Fox and Morgan. He knows he'll go down on the fraud rap – but at least it doesn't carry a life sentence.'

'What made you sure they were all wrong 'uns, Guv? All we really had to go on was Morgan's antics.'

Skelgill rounds his desk to stare at his map, hands on hips. After a few moments he taps the location of Harterhow with a forefinger – then he turns and spreads his arms. His expression if it could be put into words would say, "Who cares – we've solved it!" – and his response reflects this sentiment.

'It all makes sense now, Leyton.'

'But something kept you going, Guv.'

Skelgill makes a jerky movement with his left hand, dragging invisible factors towards his midriff. He labours under the burden of having to explain logically a process that does not lend itself to linear thinking; he does not know himself precisely what was the switch that tripped and suddenly lit up a complex circuit of uncertain connections.

'In the last few days – I don't know – maybe what we found out about Forrester kick-started it.'

'Forrester, Guv?'

'Aye – that he was living with no apparent income – and so it emerged was Derek Dudley. Remember – according to June Collins all her 'Spencer' did was loaf about. We know he was never a lorry driver. When I checked the invoices we took from his office, his last declared building project was over four years ago – so where was his cash coming from? He paid his bed and board to June Collins as regular as clockwork – and kept his real family afloat – until his disappearance.'

DS Leyton is nodding.

'Fox and Coot.'

'Aye – and Morgan. Dudley threatened to expose the three of them. As far as he was concerned he was clean – he could claim he innocently handled a series of bona fide property and building transactions.'

Now DS Jones enters the discussion.

'Guv – do you think Derek Dudley also knew about Marvin Morgan's peccadillos? That would have given him leverage, too.'

Skelgill shrugs.

'Maybe. Building that false wall – it could have been legit – to create a maintenance corridor for the plumbing in the guest room. I don't doubt it was Morgan that converted it into the secret viewing gallery – but Dudley might have known something about Morgan from his visits to June Collins's place in Liverpool – from her, even.'

A rather brooding DS Leyton is thumbing his bottom lip.

'Reckon she's in on it, Guv?'

Skelgill ponders for a moment and then begins slowly to shake his head.

'If she is, Leyton – any half-decent lawyer ought to get her off lightly – they'd plead complete ignorance of the murder and that she wasn't knowingly obstructing the inquiry. Personally, I think she's fed us a few white lies – fearing for her own safety – but that's about it.'

'I suppose it's not like she's been running a massage parlour in Keswick, eh, Guv?'

Skelgill's eyes do a little double take.

'You don't seriously think that's a B&B she's got there?'

Now DS Leyton finds himself rather tongue-tied. He glances apprehensively at DS Jones. She responds with an expression that suggests this is also news to her.

'But –'

'Leyton – have you ever seen the *Vacancies* sign on display? Or any guests, come to that.'

DS Leyton puffs out his cheeks and gives a nervous laugh.

'There's a flippin' surprise round every corner, Guv.'

As far as Skelgill is concerned this cliché sums up life as a detective. He lowers himself into his seat.

'I try to take folk at face value, Leyton – but when they're blatantly dishonest you can't help but wonder why.' Now he looks at DS Jones. 'Morgan – he's acted nice as pie – and yet was lying from the very first time I saw him.'

DS Jones nods to corroborate her superior's assessment. Skelgill continues.

'The day I went to his cottage – after the first news conference – he claimed he hadn't heard about the body being found – *Rose* this is. He said he'd not heard any news – but he'd obviously just switched off the TV in his kitchen – it's an old-fashioned set and the tube was still hot. And then he made some reference to that part of the hill – that he'd not been over there – before I'd even said where. I tell him we've found a corpse, and he starts talking to me about photographing a Sparrowhawk. And he claimed not to have a mobile – I'd barely been in the house a minute and I'd noticed a number was engraved on his dog's collar. How stupid did he think I was?'

He breaks off to hold out a hand to DS Jones. She understands she is to elaborate, and that it is probably not on the question of her superior's intellect.

'The phone – it was in the locked cabinet – we're just interrogating all the numbers in the memory through the service provider. It appears he was in recent contact with Lester Fox – and previously took regular calls from Derek Dudley.'

Skelgill is nodding.

'Morgan must have tipped off Coot and Fox about the scene of crime team. No wonder they weren't exactly surprised when I showed up. Fox and Morgan must have wondered what the bones were doing half a mile away – and then they learn it's not even their body. They'd have been frantic about whether one of them had let something slip – and Fox was obviously paranoid about letting Coot speak to us on his own. If only I'd sussed him sooner.' Skelgill makes a sharp gesture of frustration with both hands. 'Meanwhile, we're off investigating the wrong murder.'

Both DS Jones and DS Leyton inhale as if to speak – but the paradox strikes home – and a silence descends as all three detectives reflect on this extraordinary aspect of the case. There grows a palpable sense of relief – that their little group has survived the self-inflicted tensions wrought by trying to employ clues to one crime to solve another, entirely unrelated, except by coincidence of time and location. Small wonder that the strange mind of Skelgill – that frequently enlists a sixth sense to do its work – has endured such turmoil. Only now does he see clearly – his mental picture like a figure-of-eight climbing knot – in one loop the murder of Miriam O'Donoghue, in the other that of Derek Dudley – and, standing at the intersection, a forlorn June Collins. (And not forgetting Morse, the irrepressible Lakeland Terrier that surely has a bright future in the police service.)

After a minute their collective reverie subsides, and Skelgill determines this is an appropriate moment to reveal the contents of one of his carrier bags. He pulls it from beneath his desk and dumps it with a clunk on the surface; it sounds like a bottle and indeed the bag falls open to expose a magnum of fine champagne with the price ticket still affixed. He gets up a little ponderously as if he is about to make a formal announcement, and grins – rather self-consciously – at DS Jones.

But at this juncture the telephone rings. Skelgill glares at the display, intending to ignore it – however something about the number prompts him to pick up. He responds with his ubiquitous "Aye?" and then listens for a moment; his gaze falls upon DS Leyton. He places a hand over the mouthpiece and addresses his sergeant.

'That's the hospital – they want to put your wife through to you.' Now he hesitates. 'Want to take it somewhere private?'

DS Leyton is on his feet, trepidation in his eyes, his complexion suddenly pale. He glances at DS Jones, who is regarding him anxiously from her seat, and then he addresses Skelgill.

'I'll take it now, Guv.'

He accepts the handset from Skelgill and introduces himself and waits for a moment. He stands hunched and despondent. Then he makes an involuntarily start as the call is connected.

'Alright darlin'?'

He listens for a good half minute, his expression one of growing disbelief. For a loquacious fellow he is uncharacteristically stymied, and swallows successively as if there is a persistent lump in his throat. When it becomes his turn to speak he glances uneasily at his colleagues – perhaps he should have opted for privacy after all. Then he pulls himself together to deliver a decisive response.

'I'll come and get you – right now – love you, girl.'

Looking dazed he returns the handset to Skelgill – but he realises he must provide an explanation.

'Stone the crows.'

Hearing this expression Skelgill detects a hopeful straw in the wind and stretches across the desk to place a palm on his subordinate's shoulder.

'What is it, marra?'

DS Leyton gazes abstractedly at his boss and then at DS Jones.

'She's only gone and got a flippin' bun in the oven.'

In a blur of movement DS Jones is out of her seat like a jack-in-the-box to embrace her colleague – joyful tears springing spontaneously mid-flight; DS Leyton himself perhaps conceals a sob of relief in the minor melee that ensues; when they disentangle he finds Skelgill waiting to grasp his hand.

'You old devil, Leyton – no wonder you've been so dozy lately.'

DS Leyton shakes his head with disbelief.

'Cor blimey – all this doctors-and-hospitals malarkey – just 'cause she used to have a bit of a thyroid problem – an' all the time they're barking up the wrong tree!'

Skelgill gives DS Leyton a friendly punch on the shoulder.

'That's what trees are for, Leyton.'

DS Leyton produces a paper tissue from his trouser pocket and blows his nose. He emerges from behind the handkerchief with a beaming smile, pure happiness that his wife is well and he is to be a father again. Skelgill decides he should take control of the situation; he motions that his two sergeants should be seated.

'Leyton – I realise you need to shoot off – with my blessing – but bear with me for one minute.' He ducks beneath his desk and brings out the second carrier bag. He places it on the surface, but first he refers to the bottle of champagne.

'Now I did intend to make this award for an exceptional piece of detective work in bringing to book the killer of Miriam O'Donoghue.'

He glances pointedly at DS Jones – and DS Leyton claps his hands – while DS Jones looks astonished. Whether this is because Skelgill has so openly recognised her achievement – or simply that he has splashed out on such an expensive bottle of bubbly – it is impossible to tell – but she quickly adjusts her shocked features to reflect the appropriate degree of propriety.

However it suddenly dawns on DS Leyton that he has trumped her news – and that Skelgill is about to reverse his decision. He leans forward and reaches out a hand of protest.

'No – no, Guv – she must have it – no argument.'

But now it is Skelgill that holds up two silencing palms. Then he delves into the second bag and pulls out a shrink-wrapped box – it is a new compact camera. He clears his throat.

'I did have the idea – what I realise now was a ludicrous brainstorm – of starting a blog.' His cheeks actually colour a little at this and he continues hurriedly. 'I'm talking about fishing.'

'That's brilliant, Guv.'

This is DS Jones, and DS Leyton nods heartily. But Skelgill is determinedly shaking his head.

'But what came over me? Why would I want to give up all my secrets? Tell everyone the best places to fish. When to go. What to use. I'd be swamped. And now –' He thumps the desk – perhaps more forcefully than he intends and both bottle and camera jump. 'And, now, there is a far more deserving cause. To record the newest member of the Leyton clan – and one to be Cumbrian born at that.'

He tosses the box to DS Leyton – effectively forcing him to accept it.

'But – Guvnor – these things cost a small fortune – I'll pay you the money.'

Skelgill glowers disapprovingly.

'No way, Leyton – it's yours.' He gives a short hysterical laugh. 'You know I'll forget to buy a present after the birth.'

They all chuckle at Skelgill's uncharacteristic candour – the flood of self-deprecation seems to be buoying his spirits further. Now he rises and hands the bottle to DS Jones – who stands and curtseys to receive it. She admires the label and raises it for their consideration.

'Guv – shouldn't we be wetting the baby's head – or whatever you do at this stage? Surely we could all have a little sip? I can fetch cups from the machine?'

Now Skelgill's practical side comes to the fore.

'Once you open champagne you need to finish it. Take it home, lass.' He smiles a little mechanically. 'You must have someone you could drink it with.'

At this DS Jones frowns, and there is a fierce if brief glint of reproach in her eyes. She places the bottle on Skelgill's desk, halfway between them. Then she raises a hand to indicate the window behind her.

'It's going to be another lovely evening – why don't we have a picnic supper – a double celebration? We know the perfect quiet spot!' She grins; only half in jest she means Harterhow. She turns to DS Leyton. 'Maybe you could bring your wife? I could get some soft drinks, too.'

DS Leyton smiles, his expression grateful.

'Nah – nah – count me out. After all this worrying – and now the shock news – what I need is a quiet night in – get the missus her favourite takeaway to save her cooking.'

Skelgill is looking questioningly at DS Jones; she catches him doing so. He averts his eyes rather in the manner of a dog found coveting its owner's unattended dinner, that now pretends it was merely guarding it. A little smile creases her lips and Skelgill sees this and gives a helpless shrug. The unspoken exchange seems to settle something, and now they both look at DS Leyton – he is turning over the camera box in his hands, contemplating its advertised features. He senses their gaze and looks up, surprised by the scrutiny. He raises the box – but his response is not what they anticipate.

'Guv – those photographs of Morgan's – the ones you had to explain away to the Chief?' He glances a little apologetically at DS Jones. 'How did you pull that off?'

Skelgill folds his arms; he takes a moment to compose his reply.

'That morning, Leyton, the sun was behind me and I saw its reflection off a lens in the pine trees. How do you fool a person who's spying on you? Answer: do something you wouldn't do if you knew you were being watched.' Now he shrugs in an exaggerated manner, as if this logic will excuse his actions. 'I turned round and there was Jones – I just did the first daft thing that came into my head –'

DS Leyton is nodding – a little open-mouthed, it must be said – while DS Jones – perhaps she is affronted, though her expression equally could be one of approval.

'After Jones had taken June Collins away – Morgan was still watching – so I made it look like I was –'

He searches unsuccessfully for a euphemism, but DS Leyton is looking suitably enlightened.

'So you were just pretending, Guv.'

Now Skelgill makes a tutting sound with the tip of his tongue.

'Leyton – first law of the jungle – never answer the call of nature in the middle of a gorse bush. Bloke – or woman, come to that.'

DS Jones is amused – she makes a face of vicarious pain and they all join in with her mirth. Skelgill, however, adds a rider.

'Mind you, at the rate you're going, Leyton – maybe it would put a stop to the local population explosion.'

DS Leyton winks at his colleague.

'Like you said, Guv – these things happen.'

With a grunt he pitches forward and stands upright, holding the camera box carefully with both hands in front of his chest.

'On which note, I'd better do one, Guv – I'll get the missus safely home and then come straight back this afternoon.'

Skelgill points a reprimanding finger at his sergeant.

'Don't you dare come back today, Leyton – we can manage fine.'

DS Leyton shoots an apologetic glance at DS Jones, for he recognises the 'we' that means 'she'.

'Right, Guv.'

'Work out how to use that camera.' Skelgill suddenly gives a little involuntary laugh. 'Just don't take it anywhere near Harterhow tonight.'

'No, Guv.'

'Aye – and another thing, Leyton.'

'Guv?'

'Next time you have the bright idea of putting your career on the line when you think you're saving my bacon – don't.'

'Yes, Guv. And watch out for that gorse, Guv.'

***

Next in the series

'Murder at the Flood' is scheduled for publication in July 2017. In the meantime, books 1-7 in the series can be found in the Kindle Store. Each comprises a stand-alone mystery, and may be read out of sequence.

Printed in Great Britain
by Amazon